# WOLVES OF THE SEA

"Here I am!"....she cried. "If you must kill someone, kill me!"

# WOLVES OF THE SEA

BY

GASTON LEROUX

AUTHOR OF "THE SECRET OF THE NIGHT," "THE
MYSTERY OF THE YELLOW ROOM"

FRONTISPIECE BY
H. J. PECK

**WILDSIDE PRESS**

# CONTENTS

# WOLVES OF THE SEA

# WOLVES OF THE SEA

## CHAPTER I

### NUMBER 3216

"My own ambition has always been to be an honest man," said Little Buddha, casting a glance in the direction of the convict guards who, revolver in hand, were walking between the cages.

"What for?" asked the Toper.

"What for? Why, to set up as the owner of a wine shop, of course."

"We can't all keep a wine shop," said the Toper in a tone of philosophy, "life would be too easy. Every man who comes into the world has his work cut out for him. You, Little Buddha, were certainly intended to grind away in Cayenne. As Chéri-Bibi says, *Fatalitas!* What is written is written. We can't cheat Providence. Talking of Chéri-Bibi, do you know what Carrots said to me? "

" I'm not bothering about what Carrots said to you," replied Little Buddha, lowering his voice, "but it's time we began to talk seriously. Now then: Is it for to-day or is it for to-morrow?"

9

The other outlaws repeated in the same tone, gathering round Little Buddha:

"He's right. . . . Is it for to-day? . . . Is it for to-morrow?"

"Shut up!" growled the Toper. "It's for whenever Chéri-Bibi pleases. But hang it all, shut 'up!"

As a warder passed stealthily along the bars of the cage, bending his legs in order to counterbalance the rolling of the vessel which was particularly heavy that day, the Toper continued aloud:

"No, but didn't you hear what Carrots said? How silly the fellow is to talk like a preacher. He's very squeamish. The only thing that he's got up against Chéri-Bibi is robbing the body of the Marchioness. He says that cemeteries should be sacred."

"He makes us laugh," chuckled Little Buddha, who was seated on his kit bag. "The rich have no occasion to take their trinkets to the grave with them."

"You see this hand," said Carrots. "It has made as many victims as there are fingers on it. Well, it wouldn't have done that. It would loathe that."

"Chéri-Bibi did what he wanted to do. If he wasn't in irons you'd hold your jaw."

"That's a certainty."

"Ask the Kanaka [1] if he played the fastidious in the dissecting-room."

Carrots shook his head obstinately. Chéri-Bibi did

[1] Kanaka, Canaque, Kanak, a native of New Caledonia and now applied to any native of the French colonies. TRANSLATOR'S NOTE.

what he wanted to do, used the knife, was a thief—
and such a thief!—cheeked the judge and all the
Court, cleared out ordinary people, but he did not
approve of Chéri-Bibi robbing the dead. That
brought bad luck. They mentioned the Kanaka, an
ex-doctor who had been condemned to ten years' hard
labor because he would not say for what purpose he
required the strips of flesh which he had cut out of
one of his living patients whom he kept by main force
in his house, bound to a leather couch. Well, the
Kanaka drove his own trade. Dead meat or living
flesh, doctors as well as murderers gambled in it; it
didn't frighten them. And turning to the Kanaka,
Carrots added with a vicious laugh:

"They do with it what they like, and it's not for
nothing that they call him the Kanaka."

At this terrible allusion to the notorious cannibalism of the aborigines of New Caledonia, the Kanaka,
who was yellow, became green. The other, obsessed
by the one idea, continued:

"Take it from me, Chéri-Bibi was not born for that.
There were better things for him to do than that. He
showed a lack of delicacy."

"Chéri-Bibi is a giant and you are a set of pigmies,"
rapped out the Kanaka in a voice of contempt, turning
his back on them.

"That's true," said Little Buddha. "He robbed the
dead, but he did it to help the poor."

"I grant that," said Carrots, firm in his opinions,

"but that throws discredit on the trade. That's not the way to insure the progress of society. I've never read in Karl Marx or Kropotkine that you must do that sort of thing."

Carrots had not read anything at all. But he never lost an opportunity of quoting the names of great men which were bandied about at public meetings, as if these important persons shared his views regarding the constitution of society.

"Chéri-Bibi has done everything in his time," explained Little Buddha. "He even began his career by being an innocent victim."

More often than not Little Buddha expressed himself in studied language, as became a man who had been clerk to a sheriff's officer. He was nicknamed Little Buddha because with his thick-set, short-legged body as round as a barrel, his neck well sunk between his shoulders, and his arms folded across his chest, he resembled those little Asiatic gods which are to be found in second-hand dealers' shops.

"Yes, he was innocent; at least that's what he said," he went on with a sigh, "and I quoted his case in my book on the 'Reform of the Magistrature.' Oh, the rotters . . ."

Little Buddha sighed as he thought of the sentence of penal servitude for life to which "they" had condemned him for having in "an attack of nerves"— so this sluggish person declared—taken the law into his own hands in a struggle with an old woman who had refused to hand over to him the key of her cash-box.

"That's the way of the world now," groaned Carrots. "It's enough for you to have done nothing for them to send you to a convict settlement. I have 'done in' five, I give you my word. Not one more and not one less. Well, it's for the sixth whom I never saw that you have the pleasure of my company. I say what I think. I've never committed a useless crime. I've always had a conscience. I'm a miserable wretch, 'tis true; a thief, 'tis true; I've used the knife, 'tis true; but that's no reason why they should condemn an innocent man."

"That's the only thing society has ever done for you," said Little Buddha in a tone of philosophy.

"While Chéri-Bibi is always doing something for society," broke in the Toper, who was nervously following with a watchful eye the movements of the convict guard. "Did you see how he spat in the Commander's face? There's another man who gives me the hump with his doleful countenance. Do you know what he said to Chéri-Bibi?—'Do you want anything, are you ill, Chéri-Bibi?' And here was Chéri-Bibi spitting in his face! He did the right thing. We don't want pity. What we want is justice."

"Is it for to-day, or is it for to-morrow?" came from the hoarse voices of the men at the back of the cage.

The Toper growled louder than ever so as to drown their murmurs:

"If the Captain sings small to Chéri-Bibi, it's because he funks him, just as the juries were too funky to condemn him to death for fear of reprisals. Everyone funks Chéri-Bibi."

At these words the shadows at the back of the cage who were reclining on their kit bags and hammocks, which were rolled up in accordance with regulations, rose to their feet, and a humming sound, soft and rhythmic at first, but soon growing in volume, came from between decks.

> *Who is it pads the hoof in gore,*
> *And sets the dynamite a-roar,*
> *And scares all Paris more and more?*
> *Sing ho for Chéri!*
> *The guv'ment will not leave us free,*
> *From the Bois d'Boulogne to Gay Paree;*
> *Who blows the blooming lot U P?*
> *Sing ho for Chéri-Bibi!*
> *Sing ho for Chéri-Bibi!*

The Toper with a few blows of his fist and a few rough words imposed silence, rapping out in a hollow voice:

"Look out! . . . warder's coming."

"*Chouïa,* silence!" ordered the African, who was notorious for the extraordinary cruelty with which he had treated his mistress.

The overseers came hurrying up.   They were

furious. Keys grated in the locks. In the diffused
light which feebly poured in from the railed portholes,
the men could see through the bars, warders, revolver in hand, surrounding the men who were carrying the mess.

"Eyes front!"

The cage which contained the Toper, Little Buddha,
Carrots and the Kanaka was the first in the upper
gun deck next to the *Bayard's* forecastle. She was
an old cruiser which had been converted into a transport and commissioned recently to convey convicts
and persons deported from their country, from the
Isle de Ré to Cayenne, since the *Loire* alone was not
equal to the work.

The issue of rations began at this cage. As soon
as the order "Eyes front" rang out the fifty convicts
who crowded the cage leapt to their feet. There were
tragic faces among them; pallid faces, faces tinged
with green; hollow cheeks, feverish eyes. Their
heads and faces were clean-shaven, and they were
dressed alike in the same square cap, the same jacket
and trousers of coarse brown cloth, the same heavy
yellow shoes. Round their arms was a band on which
a number was inscribed, for in the eyes of the authorities these men no longer possessed a name. They
lined up, elbowing each other so as to get in position,
for they had caught sight of the second-in-command,
a terrible martinet, who sent them to the cells, and
put them in irons for next to nothing. The convict

guards were subservient tools, cursing and swearing and striking hard at the men, ever ready with their "shooters," as if the revolvers themselves were choking with the shot that filled their mouths, and longed to be relieved of their powder and their "suppressed lightning." The criminal fraternity were smartened up a little by the wards' bullying methods.

The guards enter the cages like animal tamers going among wild beasts. With revolver cocked, erect and on the alert, they encounter the eyes of each man in turn, and read in them rebellion, fury, impotent rage, and they compel them to shrink from the gleaming barrels. "Eyes front!"

The men who do not move to their places smartly enough with a click of the heels, their hands at their sides, are roughly hustled and soundly thrashed.

Nothing escaped the little piercing eyes of Lieutenant de Vilène, the second-in-command of the *Bayard*. There was but one word on his lips: "Cells." He would have broken Chéri-Bibi if he had been in the Captain's place. And nothing more would have been heard of the monster. The Captain and he would no longer have had to look after a man who had escaped from penal servitude once, from the lock-up twice, from a departmental prison thrice, and for whom doors seemed to have been built only to open of themselves, and bars erected only to support the rope or the bedclothes which set him free. They could very well have done without such a charge; and they both lived in dread of letting this terror loose on society.

However, Chéri-Bibi was in irons. At any rate that was something. And he would remain in irons during the voyage on board ship. De Vilène had made Captain Barrachon swear it. The latter had not yet got over Chéri-Bibi's gross insult to him—him who was always so considerate with the convicts and professed humanitarian sentiments.

"That will teach you a lesson," de Vilène said to the Captain.

The Lieutenant entered the cage in a fury, behind the warders, accompanied by the Overseer General, who himself had come hurrying up on hearing the unusual noise from the lower deck.

"Suppose I stop your rations. You know well enough that you're not allowed to sing," said the Inspector.

"If anyone wants to join No. 3216 in the hold let him say so," exclaimed de Vilène. "Two days in the cells for you, Corporal, for not rolling up Chéri-Bibi's hammock."

The Corporal was no other than the African and he was on the point of receiving three tubs, which were being delivered to his cage, containing rations for his hundred and fifty men, and slinging the "dishes" to the deck above by means of the chain.

When he heard the sentence he said like a school-boy:

"We're going it!"

"Four days."

He was silent. De Vilène shot a devastating look at him. He did not understand how a man with the African's record could reply "We're going it" to a naval lieutenant. He was beside himself. His wrath deprived everyone in the cage of the power of movement. The convicts around him held their breath. They knew that punishments incurred during the voyage would have a terrible influence on the treatment which would be meted out to them when they arrived in Cayenne.

"You're so happy here, you sing," snarled the officer. "Apparently because the absence of No. 3216 gives you more room."

It was true that the departure of Chéri-Bibi had given them more room for they were packed in the cage like sardines in a tin. When Chéri-Bibi was ordered below in irons, two warders, who never left him, went with him; for, of course, they did him the honor of keeping a special watch over him. To begin with, the convict guard had been doubled in the passage outside his cage; afterwards two warders kept their eyes on him day and night in the cage itself. And at the end of the passage near the hatchways, and at all the entrances leading to the cages, soldiers were posted ready to fire at the first alarm.

The Lieutenant made the tour of the cage, turning the kit bags upside down as though he scented a surprise of some sort, some malevolent trick, devised in the dreadful gloom of this corner of the infernal regions. He opened one at haphazard. He knew quite well that after the perfect search to which the men had been subjected on leaving, he would find in it only the regulation outfit; but, even then one could never be easy in one's mind, never be sure of anything with such miscreants. Finding nothing out of the way in the kit bag, he vented his spleen on the floor which he considered had not been properly swabbed.

"Who swabbed the deck?" he shouted; and turning to his escort, "For the future the cleaning for the cages will be done by men told off for the purpose. The overseer in charge of the men on fatigue duty must be satisfied that the work has been properly done, and must report to the Overseer General, who will inform me or my assistant."

Then turning on his heel he confronted the men:

"And you. . . . Listen to me. . . . The men on fatigue duty, doing their twenty-four hours service, will not be allowed to go on deck with the others for the daily half-hour's exercise. They must wait till they've finished their work. You will receive some small scrapers for this work, in addition to the swabs, for you don't wet them enough. Damme, I want your cages to be as clean as the Commander's sitting-room. Do you follow me? Do you understand—you Chouïa —you Corporal."

"But the Commander said that . . ." murmured the African with a sigh.

"There's the Commander," interrupted the Lieutenant as he thrust his revolver in the man's face.

The warders were in a state of immense elation. The Lieutenant was not the man to let the grass grow under his feet. But one of them, unluckily for him, laughed a little too loudly. The Lieutenant ordered him twenty-four hours in the cells, which would teach him to take the service seriously. It was the turn of the convicts to be delighted, and one of them cried out in the dusk:

"Bravo!"

On hearing this word of approval de Vilène, who was certainly very touchy, ordered one of the three dishes containing food for the cage to be taken away. It would make them tighten their belts. It would teach them to express an opinion when it wasn't wanted.

He left them in a silence that could be felt.

After the convict guards went out and the bars were padlocked, the men snarled and gnashed their teeth. Once more a portion of the mess was taken away from them. And appalling in their rage, they surged round the Toper.

"Is it for to-day? . . . Is it for to-morrow?"

"It's for whenever Chéri-Bibi decides."

On account of the rolling of the vessel the "dishes"—the two tubs—were suspended on a chain.

The Corporal was in charge of the first two parties of men who took their places round the tubs, and began to forage in the nauseous mixture which was simmering in them. The mess cooks kept a sharp look out on the movements of the wooden spoons plunging in this glue-like skilly consisting of odds and ends of carrots, turnips and leeks that at the finish were done to rags, or rather the residue of the stuff containing haricots so hard that nothing could soften them or make them lose their shape and identity. Each tub had, on this occasion, to satisfy the hunger of seventy-five instead of fifty men, because of the "privation." Fortunately some of them suffered from the rolling of the ship, and being in a state of collapse in the corners, near the buckets, refused to answer the call. The convicts ate their food with mouths bent over the tubs like pigs bending over troughs. As they ate they continued their growls against the Lieutenant and the convict guards; the "warders" as they called them, although these men had the title and rank of "Military Overseers."

The overseers passed and repassed the cages rapping out frightful oaths and jeers and threats. At one moment a loud clamor of slamming bars and a cry of pain could be heard from a distant cage on the gun deck. The convicts who were eating did not even look up. They knew the meaning of it. It was another old offender who had served his sentence in the cells, and on being brought back to his den had failed to enter it quickly enough. So they slammed the grille on his fingers.

The convict guards' chief sport was this crushing of fingers. Oh, the warders were swine? Wait till they had one of them in their power. "When would it be—to-day or to-morrow?" It was for whenever Chéri-Bibi decided. Nevertheless let him hurry up!

Group succeeded group round the "tubs." The men who were no longer eating watched the others eat. Each man was left his share. They showed a sense of fairness. And they stroked their stomachs with an air of satisfaction.

The rolling of the ship increased. Men slipped and lurched and cried out as others trod upon their feet. One blundering fool hung onto the "tub" and it began to bob up and down like a ship in distress. It was stopped too abruptly and there was a general shout. The haricots had made off! It was an unexpected bonus for the men who had finished their meal. They rushed forward and threw themselves upon the loathsome mess scattered over the deck.

The sea was terribly rough. The kit bags rolled one over the other; and one caught the clatter of things falling from their places between decks. A warder was sent sprawling on his face between the cages, and his revolver went off. The convicts

laughed as only convicts can laugh. The shot did
not kill or wound anyone.

"I wish it had killed you," exclaimed the warder in
a rasping voice as he scrambled to his feet.

In one cage a convict complained that salt water
had been given him to drink. And the seas still
mounted higher. . . . The waves sweeping against
the ship's waist and hurling themselves over the
prow produced a thunder like the firing of heavy
artillery.

At that moment the men who were eating at the
"chain" with the Toper were listening to him with
both ears. Carrots, the Kanaka, Little Buddha, and
the African himself neglected their soup. But they
pretended to be utterly intent on eating in the same
gluttonous fashion.

"Don't worry," whispered the Toper. "As our
curate said: 'There's a good time coming.' It was
not for nothing that Chéri-Bibi got himself put in
irons. And the reason why he spat in the
'Guv'nor's' face was that he didn't want to be
interfered with. He's got his scheme. It's a
good 'un."

"We'll leave that to Chéri-Bibi. Seems we might
in irons?" whispered Little Buddha. "I myself can
do nothing without him. I've no confidence in
anyone but him."

"That's his affair. He knows his business.
There was no way of making our arrangements so

long as the warders were in the cage watching him. That's why he got himself put in irons. Do you understand now? He can talk."

"I shall be in the cells to-morrow," said the African. "Hurry up, so that I know what's what. Is it a fact that we're all agreed on a shindy?"

"Certain," declared the Toper, nodding his head.

"All agreed to seize the ship."

"Certain."

"Is the lower gun deck in it?"

"The lower gun deck as well as the upper gun deck."

"Aren't there any police spies?"

"No, and no prison spies. All of us are in it quite openly. Ready to risk our skins if necessary. Win or die, what!"

"But what are we going to do when we've got the upper hand?"

"We'll leave that to Chéri-Bibi. Seems we might turn pirates. We can please ourselves seeing that we shall be our own masters, what? Everything in the store-room will be ours, the whole caboodle, the ship and the government's money."

"We shall be masters of the Atlantic. Let those who come up against us look out!" said Little Buddha, and playing the gentleman he went on: "What awful weather! What a hustle! You're treading on my foot, Toper. Did you ever see such a crowd packed into so small a space? We might be on the Boulevards on the fourteenth of July." And he hummed as he cleaned out the bottom of the tub:

*In Paris chock-a-block with troops.*

"Sing! Sing!" ordered the Toper. "There's the warder. Don't let him suspect that we're planning things. . . ."
Little Buddha wiped his mouth with his sleeve and finished:

> *In Paris chock-a-block with troops,*
> *Where I go for my little treat,*
> *There'll be twenty million nincompoops*
> *A-treading on my feet.*

The guard had passed. The Toper went on:
"Maybe we can go to Caracas where there's a revolution on. We could offer our services to the revolutionary army, and then it would be our turn to become the government."
"That's a good idea," said Little Buddha approvingly. "You shall be Minister of Justice and I Minister of Education. You'd see how I would educate the people. There would be no use for murderers."
"Now you've talked enough rot," said the Kanaka, who never allowed himself to take a cheerful view of anything, "can you explain, Monsieur the Toper, how we who are unarmed, locked up in cages, surrounded

by warders and soldiers ready to search us, can get hold of the *Bayard?*"

"You want to know too much," returned Carrots.

"That's a fact, he's too inquisitive," insisted the Toper. "Chéri-Bibi doesn't like it. I've told you he's got his scheme."

"Well, I tell you that without arms we can do nothing."

"I agree with the Kanaka," said the African.

"Who told you we shouldn't have any arms?"

"Where are we to get 'em from?"

"Aren't there any on board?"

"Yes, but we can't get at 'em."

"The scheme is a very simple one," the Toper let slip at last, in a tone of irritation. And leaning towards his companions at the tub he continued: "We shall have arms . . . as many as we want to make us masters of the lower deck. Do you follow me? We shall have arms . . . cutlasses, shooters . . . Excellent! At a given moment, when the cage is opened we shall make a rush at the guard, the Overseer General, the Inspector, the Lieutenant, in fact all the lot of them, and do for them. We shall open the other cages before the guards on the upper deck know what's going on."

"But the sentries will fire and the soldiers and sailors come hurrying up. We shall all be massacred."

"Silly fool!" returned the Toper in a tone of contempt. "It's certain that many of us will have to pay for it. More than one of us will get shot. But you can't make omelettes without breaking eggs, can you? The chief thing is not to funk it but to do the needful. Eight hundred pals on board will be armed. . . . We'll make a dash for the hatchways, and it's the sentries that'll pay for it. And then we can barricade the hatchways in the gangways with kit bags and any stuff we may find in the hold. . . . I tell you, there'll be a devil of a racket. We'll fight like they did in the days of the Revolution, what? It's a bad look out for the funkers. For my part I'd rather go under in the attempt than snuff it at Bré slaving away for the Government."

A murmur of approval greeted the orator's last words. Nevertheless the Kanaka did not seem entirely convinced. He was a man with the scientific mind. He mistrusted the Toper's enthusiasm, his impulsive, thoughtless temperament. Yet he realized that Chéri-Bibi had chosen him as the confidant of his plans because, owing to his herculean strength, his brutality and his exploits, the Toper exercised a real influence over the convicts; and Chéri-Bibi was confident that he would not betray him but would make short work of those false friends who when they had knowledge of his intentions did not regard them as wonderful.

"The proof that we shall have arms when *he* likes," went on the Toper, getting up, a movement which was followed by the gaze of all the convicts who had been furtively watching Chéri-Bibi's lieutenant as he talked, "the proof is that he wants us all to-day, in a body, to drink his health. We've had enough water. Come on, Carrots, have a look at the bottom of your bag."

Carrots did as he was told and almost died on the spot from shock as his fingers came in contact with the agreeable chill of a glass bottle, and pulled it out with a trembling hand. All the men stared at it with the exception of the Lamb. There is always at least one Lamb in each cage who does not want to know anything of what is happening round him, and whose hypocritical attitude is allowed to pass because more often than not he is in a state of despair that prevents him from eating, and willingly foregoes his rations. With the exception, therefore, of the Lamb and the Toper, who started off on a tour of the grille just to keep the "deputy warders" under observation, every man had his eyes fixed on him, even the sick who pulled themselves together in order to see and understand. . . . Was it then indeed true? . . . A bottle. . . . A really big fat-bellied bottle. . . . A beautiful tickler. . . . A liter such as they had not seen for many a long day, for they were not entitled to buy luxuries at the canteen like the old offenders who were allowed to have money and the happiness that money can buy They all stood up in spite of the pitching and rolling and their illness. . . .

Clutching one another, with a tremulous movement of the fingers, their eyes starting from their heads, they stared at the bottle.

Carrots, who trembled so greatly that he was afraid of dropping it, held it tightly clasped in his arms; and then he opened it with eyes closed, nostrils dilated and face transfixed. The bottle contained rum. They would be able to have a tot of rum. The mere thought of it excited their thirst. Men who no longer had the right to anything save blows and kicks like wild beasts, and to starve to death, suddenly saw the light! A bottle of rum! What a miracle and what a mystery. It was Chéri-Bibi's doing. He alone was capable of such a stroke. He alone could explain the inexplicable—how this wonderful thing had come about in spite of perpetual searches and frightful and continuous supervision. The man who had smuggled in this bottle of rum would also smuggle in arms. That could be depended on. There was no longer room for any doubt. And the men in all their varied brutality passionately vowed themselves to him.

"What a piece of luck the Lieutenant didn't fix on Carrots' kit bag," said Little Buddha.

"It proves that Providence is with us," declared the Toper. "Come on, there's a drink all round. There isn't enough in this one for all of us."

He took four large bottles of rum out of the bag at the moment when he felt that there would be a scrimmage round Carrots' bottle, which would not go far among so many. Then there was a gloomy and mute delirium. They drank, they gurgled and choked with joy, their heads thrown back a little, transported by the flow of the burning spirit. Those who had not yet drunk waited, their hands outstretched, their fingers bent, growling impatiently, gasping painfully and heavily for breath. The Toper kept order, and when the warders walked down the alley-way he put the bottles out of sight. And then once again the men made a rush at them. When the unclean kiss on the mouth of the bottle continued too long, men cried out in muffled and threatening voices: "That'll do!" and the drinker gave up the bottle with flaming eyes. When the bottles were empty there was at first a silence, a sort of physical exhaustion to which they yielded with one common accord. And then suddenly the same impulse of gratitude leapt forth from all their throats. And the hoarse voices rang out:

> *The guv'ment will not leave us free,*
> *From the Bois d'Boulogne to Gay Paree;*
> *Who blows the blooming lot U P?*
> *Sing ho for Chéri-Bibi!*
> *Sing ho for Chéri-Bibi!*

The guard in hot haste leveled their revolvers through the bars, and the Captain and the Lieutenant rushed up with a number of soldiers before the men

could be made to stop their singing. The whole
cage, when silence was restored, was condemned to
three days bread and water diet. A warder discovered the empty bottles. Lieutenant de Vilène
went pale with rage:

"Who made you a present of these?"

There was a silence.

"Who made you this present?"

Then the convicts in unison shouted:

"Chéri-Bibi . . . Chéri-Bibi."

The Captain, noticing that they were in a state of
mad excitement due to the rum to which they were
unaccustomed, and wishing as far as possible to
avoid further trouble, ordered his men to retire.

"You must make an inquiry," he said to the
Lieutenant when they were in the alley-way, "and
if the guards are at fault, punish them severely.
Bottles of rum in the cage! Why, there might have
been arms. Oh, we've got to find out all about
it. . . . It's inconceivable."

"Absolutely. But what is more inconceivable
still, Captain," replied the Lieutenant, "is why the
juries did not condemn all these miscreants to death.
If they saw them as we see them, it is quite likely
that they would regret their weakness . . . not to
say their cowardice. When I think that they did not
dare to strike at Chéri-Bibbi. . . ."

"Yes, it's monstrous."

The circumstances of Chéri-Bibi's last trial were

indeed monstrous. To begin with, two of the jurymen whose names were in the ballot, and who in
spite of their efforts were not challenged, had simply
fainted, and they had to be brought to by massage
before they returned to a sense of their duty to
society. They requested the President of the Assize
Court to afford them police protection to their homes
after the trial, and to instruct the detective service
to continue to guard their precious lives; and finally
they returned a verdict of guilty with "extenuating
circumstances," finding that Chéri-Bibi was only in
part responsible and thus saving his head. The case
was, moreover, conducted with a remarkable lack of
firmness by the President, who was so polite that he
seemed to be asking the prisoner's pardon for taking
so great a liberty as to try him. The state of mind
of the Seine Assize Court at this period may be
gathered if we recall that on the very morning of
the trial, the wine shop in which the waiter served
who betrayed Chéri-Bibi and handed him over to
the police, was blown up like a box of fireworks.
It was a warning that the jurymen had taken to
heart.

"Let's go and see him," said the Captain, who
descended the ladder leading to the lower gun deck.
"This Chéri-Bibi prevents me from sleeping," he
confessed.

They went along the lower gun deck, between the
cages. On the upper deck, thanks to the portholes,

it was possible to see almost distinctly, but the
second deck was like night with a few dim red
gleams from lanterns that swung with the rolling of
the waves. Only the iron bars shone, and behind
them, looming in the darkness, the faces of demons
appeared, like the hideous faces seen in nightmares,'
and they stared at the warders as they passed,
revolver in hand. The two officers merely walked
through the alley-way and went below to the third
deck. As soon as they descended to this inferno
the obscurity became impenetrable. In places they
had to grope their way step by step, leaning against
the iron walls behind which they caught the sound of
wails or curses. They reached the alley-way in which
lay the cells under a military guard. At the far end,
at the very back of this hell, a warder opened the
door for them. And they went in accompanied by
a sailor carrying a lantern. Two deputy convict
warders—guards whom the convicts placed even
below the warders—rose to their feet at the entrance
to the cell and gave the salute.

Some object was crouching in the gloom of the
background.

For a few moments the two officers took stock of
this object which did not stir. Was it dead? Was
it alive? The Captain, heavy of heart, much concerned, determined to make sure.

"Aren't you ashamed, Chéri-Bibi, to have spat in
the face of your Captain?" he said.

The still motionless object possessed a voice, and a hoarse voice replied:

"You were wrong to take it as a personal insult."

When Captain Barrachon, worthy man, who asked only to live in peace, and to whom by a frightful stroke of fate the duty had fallen to take this cargo of malefactors to its destination, heard Chéri-Bibi's reply he turned giddy: "You were wrong to take it as a personal insult!" He had to hold on to the bulkhead so greatly was he moved. It was really too much. Chéri-Bibi was obviously making fun of him. The little spirit which the practice of his social and humanitarian theories with his subordinates had left the Captain received a rude shock. He realized that de Vilène was undoubtedly right in treating these miscreants as wild beasts who had nothing in common with ordinary human nature. And what the past crimes, the blood-stained notoriety of Chéri-Bibi failed to achieve, namely, make him forget that a man, however low he may have sunk, still belongs to the human family, the convict's mockery had accomplished in a flash. He bitterly loathed all those wretches, and he could not forgive them for making him believe for an instant that he could win them by fair treatment and make better men of them. Why, he had never lost an opportunity since the vessel started of showing Chéri-Bibi that his heart was not steeled against the evils of the prison system, by granting some relaxation of the terrible regulations,

by improving the convicts' daily fare, and by
interesting himself in their general welfare. He
allowed them now and again an additional short
exercise on the upper deck with the sole object of
preventing them from stifling to death in their cages.
And this was his reward! Chéri-Bibi spat in his
face and told him not to regard it as a personal
insult. . . . Yes, yes, de Vilène was right . . . it
would teach him a lesson . . . it would teach him a
lesson. For the future he would be pitiless and he
began:

"Chéri-Bibi, you are a reckless fellow."

The object squatting in the dark corner chuckled.

"Consider that I spat in the face of society. It
was not intended to annoy you personally, Captain."

He heard the hoarse, husky, forbidding voice, the
manner of saying "Captain." How could one pity
such wretches? If only he did not get loose. He
would be capable of anything, anything. He had
already proved that he was capable of anything, but
after Captain Barrachon had spoken he meant that he
was able to do anything against him; in other words,
entail upon him all the anxieties that would follow
his escape, to say nothing of the crimes that he would
commit aboard ship. The man who devised a scheme
for blowing up the Law Courts would certainly see
nothing out of the way in shooting Captain
Barrachon.

Prudence was the watchword. Chéri-Bibi should

remain in irons until the end of the voyage.  He told him so.

"That's all right," replied the voice.  "I prefer you like that.  You disgust me less."

"Bring your lantern nearer," the Captain shouted to the sailor.

He examined with minute care the irons, called bars of justice.  They consisted of a long rod of over an inch in diameter with fetters attached which kept the legs crossed, and, if needs be, the arms as well.  In Chéri-Bibi's case the arms were crossed.  When the shackles were once fitted to the limbs, they were threaded to the rod, and let down to the spot which they were intended to occupy.  Afterwards the end of the rod was closed by means of a large padlock which served as a bolt.  An iron pad covered the other end of the rod, to prevent the fetters from slipping off.

Captain Barrachon made sure that the bars and shackles were in position and Chéri-Bibi's limbs also. The lantern did not cast any light upon the lower part of the object crouching in the dusk; the object whose wheezing and hateful breathing could be heard though its face could not be seen.  The Captain took the lantern from the sailor, and felt no inclination to throw its rays upon Chéri-Bibi's face, which always perturbed him.  He could look at the hands and feet in their irons; but he would not look at the face, the hideous face. . . . He could not bear to see it.

. . . He shuddered at the thought of the terrible expression which it must wear since he had ordered him to be kept "in irons for the rest of the voyage," for, after all, it was as though he had sentenced him to death.

The lantern was clear of the rod and was held over the padlock, which was properly fastened. It was a sound, heavy, thick, honest padlock of which the Captain held the key, the only key, in his pocket. And he stood up with a sigh of relief. He was more easy in his mind now that he had examined the irons.

"I've always regretted," he said to the Lieutenant, "that these irons which recall the Inquisition and the gloomy Middle Ages, are used in our navy to punish the slightest breach of the regulations or of discipline. But really I'm not sorry that we still have these last vestiges of barbarism at our command when we have to deal with a convict like this."

"Shut up!" said the voice in the dark.

"Do you hear him? 'Tis crime itself that is speaking," said Barrachon, incensed. "Crime in all its impudence and horror. Crime with no name to it."

"Yes, for it's called Chéri-Bibi," shrieked the voice proudly.

"This wretch respects nothing. Perhaps he has parents who are mourning over his misdeeds, but he

is as oblivious of them as he is oblivious of the crimes
themselves."

"I've weakened my memory by excess," replied
the voice.

"Let's hurry away," exclaimed the Captain, "or
I shall kill him and regret it all my life."

"And I . . . I should congratulate you all mine,"
replied the Lieutenant.

The Captain turned to the two men whose duty
it was never to lose sight of Chéri-Bibi.

"I've ordered the guard to be relieved every hour.
It will be less of a strain. You know your instructions. . . . You must never speak or answer No.
3216."

At that moment a dismal sob came from the darkness. It was so terrible and so mournful that both
officers were singularly impressed. The Captain was
at the end of his endurance. He lifted the lantern to
a level with the face of the man who was crying.
And all five—the two officers, the two warders, and the
sailor—started back appalled, for they had before
them a man who was laughing. The men would
never forget the abominable spectacle, this bitter
laughter in the red gleam of the lantern, this
monstrous grimace of the man who mocked them by
laughing from ear to ear because they believed for
a moment that he had moaned and felt compassion
for his suffering. The Captain let the lantern fall,
and it shattered, and the light went out, and the

loathsome object faded in the darkness.   Barrachon, stifling, staggering, opened the door of the cell and took refuge in the alley-way.

"He laughs!" he muttered, overcome with a fit of shivering.   "The monster must have laughed when he committed his last murder."

The door was not yet closed, and Chéri-Bibi heard the Captain's word.   And the hoarse voice over-took Barrachon as he fled:

"You're wrong in thinking it made no difference to me.   That very night I had to take a mustard foot bath!"

Barrachon and de Vilène pressed their whole weight against the door to shut out the sound.

Then they mounted the steps of the inferno which above and below and around them seemed once more to be filled with a general shout.   The convicts would. not keep silent unless they saw a non-com-missioned officer or an officer.   From cage to cage, from cell to cell, from lower deck to upper deck ribald songs, insults, curses, challenges, obscenities were being bandied about; but the Captain and the Lieutenant could think only of Chéri-Bibi.

"Luckily for all of us he'll be dead before the voyage is over," said de Vilène.

"Why should he be?" asked Barrachon, stopping short with one foot on the last rung of the ladder which ran up to the second deck.   "Why do you want him to die?"

"He won't be able to hold out to the end with those irons on. His hands and feet are already bleeding."

"The devil they are!" said the Captain, thinking out aloud. "That's a 'question of conscience.' "

"Is there any question of conscience concerned with men like that? We must have more pluck than jurymen, that's all. . . . Hark!"

The vessel re-echoed with the convicts' doleful singing.

"There's no hope with that scum," went on the Lieutenant. "Oh, if we made up our minds to it! A little blood-letting would soon bring them to their senses."

Before the Captain had time to reply a big white body came tumbling against him, grabbed him as it passed, made him slightly lose his balance, continued its course swiftly down the ladder, heels uppermost, and would have rolled to the bottom of the hold if the Lieutenant had not quietly caught it midway. The officers recognized the cook's mate, who had obviously not found his sea legs. From the beginning of the voyage the lurching and wallowing of the ship held him at their mercy. The unfortunate man could not stand upright. Because of this fact and his thinness he was the sport of the warders and the sailors, who nicknamed him the Dodger.

"What are you doing here?" asked the Captain.

"You see for yourself, sir" the Dodger replied
in a serious voice. "I'm collecting my dishes."

As a matter of fact, men were following him with
the convicts' mess tubs. He caught hold of the rope
of the ladder and added:

"Do you know, sir, that the cook has been working it out in the store-room with the Inspector? Not
a single bottle of rum is missing."

At that moment a more than usually sudden lurch
of the vessel made him let go the rope and he went
flying down to the deck below.

"I never heard of such a thing," groaned the
Captain.

"I swear that I'll clear the matter up before the
day is over," said de Vilène. "The rum must have
been sold to them by the overseers."

When the announcement was made by the guard
that the two officers had returned to the lower deck,
the singing ceased, to be taken up again as soon
as the Captain and Lieutenant had passed. And
it was the turn of the upper deck to smother its
clamor.

"Here's the Cap'n and the Second!"

The signal passed from cage to cage. The two
officers halted for a moment before the "financier's
cage." Not that a special compartment was set aside
for financial gentlemen, but the cage owed its name
to the great number of fraudulent bankrupts and
swindlers who had misappropriated funds who were

present, cheek by jowl with the usual number of common rogues. For that matter they were all dressed alike. Thus it was impossible to distinguish the small fry, the society sharper, the solicitor who was once held in honor in his county, the fraudulent banker who had surprised the town by his display, nor those popular cracksmen with a sense of humor who when they came before judges and juries excited the admiration of certain ill-balanced young persons. Spiritless, dejected, cast down amidst this confused jumble of the tagrag and bobtail of crime, they were no longer recognizable with the exception of the Top, who every now and then, when least expected, gave vent to a sharp, shrill chuckle which vibrated like a pea-whistle, and had the effect of driving the overseers almost crazy.

The officers afterwards passed on to another compartment, the cage for women, containing some forty old incorrigibles who, as soon as they caught sight of the Captain, began to bewail their fate and to groan in the most heartrending manner.

"Have you done sniveling?" snarled one of them, whose white face and flaming black eyes were glued to the grille.

Oh, she was not the one to whimper was not the Countess. Always in a passion, always in rebellion, she never ceased to stride round her cage like a wild hyena, scattering with a blow from her paw anyone who might stand in the way of her perambulation.

The other women dreaded her, for she was cruel, and of great strength, and used her teeth. She was extraordinarily beautiful. And they called her the Countess because she had assumed towards them from the beginning the airs of a great lady.

And then one day she started to talk slang as if she had been used to it all her life, and she dominated them by her brazen effrontery. The Countess was the Kanaka's wife and was condemned at the same time as that peculiar doctor for deeds which the indictment itself dared not describe. They were suspected of cannibalism.

Barrachon and de Vilène stood before this beast of prey clinging to the bars of its cage.

"What do you want, Captain? Do you want me to make love to you?"

The Captain uttered a cry of pain, for the Countess suddenly stretched out her claw and seized him by the chin.

"I've got him by the beard . . . I've got him by the beard!"

The Lieutenant had to strike her a violent blow with the butt end of his revolver before she released her hold. She flung herself back, whining like a beast in a menagerie mastered by the prong of its keeper.

The Lieutenant ordered her to be taken to the cells at once.

"Oh, let's get out of this," gasped the Captain.

"Let's get up to the light of day. We must leave these cursed places."

De Vilène shrugged his shoulders and followed him. The Captain's weakness and his bombastic manner of expressing himself irritated him. Barrachon could endure it no longer nor could he master his disgust. He glided between the last cages as though he were running away, and heaved a sigh of relief when he placed his foot on the deck, notwithstanding that, down below, the inferno re-echoed once more with its terrible songs.

"But why are they singing? We've never heard them sing like this before," he said to the Lieutenant. "Something is happening that we know nothing about."

"Convicts are fond of singing," answered the Lieutenant, smiling coldly. "Do you know the derivation of the word *chiourne,* convict? It comes from the Italian *ciurma,* which itself is derived from the Greek *keleusma,* and it means the Song of the Rowers. What is there more agreeable in the world than the Song of the Rowers?"

The Captain made off. He locked himself in his cabin. He was assailed by the gloomiest forebodings. He was especially perturbed by the mystery of the bottles of rum. Fortunately he had a considerable armed force under his command. Had he made sufficient use of that force? Had not his own weakness produced, by degrees, the state of mutiny into which his extraordinary cargo had fallen? If he had dared to let his men use their weapons once or twice, as was his right, there would have been no more singing in the cages. And then he asked himself: "After all, why should I prevent them from singing? Why?" And he realized that it was not the singing that worried him, but someone that was at the bottom of it all, someone in the vessel, and that someone was no other than Chéri-Bibi. He had confessed to his lieutenant that the man prevented him from sleeping. As he reached this point in his reflections, there was a loud knock at his door and Lieutenant de Vilène came in as pale as death.

"What's the matter?" he asked in a voice that failed him somewhat, for he was already convinced that he was about to hear of some terrible misfortune.

"The matter is that No. 3216 has escaped," replied the Lieutenant quickly.

"Chéri-Bibi?"

"Yes. Chéri-Bibi is not in his cell."

The Captain partly turned round and dropped onto the sofa.

"But look here," he exclaimed with a start, "you don't mean to say so. What about the warders?"

"Both of them are dead. The relief guard found them behind the door of the cell strangled. The irons are still padlocked, and Chéri-Bibi has disappeared."

# CHAPTER II

ON hearing the Lieutenant's last words the Captain made sure that the key of the padlock was in his pocket and ran towards the cabin door like a madman. De Vilène stopped him.

"Wait a bit, Captain," he said. "Don't go out in that state. We've the greatest reason to conceal this matter as far as possible. Chéri-Bibi can't be far away; he can't escape us; we will catch him again, but let's try to lay hands on him without rousing anyone's suspicions. As you said just now, things are happening that we know nothing about. I've not said anything to the Inspector yet, but he has just made an alarming report on the state of mind of the convicts in the lower decks. Something is in the wind, and the disappearance of Chéri-Bibi is perhaps only the beginning or the signal of the affair. At my request the Sergeant and the two warders, who alone know the truth, have sworn that they will not breathe a word to a soul. Let's make our investigation alone without seeming to do so. Afterwards we will come to some decision. To act otherwise will be to encourage the convicts and perhaps to frighten our men

46

out of their wits, for they have a terror of Chéri-Bibi."

"You're quite right," acquiesced Barrachon. "We must be calm. . . . But it's awful."

"Let's quietly go down to the cell," said the Lieutenant, "and we'll see for ourselves. I have my little dark lantern in my pocket. Chéri-Bibi must be in the hold. We'll see from which side he escaped."

"What about the dead warders?"

"They're still in the cell. My opinion is that they should not be moved to the sick-bay until to-night."

"Oh, it's terrible," groaned Barrachon, beside himself. "How can such things be! . . . Let's go."

They left the cabin, affecting as far as possible an air of unconcern.

"I've doubled the sentries on the pretence that the convicts are in an ugly frame of mind, and on the off chance I've placed overseers near each boat," said the Lieutenant.

"You're perfectly right; but he won't risk coming on deck in broad daylight."

"You can never tell with a man like that. He is armed now, for he took the revolvers and cartridges from the murdered warders. We must be prepared for everything."

They once more made their way down to the lower decks. It was an extraordinary thing, and seemed to them of ill-omen, but an incredible silence prevailed in the cages. Not a voice, not a word could be heard.

Not a hand or a foot stirred, though the wind had suddenly died down and the vessel was sailing on an even keel. The convicts, motionless behind their bars, stared at the officers as they passed. Nevertheless a curious chuckle came from the "financiers' cage" as they crossed the lower gun deck. De Vilène turned round. The laugh ceased. A warder behind them shouted through the bars of the cage to the Top:

"Have you done setting everybody at defiance?" And he added: "I don't know what's the matter with them to-day. A moment ago they were making a devil's row, and now we hear nothing but this idiot's laugh."

The officers descended to a lower deck.

In order that the reader may understand the events which were about to take place within the particular compass of a troop-ship commissioned to take convicts to the penal settlement at Cayenne, it may be useful to picture in its general features the plan of the *Bayard.* Five parallel lines ran the full length of the vessel. These were the five decks, which were in each case nearly six feet apart. On the first deck stood the central superstructure, deck houses, bridges, masts, funnels and the other external works part and parcel of the life and navigation of the vessel. On the second deck were the officers' cabins and berths, the staff quarters and the ward-room, and the passengers' and government officials' cabins. On the third deck, in addition to the crew's and warders' quarters, one saw numbers of men packed and huddled together in cages, each man allowed a space of under two feet square in which to move; heavy iron railings against which pallid men were seated, fiercely picking up crumbs of bread which were barely enough to assuage a hunger still left unsatisfied by dry or rancid vegetables and uneatable meat. On the fourth deck was the same picture, but the men's faces were leaden-colored because for the most part they were no longer hungry. They were down with a fever which follows the continuous breathing of a vitiated atmos-phere, for the air was freshened only through the ventilator which ran up to the prow. Thus they suffered not only from insufficient food but from abso-lute lack of air and light. On the fifth deck were the cells and the dark holds, filled with casks and pro-visions which was the domain of the ship's stewards and the commissariat. Below the fifth deck were the store-rooms.

"If he's managed to slip into the holds or the store-rooms, we shan't find him again very soon," said the Captain.

"We'll ferret him out. Why, he can't be far away," replied de Vilène. "The main thing is to know which way he went. He won't be able to move ten yards without running up against a warder. We must be prepared for anything that might happen."

They cocked their revolvers. The Lieutenant

switched on his dark lantern and they opened the door of the cell, closing it at once behind them.

The two dead bodies lay on the deck with their tongues hanging out, and their eyes starting from their sockets, and each one had a bootlace round his throat. After examining them for a moment, Barrachon rose from his stooping posture and shuddered.

"Oh, the scoundrel, if he falls into my hands I will shoot him as I would a mad dog."

De Vilène examined the irons. Barrachon bent over beside him. The whole thing was a great mystery, entirely incomprehensible. The rod was still locked, the bloodstained shackles, the bar, the padlock were in their places just as they were when the Captain verified them a little more than an hour previously. And he had not let the key out of his possession for a second. But their bewilderment was nothing to the feeling of stupefaction which followed. There was no clue in the cell that could explain the flight. From which side had the prisoner got out? It would need a very clever person to offer a reasonable surmise. The walls were nowhere broken through. The decks above and below were intact. The heavy fastenings inside and outside the door had not been tampered with. And Chéri-Bibi could not have escaped by a door outside which a guard was continuously passing to and fro. Moreover, he could not have wormed his way into the closed alley-way, where he would have stumbled against half a dozen other guards. How had he made his escape?

"It's enough to send one off one's head," muttered the Captain. "However much of a scoundrel he is, he is not the devil."

"Yes, he is the devil," declared de Vilène. "But that doesn't help us for all that."

They determined to question the warder, and they beckoned him to come to the cell. The man at once stumbled against the dead bodies. He started back in dismay.

"These are your comrades. Chéri-Bibi killed them," said the Captain.

"Poor fellows!" he said in a choking voice "They were expecting it."

"What do you mean, 'they were expecting it?' "

"When they came on guard Chéri-Bibi said to them: 'Oh, it's you. It's a bad lookout for you.' And before I locked them in they said to me: 'What's he up to? He's going to play some dirty trick on us.' I laughed at them and had a look at the irons. I pointed to their revolvers and I said: 'What are you afraid of? He has his paws in a trap, and you are two against one.' And then I locked the door."

"Didn't you hear anything?"

"Not a sound. No one stirred. They didn't cry out. There wasn't so much as a breath. . . . Oh, the poor fellows! . . . But how did Chéri-Bibi get out?"

"Listen, Pascaud. I trust you," said the Captain. "If it were not you, I should believe that you were an accomplice."

"Accomplice of what, Captain? . . . There's no possibility of being an accomplice here. We watch each other. We are all of us after each other. I've not left the alley-way; the warders can tell you so. And even if I'd opened the door to Chéri-Bibi, it wouldn't explain anything. I haven't got the key of the irons. And how did he kill two men who were armed, men who were watching him, please believe me? Do you suggest that I killed my comrades? If so, you should say so."

"Silence, Pascaud. You know very well that that's merely a manner of speaking. We don't know how he got out."

"No; but I had to say something," returned the warder. "He wasn't carried off by the wind, what? Well, devil take it, it's a nice thing."

He too searched the cell for an outlet, a hole of some sort. . . . And like the officers he found nothing.

"It's past belief," he said, more amazed than frightened. "Well, shall I tell you what I think? The men above in the cages knew about it beforehand. . . . I'm sure they got wind of it. Take it from me, they've been expecting it. They've been too pleased

with themselves, having the time of their lives during
the last forty-eight hours. And as I said to myself
this morning, it's not natural; they're faking up
something. Keep your eyes open! . . . And if
you'll allow me, Captain, I'll make a suggestion.
We can get to know things through them. We
must listen to them, that's all."

"They're holding their tongues above now," said
the Captain in a hollow and threatening voice.

"Oh, let 'em have a walk on the upper decks without rousing their suspicions. Believe me, that's where
the exchange of secrets takes place. . . . I have an
idea that they communicate with one another when
they're on deck. . . . At any rate they exchange
letters there, you know. . . . And I swear, Captain,
that in most cases it's not our fault. It's the sailors'
fault."

"How do you mean? Look here, explain yourself. What you tell me is very serious."

"Isn't the death of our comrades serious? . . . I
say again that the sailors and the women are to
blame. Now you've got it, Captain. . . . I tell you
that the men and the women are exchanging love
letters all the time. They give the glad eye on deck,
and write to each other below just as I say. And
the sailor is the postman. A scrap of paper is
quickly thrown or slipped between two bars, you
know. . . . And the women pay for the sailor's
complicity."

"What do you mean?" asked de Vilène, who had always suspected something of the kind but had not been able to catch them in the act in spite of extreme vigilance.

"What do I mean? . . . Well, the cells have something to do with it, I assure you."

"The cells!"

"Yes, the women's cells. . . . There are women who get themselves sent to the cells so as to be able to talk more freely."

"Let's have this out. . . . Speak more plainly."

"Well, it's like this. Their game is a very simple one, and they play it under our noses. When the sailor and the woman, thanks to those scraps of paper, have come to an understanding between themselves, the woman knows what she's got to do . . . get herself sent down for insubordination, that's all. . . . Now the cell remains unlocked when no one is in it. So the sailor finds his way into it, and lies down in the corner containing the sleeping-bench, or rather, under the head-rest. It's as dark as pitch. The woman is brought in and locked up with the sailor. The thing's not so very hard to manage."

"You, Pascaud, you knew about it and you did not report it! You deserve a week in irons," growled the Captain.

De Vilène checked him in his sudden fit of severity.

"What this man says is very important. . . . How did you discover all this?"

"Oh, I saw it for myself, and I wasn't overproud of it at the time, I can assure you, Captain. It happened three days ago. I was on my rounds seeing to the cleanliness of the ship, a duty that is only done every three days. I and my men had got to the cells, and I pinched an offender who was still in the corner."

"Why didn't you bring him before me?" demanded Barrachon.

"Well, sir, because as it happened it was a military overseer this time."

"A military overseer! All the more reason for reporting him. You are a sergeant. You deserve to be reduced to the ranks. Give me his name at once."

"Yes, sir. His name is Francesco and he's a Porto Vecchio man."

"Francesco? Do you know him, de Vilène?"

"Yes, Captain," replied the Lieutenant. "I know him. Here he is." So saying, de Vilène pointed with his foot to one of the bodies on the floor of the cell.

"He has paid the penalty," groaned Pascaud. "Now I can give him away, poor fellow. But you may be certain that he would never have done it if the sailors hadn't shown him the way. He wanted to take advantage of the opportunity like the others. Oh, it's awful. How can such things be. . . . And now he's punished for it. I said to him: 'Mind what you're doing, Francesco, it'll bring you bad

luck to have anything to do with the prisoners.'
But he was that way inclined, and liked to show off
when his duty took him near the women's cage.
Look here, there was one to whom he never failed to
say a pleasant word and to show some indulgence.
I can tell you about it now that he is dead. It was
that black-eyed she-wolf, you know, the Kanaka's
wife. But of course you don't know her. . . . Well,
they call her the Countess. By the way, she was sent
down to the cells only a little while ago."

"The woman who made a grab at you, Captain,"
said de Vilène.

"Oh yes, a regular she-wolf."

"But I say," exclaimed Pascaud, "he must have
heard something. She's in the next cell."

On the Captain's orders they at once left Chéri-
Bibi's cell and entered that of the Countess. No
sound came from the cell, nor did the prisoner show
any sign of life. They were astonished, and it was
with growing anxiety that they threw a light in the
corners. The Countess was no longer there.

"Well, this is about the limit!" exclaimed the
Sergeant.

The Lieutenant did not say a word, but carefully
pushed aside the plank which was used as a sleeping-
bench, and a flash of light from his dark lantern,
turned towards the deck, showed the Captain a gap
large enough to permit anyone to slip through.

Barrachon and the Sergeant were about to utter an

exclamation, but the Lieutenant, with a quick gesture, stopped them.

De Vilène at once put out his lantern and the three men left the cell on tiptoe. Quietly they locked the door. The guards on duty in the alley-way were greatly perplexed by these various movements, and halted in their everlasting march up and down.

"Keep moving. What are you standing there for?" whispered the Lieutenant.

The men once more started to pound the deck with their heavy tread.

Barrachon realized the position. The convicts must not suspect that they were discovered, if it could be avoided. The three men were at one in agreeing that Chéri-Bibi and the Countess had escaped through the hole.

They could not imagine how Chéri-Bibi had shaken off his warders, or how he had joined the Countess; but they felt certain that both convicts had gone down that way. And they concentrated their thoughts on the problem of how to catch them again. The cavity ran down to the old small arms magazine which had been transformed into a goods hold, and almost entirely filled with bales intended for merchants in Cayenne. Though the convicts might find places in which to hide themselves, they would not be able to hold out for any length of time, because they would inevitably be surrounded and discovered.

They would attempt to take the convicts unawares by using the ladder which led direct to the storerooms, for they must not think of descending through the hole. Otherwise the entire crew would have to go through the mill and be killed one by one. Chéri-Bibi was not in the habit of doing things by halves.

The Captain, impelled by the necessity for action, desired to descend the ladder at once, but de Vilène persuaded him to listen to reason, and a body of ten warders were brought along, without any attempt at secrecy, by Pascaud, who went to fetch them as if he wanted them for some ordinary duty.

He merely told them to go below with their rifles, an order which did not excite any surprise inasmuch as all the men in this floating barracks were armed. The convicts watched the men pass as though it were an everyday sight, without expressing the slightest astonishment or the smallest curiosity. But in the financiers' cage the convict called the Top, of hilarious temper, and a fraudulent banker by trade, gave utterance to the fantastic and insufferable chuckle which always maddened the guard. The Captain told the men the truth. They gazed at each other with terror in their eyes. They would have to fight Chéri-Bibi, who was armed and had taken refuge in the old small arms magazine after murdering two of their number. They were, without doubt, burning for revenge, but what a piece of work it was! How were they to set about it? The very simple plan, the too simple plan, which the Captain explained to them, was received with a wry face. If Chéri-Bibi were discovered, and gave himself up without resistance, his life was to be spared! He would be tried in accordance with the regulations, and executed in accordance with the law. If he defended himself, then, of course, he was to be given no quarter. He was to be shot on the spot.

"Have you anything else to suggest, my dear de Vilène?" asked the Captain, turning to the Lieutenant in accordance with his usual custom and system of consulting the junior officers on the measures, even of the gravest kind, which had to be taken in common.

It was not that the worthy man was lacking in initiative or feared to assume responsibility; but he wanted everything that happened on board between him and his subordinates to be done, as he said, "on a family basis," and "under the auspices of an entirely paternal discipline."

De Vilène was boiling with impatience. He felt with reason that they were wasting time, but since his advice had been asked, he gave it.

"It's not a question of Chéri-Bibi probably defending himself, he will certainly defend himself. What has he to gain by sparing us? Absolutely nothing. His fate is settled in any event. He is a wild beast at bay. Before he is killed he will be intent on one thing only—shooting down as many of us as he possibly can. Don't let us, therefore, play his game by exposing ourselves to his shots. My opinion is that as soon as we open the hatch we should sweep the field by firing, as quickly as possible, a volley round the ladder and then rushing down into the hold."

The Captain replied:

"I shall lead the way and call upon him to surrender, and you must follow me."

"Very good, Captain."

The convict guards were literally trembling at the thought of the adventure, so greatly had Chéri-Bibi spread terror among them.

De Vilène had already ordered them to bring torches and lanterns, so that each man should be able to light his own way.

Taking Pascaud aside he said:

"You are posted on guard here and must stay here. Watch the hole quietly with a couple of men. If Chéri-Bibi and the woman try to come up this way, shoot them."

Pascaud replied in a gloomy voice that the Lieutenant could rely on him.

At the moment when they were about to uncover the hatch, the Captain informed the men that Chéri-Bibi was not alone, but was below with a woman whose life it was desirable to spare.

"Not a bit of it!" growled the convict guards

when they learnt that they had the Countess to deal with. "She is probably more to be dreaded than the other."

In the midst of perfect silence they removed the hatch over the ladder. The Captain descended the first few rungs, holding on with one hand and carrying his revolver in the other.

"No. 3216, I call upon you to surrender!" he shouted in a dull voice.

The light from the torches illuminated only a small part of the hold, but they were able to distinguish bales in monotonous heaps carefully stowed and trimmed on either side of the little wooden gangway, called the platform deck of the hold, which led to the ladder. A few yards away the darkness was impenetrable, and throughout the hold an awful silence prevailed. Nothing broke the stillness, not even the sound of men breathing at the top of the ladder. The life of every man seemed suspended over this cavity, this mysterious abyss, where death was already casting its shadows.

The Captain remained there, unprotected, his body presenting itself to the shots of the terrible Chéri-Bibi and the she-wolf who was with him.

"Look out!" cried the Lieutenant suddenly. "Look out, Captain. Something stirred over there behind that bale."

There was no need to order the men to fire. A tremendous report rang out in the hold. The warders had aimed their rifles over the heads of the two officers in the direction of the bale to which the Lieutenant had pointed.

The Captain and the Lieutenant leapt down the ladder. The men scrambled after them. And for a moment they stood in a group behind the Captain, who stopped them with outstretched arms.

The torches held aloft by the men threw back the darkness a few yards on the main gangway above the deck.

And as soon as the noise and reverberation of the heavy explosion died away, the obscurity once more became hushed and mysterious and menacing.

Then Barrachon repeated his summons.

"No. 3216, will you surrender?"

But whether it was that he refused to surrender or could not hear, No. 3216 did not answer.

"Forward!" ordered the Captain. "Search everywhere."

The guards followed closely on the heels of their officers.

In reality the examination of the hold was not so complicated as at first sight might have been thought. The merchandise was stowed away so symmetrically that it was impossible to slip one's hand in between two bales or two boxes. The trim of the hold had been scientifically effected so as to prevent any sort of accident to the freight.

By de Vilène's orders—he himself was on his feet

—the men went down on their knees on the platform-deck of the hold, crawling on all fours like animals over the wooden hatches on the floor of the ship. The platform ran crosswise, two branches going from port to starboard and two others running from fore to aft. It did not take long to search the unoccupied space in the fore hold. They saw nothing, were stopped by nothing.

"They must be here," muttered the Captain. "They can't have got away, unless they've gone up through their hole."

"That's impossible," declared de Vilène. "Pascaud is on the lookout above with two men."

"Then they can't have escaped. We must search again. The store-room has no other outlet. It is absolutely closed. They must be here."

Several bales which seemed to jut beyond the trim of the hold were moved, but nothing suspicious was discovered, and they were replaced in their positions. A few casks were likewise clumsily rolled aside. Nothing was behind them.

De Vilène displayed the greatest energy, and rummaged in the darkness with systematic thoroughness. His search was no more successful than that of his men.

Suddenly a pistol shot echoed, and a bullet whistled past the Captain's ear. All the men fired, and there was a terrific uproar and confusion. What were they

firing at?   In what direction?   It was a veritable
miracle that no one was killed on the spot.

Nevertheless a man lay groaning in the hold. They
rushed up to him.   He had received a bullet in his
arm; a bullet fired by a fellow-warder.   He explained
that it was he who had fired the first shot; and the
bullet must have rebounded past the Captain. What
had he fired on?   He could not say exactly; apparently a shadow had slipped between his legs, the
shadow of a huge rat which disappeared under a
plank.   Then it was discovered when the plank was
pulled up that it opened on to the main bilge.

"Hang it all!" exclaimed the Captain.   "They've
had the cheek to make off that way."

This main bilge, the well-room of the ship, was
at the bottom of the hull, and consisted of a narrow
gut or channel into which flowed all the water on
board.   As soon as it was full, it was emptied by the
pumps.   At that moment it was but half full.   Even
for a man who was called Chéri-Bibi to have dared to
use such a method of escape, showed that he was
conscious that death was on his track.   The Captain
was in a state of despair.

"Now they're able to go wherever they please," he
said to de Vilène in a mournful tone.   "From this
well, such devils as they are will be able to communicate with every part of the ship.   The fact that they
will have to remove the hatches won't worry them for
long, and they will go where they please.   Where

shall we look for them? The fore hold, the after hold, the store-rooms? They'll go from the old small arms magazine to the coal bunkers. They'll be walking about among us as if they were in their own homes, and we shall be utterly nonplussed."

"If they are in the bilge, which is not yet certain," replied de Vilène, "we can send them a few volleys from our revolvers on the off chance."

Flattening himself against the hatch he discharged his revolver and then waited, his ears on the alert. He caught only the sound of the plashing of the water, and rising to his feet said:

"It's quite simple! We should have to unload the entire cargo to find the pair of them!"

He mustered his men near the ladder. The man with a bullet in his arm was whimpering like a child. The Captain ordered him to be silent.

"You're going to the sick-bay, my lad. You will be asked a lot of questions. For that matter everyone must, by now, be aware of the facts. You must tell those to whom you have anything to say that Chéri-Bibi is dead. . . . Do you understand, all of you?"

"Yes, yes," replied the warders. "You can rely on us, Captain. The convicts will be only too delighted to hear it!"

# CHAPTER III

BARRACHON left six men in the hold, two of whom were ordered to stand by the hatch over the bilge.

"If they're not already dead they'll soon be drowned," said a warder who had closely inspected the level of the water. "There's hardly enough room for them to hold their heads above watei and to breathe."

"To my thinking they won't get out of it," said another. "What do you expect them to do? They can't climb up through the pump-pipes."

The Captain and the Lieutenant joined Pascaud in the cell from which the Countess had disappeared.

"Well," said the Sergeant. "What's the result?"

"Nothing. We haven't found him," returned the Captain after dismissing the men. "The only thing is that the guards are spreading the report that Chéri-Bibi is dead so as to prevent people on board losing their heads."

Pascaud expressed the opinion that it was the right thing to say to keep the convicts quiet.

"Have you discovered anything?" asked de Vilène.

The Sergeant shook his head.

"I can understand," he said, "how she escaped seeing there's a hole, but we ought to find out how Chéri-Bibi managed to get out. Now, you know, I've groped about everywhere. There's no communication between the two cells, not the slightest. Chéri-Bibi's cell is as solidly closed now as it was when he was in it. So what does it mean? It's a conjuring trick or witchcraft—you can't get away from that. . . ."

In Chéri-Bibi's cell they were once more confronted by the dead warders and the problem which they presented. And they were no further advanced in its solution. After throwing a net over the two bodies and leaving a couple of lanterns near them, like burning tapers in a mortuary chamber, the Captain and the Lieutenant went on deck. No one on the *Bayard* spoke of anything but the tremendous event: the death of Chéri-Bibi. He had been shot point blank in the hold in attempting to escape with the Kanaka's wife, an old offender. She was wounded; details were given.

She had defended herself like a lioness. The Countess, indeed, in the imagination of those on board, changed her animal personality according to circumstances; now she was a she-wolf for cruelty, now a tigress for ferocity, and now a lioness for courage.

It was chiefly among the government officials who were returning to their posts, and the warders' families, who all gathered together in the daytime in the after part of the vessel, on the poop, that gossip on board reached unending lengths. That day young women ceased to sing, and children to play, and Chéri-Bibi's name was on everyone's lips. The poop was, in general, the one cheerful spot in this floating citadel in which, everywhere else, one caught sight only of grilles, rifles, revolvers, and uniforms, and caps with more or less gold lace on them. The tidings of Chéri-Bibi's death were welcomed with special delight. So much had been said about the villain that the ladies were glad for themselves and for their husbands' sake that they were rid of him.

They were well acquainted with the convicts' little peculiarities, for they scrutinized them with curiosity when they came on deck, in batches, to breathe the sea air, and walk in a circle on the fore "quarter" under the perpetual menace of the rifles. They would not, to be sure, have mistaken the Top for Little Buddha, although both men were as round as tops and were dressed alike; and they "knew the facts" and the "antecedents" of each man. They were rather proud of traveling in the same ship with "notorious persons whose names had figured in all the newspapers." They exchanged views as to which man looked most to be feared or most to be pitied. The Toper and the Kanaka had for long excited their attention, which had now died away. Chéri-Bibi was the only man in whom their interest had not grown stale. But he was never to be seen.

Chéri-Bibi persistently declined "to take the promenade on deck," and showed such obstinacy that the guards had ended by leaving him alone. Chéri-Bibi spurned the Captain's favors. Chéri-Bibi remained lolling in his cage or cell, refusing to show himself. And now the gossips, notwithstanding the acute desire that had possessed them, would never see him. He was dead.

When the Captain and the Lieutenant crossed the deck to reach the chart-room, to visit the Navigating Officer, Sub-Lieutenant Kerrosgouët, the ladies would gladly have cheered them. But they, too, had some sense of discipline, and they kept silent. They would have liked to know what the men were saying below in the convict prisons—the cages were so called in official language—but the convicts were saying nothing at all. The silence was maintained.

And it was this strange silence that formed the subject of discussion between the Captain, the Lieutenant, the Navigating Officer, the Inspector, and the Overseer General in the chart-room where they met together to hold a council of war. Barrachon chose this spot in preference to any other because from its position he overlooked the entire ship, and could plainly see through the scuttles what was occurring on deck.

The Navigating Officer, the Inspector, and the Overseer General learnt the truth with alarm and dismay. Chéri-Bibi was not dead. Chéri-Bibi was free somewhere in the ship. It was too late that day to open the hatchways and the hatches over the hold, as the Captain suggested, and send all the available guards and armed sailors below, so as to engage in a swift and general chase which could not fail, in the end, to produce a satisfactory result. The plan would be put into operation, at the earliest hour, the next day. Meanwhile they decided that during the night sentries should guard every entrance, every ladder, every passage, even those which led to the passengers' and officers' berths, and that fifty warders, revolver in hand, should pace up and down outside the cages on the lower and upper gun decks until morning.

"If there are any convicts who doubt Chéri-Bibi's death, these measures will keep them quiet," observed the young Kerrosgouët.

"Oh, we can't teach them anything!" declared the inspector. "They know all that there is to know now, simply because they know all that goes on before we do. In my opinion, they're waiting in silence for something to happen; something that we know nothing about."

"They give me the same impression," agreed the Overseer General. "I've never seen them like this before. They are acting in the cages in accordance with some prearranged signal. One would think that they were afraid of producing an outburst before they are ready for this thing that we know nothing about."

"What can they do?" asked de Vilène. "We should shoot them down like rabbits."

"It would give us a lot of trouble afterwards," interposed the Inspector.

"Well, Monsieur, it would certainly have been more to the point if a better watch had been kept on them before now," muttered Barrachon.

Without mentioning Pascaud, the Captain revealed the trick of the correspondence that was carried on between these delightful people in which sailors, women, and love were intermingled. He was glad to put before him the case of Francesco of Porto Vecchio, caught in the act.

"Oh, we shall never prevent them from writing to women," said the Inspector, whose face became scarlet under the reproof. "I don't know how they manage it. They haven't any ink or pen or paper or anything. Moreover, they are searched again and again. . . . And that doesn't prevent them from writing . . . and nothing prevents them from buying bottles of rum! We saw that only a few hours ago. . . . This is not the first time, Captain, that I have been utterly nonplussed. You don't know how Chéri-Bibi got out, and I don't know how the bottles of rum got in! See! . . . Watch them now, they look as if butter wouldn't melt in their mouths!"

He pointed through the scuttles to a few convicts whose turn it was to take the air and who were dolefully promenading the deck.

As it happened the Toper, the Kanaka, Little Buddha, and Carrots were together. During the few minutes in which they were permitted to stretch themselves on deck under the watchful eyes of the guards, they at first yawned enough to put their jaws out of joint, and then talked "philosophy." Were they conscious that the guards were listening to every word they said? The news of Chéri-Bibi's death, which had been cried aloud by the guards from deck to deck, could not have left them so utterly indifferent; and yet the Kanaka said in a casual tone:

"How sad it must have been for our poor Chéri-Bibi to die without seeing the penal settlement again. He was mentioning it to me only a few days ago, and spoke of the delight it would be to him to visit once more the land where for the first time in his life he enjoyed a little rest."

"If he were as happy as all that," said Carrots, "I don't see why he left it."

"It was gold that did it," explained the Kanaka. "He told me about it, and I'll give you the story, because, after all, it will put a little pluck into those who are fond of the precious metal. It appears that at Guiana there's a gold mine, the existence of which is known only to the prisoners. The Government has done its utmost to discover it, but don't they wish they may get it! Meanwhile the old offenders work the mine in common. Each man slips away in turn, goes and works at the mine, comes back with the gold, and stands treat to the whole community.  Of course when the man returns he can't avoid a few days in prison.  But what does that matter if he is rich?  Well, one day Chéri-Bibi came back very rich; so rich that he was able to buy a small boat and the consciences of a couple of warders.  In this way he reached Maroni river, and managed to return to France, where, he said, he found things deadly dull.  He wanted to become an honest man, and he couldn't do it!  And then he'd spent all his money.  So he worked to be sent back to his pals again.  But it's all over.  He'll never see them any more.  Poor Chéri-Bibi!"

The others took up the refrain and sighed:

"Poor Chéri-Bibi!"

"What poor devils we all are!" broke in Little Buddha after a moment's silence which was apparently devoted to the dead man's memory.  "He was in the prime of life."

"As strong as a lion," suggested the Toper.

"As strong as a lion.  And yet he didn't know how to control his temperament."

"We are all at the mercy of our temperaments," said the Kanaka, the ex-trader in dead bodies, in the manner of a lecturer.  "You, the Toper, you suffer from irritability.  That's the temperament which is characteristic of dangerous and caustic persons who do great things in the world.  Your works have been crimes, but you are not to blame for them.  You can say that from me to the Great Judge when the time comes for you to give an account of yourself. You, Little Buddha, you suffer from sluggishness; in other words, you were born lazy and a pessimist. There's no hope for you, poor boy, with such bad luck, for you know as well as I do that idleness is the mother of all the vices. As to Carrots, he is of a sanguine temperament; he has strong, fiery, impulsive passions, and a temper hard to subdue. And, in fact, there's only one thing that is in his favor, and that's his bad character."

"How well he can hold forth," observed Carrots. "But, I say, my dear old medicine man, have you heard the latest? They say that the Countess has bolted with the 'boss.'"

"If it pleases him I've no objection," returned the Kanaka unconcernedly. "There's been a coldness between madame and myself for some time."

At this moment the Toper was lying at full length on the deck, seemingly dozing off into a sleep; but his hand was under his cap, which had been flung down beside him, and he was taking a deal of trouble to slip a tiny note, that did not take up more room than a postage stamp, into a crevice between two battens of the deck. When the operation was completed, he rose to his feet in the most natural manner; for the convicts were returning to the lower decks, urged forward by the guards, who drove them before them like cattle.

The men were extraordinarily docile, notwithstanding the hard words, and still harder blows from the butt-ends of revolvers, which they received from the warders. Little Buddha became quite poetic. He said to a young chick that stretched out its beak between the bars of the hen-coop:

"You are very fortunate, for you can see the sunrise every day!"

"Try to continue to do so!" the Kanaka thought it well to add.

And when on their way below, the ex-doctor and the ex-clerk to a sheriff's officer treated each other with elaborate courtesy with their "After you," they each received a kick which accelerated their movements.

"That's to help you to come to an agreement!" said the warder, thrusting his revolver in their faces, for they turned round furious at so gross an insult. "Well, what's the matter?" said the warder. "Do you want to send me your seconds?"

The entire batch of men burst into laughter.

"You see how nicely they behave now that Chéri-Bibi is dead," said a warder. And he slammed the door of the cage with a bang on Little Buddha's fingers. Little Buddha, swelling with pleasure, eyes upturned, had cleverly taken away his hand; but only just in the nick of time!

"Another day, dear friend," said Little Buddha

to the guards. "Good night, dear friend. Pleasant dreams!"

He hung up his hammock, begging his neighbor not to "give him the hold," which was an expression used to describe the trick of unfastening the hammock so that the sleeper should fall to the deck—for he wanted to see the brightness of the morrow in good health.

Meanwhile an event of some interest was happening on deck at the very spot which the convicts had just left. The Navigating Officer, M. de Kerrosgouët, was walking with a reflective air round the hen-coops and the cattle-pens, now raising his eyes aloft studying the weather, and then letting his gaze stray to his feet in the attitude of a man in deep thought. A light breeze was still blowing, although, unfortunately, it came from the northwest, but that was a detail which was hardly likely to cause the officer any concern. So why was he there? He ought to have been in the chart-room. Suddenly his preoccupation seemed to vanish; he pulled himself up in his walk, and quickly, casually, after stopping a moment at the sight of some sailors slaughtering an ox which had negligently broken a couple of its legs during the rough weather, he returned to the chart-room which his superior officers had not left, for they had been watching his various movements through the scuttles.

"Well?" said the Captain.

"It's done. I was right. The man called the Toper slipped a piece of paper between two battens."

"Why didn't you bring it to us?"

"Because we can always get it from the person who comes to fetch it."

"Exactly," agreed the Lieutenant. "Let's break up, and let each man go on his business as if Chéri-Bibi was in his cell, or if there were no such person."

"I will stay at my post to see the last act of the farce," said Kerrosgouët.

But as they were about to separate their attention was attracted by the vision of a newcomer who was walking the deck with a thoughtful expression, as Kerrosgouët had done a moment before, and was now and again looking about as if in search of something. Their astonishment knew no bounds, for the newcomer wore a cornette, the large white cornette with turned back wings of the Sisters of St. Vincent de Paul, and under this white cornette they could distinguish the pale, sad, gentle and innocent face of Sister St. Mary of the Angels.

This sister of mercy, whom the Government had permitted to sail for Cayenne where Sister St. Mary had courageously asked to serve in the hospital so as to be near the most miserable among men, was admired by everyone on board—crew, passengers, convicts.

Her lovable disposition, in spite of a touch of sadness which never left her, the frequent little services which she rendered the wives and families of the warders, her solicitation with the authorities on behalf of convicts who were at death's door from heat or hunger or thirst in the cells or cages, not less than her gracious beauty, quickly made her popular. Nevertheless when Sister St. Mary failed to soften the rigidity of the discipline on board, she was the first to submit to its necessity, however hard it might be for the miserable wretches whom this saintly girl so greatly pitied. Could it be possible that in these circumstances the virtuous St. Mary of the Angels had secretly entered into correspondence with a man of the loathsome character of the Toper, and this, too, at a moment when it had become essential to exercise a greater measure of severity with the convicts?

The idea was so utterly inconceivable that the officers would not have believed it had they not witnessed the incident with their own eyes.

The nun, after a last glance round her on this deserted part of the deck, stooped quickly, pretending to pick up some object which had dropped from her wide sleeves. Now those sleeves, like the Toper's cap, remained a sufficient time on the deck to enable the small hands underneath them to move freely.

Sister St. Mary had never walked so quickly, but was no longer of the beautiful pallor which gave her, under her white cornette, so much charm; a color suffused her cheeks. She made sure that no one had seen her stoop, and she went off, gliding over the deck with a fleetness which seemed still further to be assisted by the fluttering white wings of her cornette.

Nevertheless she was obliged for a moment to turn round, for she heard footsteps behind her. She recognized the Captain, bowed to him, and hurriedly went on her way.

Sister St. Mary had never walked so quickly, but the footsteps followed close behind her. Thus she reached her cabin, which was in the after part of the vessel, somewhat out of breath. She opened the door, and without turning round, tried to close it, but a hand interposed and a voice said:

"I beg your pardon, Sister."

The nun once more changed color. She was now ghastly white. She stared at the Captain haggard-eyed, and could scarcely stammer:

"What do you want me for?"

"I want the letter that you picked up on deck."

"I didn't . . . I didn't pick anything up," she said, almost fainting. "I assure you, Captain, that I don't know what you mean."

"Yes, you do, Sister, and I am shocked to hear you tell such a falsehood."

She drew back as if she intended to shut the door. . . . The Captain advanced a step.

"Heavens!" she cried. "You're not coming in here."

"Not if you give me the letter."

She drew back still farther, and owing to the size of her sleeves the Captain could not see what she was doing with her hands. Then he made up his mind. He boldly went into the cabin, leaving the door open.

The nun leant against the wall to prevent herself from falling.

"Listen to me," said the Captain. "Unless you do as I tell you, and give me that note written by a convict, I shall be compelled to order a Sister to take it from you by force."

She did not reply. The Captain went on:

"You don't want me to do that, I presume? But what is it you do want, after all, by communicating in this way with convicts without our consent and in spite of us? Do you know that it is a terrible offense which might bring down on you the most disastrous consequences?"

Her eyes, which at first flashed in anger, now became soft again.

"I know what I owe to your character, to the mission to which you have devoted yourself . . . but, Sister St. Mary, you must understand that there are certain things that I cannot allow. I must not, I will not, for instance, admit that breaches of discipline may be made under the guise of charity. . . . Why are you so obstinate? Be careful! . . . I may soon find myself compelled to believe that there is in this something more than an indiscretion due to your zeal as a Christian. . . . For, after all, you told me a lie. . . . Let us call things by their proper names . . .

and since you lied to me, you must have had some serious motive for doing so. . . . Give me the letter."

"I haven't got it. I . . . I haven't got it. . . . Monsieur, please . . . take my word . . . and leave me."

She fell inert at his feet. Her knees sharply struck the deck. But the Captain was in no mood to pity her.

"You are covering up your hands. Show me your hands. Can't you understand that your attitude gives me every reason to suspect the worst? During the last few days we have been trying to discover how it is that the convicts know everything that happens on board, every step that we take against them, to insure our common safety. We are trying to find how they communicate with one another from cage to cage, from deck to deck, and manage in this way to plan some mysterious plot, the nature of which we do not know but the menace of which we feel. . . . Who tells them what they want to know? . . . Who is their tool? . . . Is it, by chance, you, Sister St. Mary of the Angels? . . . Oh, unconsciously, I wish to believe, and so that I may believe it, I must have that paper."

He suddenly caught hold of her hands and snatched it from her.

It was an insignificant scrap of paper on which was written simply:

"Chéri-Bibi is not dead."

The Captain, more amazed than he could say, read

the short sentence out loud. The Sister heaved a sigh, and collapsed on the floor of her cabin in a dead faint.

"What can Chéri-Bibi have to do with her?" he said to himself. "It's most extraordinary."

He called the women, who came hurrying in and set about trying to bring Sister St. Mary to herself. In distracted tones they asked the Captain what had happened to the Sister, but he went away, completely absorbed in thought, without making any reply.

Chéri-Bibi was not dead. Everyone on board knew it now. , Everyone was fully aware of the frightful tragedy that had taken place, and when during the evening a funeral stretcher, over which a sheet had been thrown, was brought up from the lower deck, everyone knew what was underneath it. Moreover, the two murdered warders had wives and children, and no attempt was made to hide the calamity from them any longer, and the sound of their moans and their cries of despair soon reached the little colony of warders' families.

Curses were uttered against Chéri-Bibi, and a feeling of terror seized everyone. The darkness of the night increased the apprehension. Those who could, locked themselves in their cabins, but no one slept, and men and women stood by their weapons until daylight.

Where was the ruffian? If he could vanish in this way it was reasonable to suppose that he could appear at will.   Everything was possible to him.   He was dreaded as though he were some specter for whom natural and human laws did not exist, and who could prowl about everywhere without encountering the obstacles which would stand in the way of other living persons.

The sailors themselves were not more easy in their minds.  At their stations, and in their mess, they talked of nothing but the amazing prisoner who had managed to break loose from his irons.   Their super-stitious instincts, for many of them were Bretons, had full play, and since it was impossible to explain his escape in any "Christian" way, it was obvious that he was in league with the devil.

It was no use doubling the guards and placing sen-tries on every hand, for the men feared that he might at any moment take it into his head to commit some fresh murder and to disappear once more.   Chéri-Bibi represented evil itself stalking on earth; and here he was roaming freely about the *Bayard* with the woman of the fiery black eyes.

A door opened and each one turned round with a look of fear, the conversation was hushed, and they held their breath.  And then a sigh of relief went up from every breast.   It was the Dodger who was bring-ing in the food.

The Dodger was, moreover, the most "funky" of all.   He made his friends go with him to the lower decks armed to the teeth, and told stories that were enough to make the bravest shudder. He thought he saw Chéri-Bibi everywhere, and he cried out like a child at his own shadow which the light of a lantern suddenly threw out before him. He arrived, out of breath, dropped on to a seat, and placed his hand upon his fast-beating heart.

"Oh, my boys . . . my boys . . . I'm certain it was he . . . I recognized his eyes . . . there, just now, on deck, and then he was gone. . . . Whosh! . . . he disappeared. . . ."

On deck the men were far from being comfortable. Those who were on duty or formed the night watch saw Chéri-Bibi in the most natural shapes which loomed in the cloudless night in the corners of ladders, the poop decks, the gangways and even under the davits of the boats. Some old sailors, carried away by the excitement of their own fears, spent their watch telling startling ghost stories. . . . The shadow of the phantom vessel was dancing in the sea, and the shadow of the *Flying Dutchman* sped under the moon.

And only in the cells did men sleep in absolute peace and quietness.

The *Bayard* was then in Latitude 32.20° north and Longitude 24.50° west of the meridian of Paris. She had passed Madeira and the Peak of Teneriffe on her port quarter, and, leaving the African shores behind, was heading straight across the Atlantic.

# CHAPTER IV

THAT Chéri-Bibi had found accomplices on board, the Captain was bound to acknowledge, but that Sister St. Mary of the Angels should be involved in the criminal's escape was beyond his comprehension. Though this last point was one which greatly harassed him, he had no intention of wasting time by investigating it at that moment.

The main thing, to begin with, was to recapture the scoundrel, alive or dead, come what may, and he would afterwards endeavor "to explain the inexplicable." In order to carry out his project, Barrachon determined to "turn everything upside down in the old tub."

There is no need to describe in detail an undertaking which was without result. It was in vain that they searched and inspected the vessel from mast to keel, and that numbers of armed military overseers and sailors crowded into the hold with, as it were, the courage of despair and thirsting for revenge. Nothing was discovered.

The main bilge-well itself was entirely emptied. It was hoped, in the end, that the scoundrel and the terrible woman who was with him in his mad adventure were drowned, but unfortunately the searchers were soon undeceived. A plucky cabin boy, who made the dangerous venture of entering the well, came back without having seen the least thing. Chéri-Bibi and the Countess could not be found.

"I will have the coal bunkers cleared. I will have the hold cleared, and all the goods turned out and put back again. I swear that we'll find him," shouted the Captain, who had lost all his pleasantness of manner. He renewed his oath over the bodies of the hapless warders, which were "thrown to the sharks" in a sack after a moving religious service at which all on board mingled their prayers and tears, save Sister St. Mary of the Angels, who did not put in an appearance.

At lunch, after this sad ceremony, when the principal persons on board were brought together under the Captain's presidency, the Sister's absence was mentioned, and the warrant officers who were present the night before, and witnessed the little scene from the chart-room, which overlooked the deck, expressed their astonishment.

The Captain did not tell them of his interview with Sister St. Mary, and he kept the Toper's writing to himself, attributing the nun's absence from the service to her indisposition. Sister St. Mary's attitude, however, perplexed him as much as anyone, but he determined not to let it be seen, for he considered that

quite enough mysteries were being talked about on
board.

And then he intended, after lunch, to visit and question the nun once more, and he believed that this time
he would succeed in "pumping" her. Fully resolved
to spare no one, and perturbed by the responsibility
that he would incur if he failed to capture Chéri-Bibi,
he replied to the questions which one and the other
put to him by grunts.

He wondered why the Lieutenant had not yet joined
him at table. He was told that the officer must have
been detained in the execution of his duty. . . . Afterwards there was a depressing silence; for the
thoughts of all of them were centered on Chéri-Bibi
and the Countess.

"The end of it will be that they'll both die of hunger
and thirst if they don't show themselves," groaned the
Overseer General.

"I don't think so!" said the Inspector. "If they
are in any of the holds they'll find a way of getting
some sort of food. There are provisions in the holds,
nice things. In my opinion they have enough friends
on board to be able to get water."

"Then such men will suffer for it," declared Barrachon. "Whoever they are, they must know that
they'll be shot at the same time as Chéri-Bibi. Any
man who assists the scoundrel in the slightest degree
will be served like him."

"What about the woman if we find her?   Will she be shot, Captain?"

"Do you imagine that I shall stand on ceremony? Shot or hanged, they will not escape punishment. But where is M. de Vilène?   Has anything fresh happened?   De Kerrosgouët, go and see."

The Sub-Lieutenant left the table, and returned in a few minutes.   He had not seen the Lieutenant, but had been told that he was below in the cages.

"He is no doubt devoting himself to a supplementary inspection," said Barrachon.   "Perhaps he is having the kit bags ransacked.   He's got that affair of the bottles of rum on the brain.   He was speaking to me about it again this morning, and said he wouldn't feel quite easy until he had cleared things up."

De Kerrosgouët sat down again.   The dishes were passed round, but once more the conversation languished.

At dessert the Captain broke a glass while emphasizing that Chéri-Bibi must be somewhere or other. His opinion was shared by the company.   Nevertheless the Overseer General said:

"Of course he is somewhere, but perhaps after all he is not on board."

And he diffidently put forward the theory that the awful couple had left the *Bayard*.

"What do you mean?" asked Barrachon with a

shrug of his shoulders. "None of the boats are missing. . . . And we should have seen them."

"They may simply have thrown themselves into the
sea."

"But how?" Barrachon burst out again. "It would
be known. Every means of egress below is barred,
and if they had come up on deck we might, perhaps,
with all the wealth of sentries on the watch, have seen
them! . . . Absurd! Let's argue the thing out, but
let's talk sense."

The Overseer General apologized, but he made the
mistake of adding:

"It's a great pity."

"What's a great pity?" asked the Captain in a tone
which became more and more abrupt.

"Well . . . it's a pity that they haven't left the
ship. It would have been a good riddance."

The Captain gave a start.

"You think so, do you? Well, allow me to tell
you that you have a strange notion of your duty. As
far as I am concerned, Chéri-Bibi was confided to my
care. If I don't see him again, living or dead, I know
what the alternative for me will be."

The Captain spoke in such a tone that the others
were very disagreeably impressed. They shivered to
the very marrow. They already saw, in imagination,
the worthy Barrachon blowing his brains out. And
what endless trouble for them afterwards! What a

terrible responsibility! They would not forget No. 3216 in a hurry!

Meanwhile the Lieutenant was still absent. When coffee was served Barrachon was in a state of alarm and at the end of his endurance. He left the mess to look for the Lieutenant himself. De Vilène might have discovered something fresh.

But the Captain's anxiety only became deeper after he had searched the upper and lower decks. He could not find de Vilène anywhere. And no one had seen him for more than an hour. Some of them thought that they noticed him going below to the cages, but the convict guards stated that he had not visited them.

When the officers joined him the Captain was in an agony of suspense. Every man set to work and the search proceeded with greater energy than ever. Nothing was found in de Vilène's cabin which could put them on the track. The crew were now fully aware of his strange disappearance, and men as well as officers endeavored to probe the mystery. They shouted the Lieutenant's name throughout the ship. It might be that he had been taken ill. It might be that he had suddenly met Chéri-Bibi and was killed.

After vainly searching for him living they sought to find his dead body.

But they were unable to find him living or dead. And a general consternation swept through the ship.

Then every man on board, from the passengers to the least important merchant, was seized with a peculiar agitation which originated in fear and reached its climax in frenzy.

Literally they became desperate. And no wonder! The Captain had the work of the world to keep the fury of these men within bounds, for, without the least excuse, they wanted to break the heads of the old offenders. Revolvers were continually being pointed at them through the bars. Threats of death were uttered every moment, and yet the convicts had never behaved themselves so well. Even the Top had ceased his hateful chuckle, for he realized that if he laughed again it would be for the last time.

The Inspector and the Overseer General, overwhelmed by the Lieutenant's disappearance and wondering if their turn might not come soon, resolved to link up their duties and to work together.

A desire to be revenged on something or someone impelled them to ask the Captain to place the men in the cages on a "bread and water" diet, and to abolish the exercise on deck.

But Barrachon, who had been to his cabin to plunge his head into a basin of cold water, for he feared a stroke of apoplexy, came out with a gleam of sanity and refused to listen to any such dangerous measure.

Every revolver was taken out of its case. Even the women on the decks were armed, and no one went alone into the alley-ways although sentries were posted in them at specified intervals.

The new and appalling incident of the Lieutenant's

disappearance caused the Captain to forget for the moment the strange conduct of Sister St. Mary. But she herself was soon to remind him of her existence. It was an amazing thing, but this saintly girl who had not been seen during the whole day, even at the burial service, showed herself on deck, as on the day before, when the Toper's horrible gang was brought up.

Barrachon caught sight of her when she appeared, and stood watching her without letting himself be seen.

She reached the guards, dragging herself along by the port-hole, and here, leaning against the ship's side for support, she began to tell her beads. She seemed so weak that the Captain expected to see her collapse at any moment on the deck, as he had seen her, the day before, fall in an inert mass in her cabin.

She was of a death-like pallor, but her eyes were extraordinarily bright. She was praying, and her gaze was fixed on the Toper, who had just taken up the position of the day before and was apparently preparing to "post" his letter.

Thus Barrachon comprehended the object of which Sister St. Mary was on deck. She had come up to warn Chéri-Bibi's friend that he must put an end to the correspondence.

It was this message, to all appearance, that was expressed so eloquently by her eyes, her wide, beautiful flashing eyes. It was this that was indicated by the slight movement of her head from right to left and left to right, a telegraphic negative. No more letters must be slipped between the planks. And it was this that the Toper understood, for the ruffian scrambled to his feet when he saw the Sister, and placed his hand in his pocket.

Barrachon at once showed himself, and at a bound was at the side of the guards.

"Search that man," he cried, pointing to the convict. "At once . . . at once. . . . Seize him by the arms . . . seize him by the arms."

Two military overseers rushed at the Toper, but he quickly shook them off and was fumbling in his pocket for the paper, meaning to put it in his mouth.

"The paper . . . the paper, . . ." shouted the Captain. "Seize him by the arms."

The convict was of herculean strength, and clutching one warder by the throat and getting free from the other, swallowed the paper. The first guard was gasping for breath, and unable to carry out the Captain's orders.

"Fire . . . fire, man," he shouted.

The Captain himself leveled his revolver, but it was a guard who fired the shot straight at the Toper's heart.

Nevertheless the convict did not receive the bullet. Sister St. Mary of the Angels had thrown herself into the fray, and lifted her shaking arm towards the weapon which hurled forth death. The shot passed through the poor girl's hand and shoulder, and she sank in a huddled heap on the deck. The Toper, meantime, stood quietly with folded arms; and while Sister St. Mary was being carried off to the sick-bay, the Captain gave orders for him to be taken to the cells and put in irons. He was led away there and then. Barrachon, the Inspector, and the Overseer General went below to the lower deck with the procession of guards and their prisoner.

The Captain was determined to question the Toper at once, for he would be tried the next day by court martial, and undoubtedly shot for mutiny and attempted murder of a warder. It was the moment, if there ever was one, to make an example.

When they reached the alley-way in which the cells were situated, Sergeant Pascaud declared that there was but one cell available, since it would not do to put the Toper in the cell from which the Countess had escaped. The cavity had not yet been blocked up. The only remaining cell was that in which Chéri-Bibi had been placed in irons, and in which were found the bodies of the murdered warders. Barrachon gave orders for the cell door to be opened, and Pascaud opened it.

The guards on a sign from the Captain were preparing to put the Toper in irons, an operation to which he offered no resistance, when they started back, uttering an exclamation. They could see something there in the darkness; a figure was lying there. A man in irons was there.

The object could be seen only vaguely in the dim light, and the guards might have thought that Chéri-Bibi had miraculously returned. The Captain, the Inspector, and the Overseer General darted forward, and lanterns were brought nearer. There was a simultaneous cry: de Vilène!

Yes, the object that lay there was indeed no other than Lieutenant de Vilène, the second-in-command on board, and his feet and wrists were imprisoned in Chéri-Bibi's irons in place of Chéri-Bibi himself. . . . Moreover, the Lieutenant had assumed a dark hue and there was not the least sign of life about him. . . . A stout gag was bound over his mouth, nose and eyes.

The gag was at once removed, and men carried the Lieutenant into the alley-way and made him breathe; at least they endeavored to restore his breathing. For some moments it looked as if he were a dead man.

At length his breast heaved, and a deep sigh proclaimed that life had returned to his motionless body.

De Vilène gazed around him with a dazed look and said:

"Captain!"

His life was saved. But it was a narrow escape. He confessed as much.

"Oh, I thought it was all over with me," he said.

While they were lavishing attentions on the Lieutenant, to whom they gave a glass of rum brought by one of the guards, Barrachon went back to the cell, and the other officers followed him in order to verify the miracle once more.

The cell was still completely closed like a box, and it was impossible to conceive by what artifice a man could get out and another man get in without passing through the door. Barrachon vented his rage on the walls, which he struck with his fists without being able to solve the mystery. There was but one key of the padlock, and it was said to be the only key that would unlock Chéri-Bibi's irons.

Now Chéri-Bibi had divested himself of the irons and fixed the Lieutenant in them, and locked them afterwards without using the key. Sergeant Pascaud, who was absolutely bewildered and still more cast down than the Captain when he learnt of the escape of No. 3216, exclaimed:

"Upon my word, Captain, I've only once in my life seen anything to be compared with it. It was at the end of a performance by some jugglers in a café in my village. One of the men was shut up in a trunk, which was padlocked, bound with ropes, and sealed with red sealing wax by persons present. We took care to fasten the ropes ourselves in knots which we learnt how to tie from sailors. Well, a covering was thrown over the trunk, and the jugglers counted ten. When the covering was taken off our man was free, with nothing to hamper his movements, standing by the side of the trunk, which was still closed, tied firmly, sealed and padlocked. Do you know what I think? Chéri-Bibi may have been a conjurer at one time. He must know the tricks of all the trades, must that particular bird."

Meantime the Lieutenant was taken to his cabin, where the Captain joined him. He was ravenously hungry and thirsty, and food and drink were brought in. He was able to speak. And he told a story which was somewhat vague but extremely formidable, and gave those who were present food for thought regarding the extraordinary power of the diabolical Chéri-Bibi.

The incident happened in the morning immediately after the burial service. De Vilène, in common with the Captain and everyone else, was astonished that Sister St. Mary was not present during the reading of the prayers for the dead. Was she ill? He determined to make inquiries, and proceeded to the nun's cabin. He had nearly reached it, and was turning the corner by the canteen when he was seized from behind with incredible swiftness and violence.

He could not make a movement nor utter a cry. A gag was suffocating him, and at least four men— de Vilène estimated that his aggressors consisted of not less than four men—reduced him to helplessness. Tied up as though he were a bundle, and unable to grasp what was happening, he did not know where they were taking him, nor could he say, even approximately, where they placed him for the time being.

But he knew that they left him for a while to himself; and they even took the precaution to loosen slightly the gag which covered his nose so that he might not suffocate on the spot. Nevertheless, the place could not have been far from the cook's galley for the odor of cooking reached him. True, the decks were impregnated with this odor toward lunch time.

At length men came to fetch him. They carried him some distance; then they fastened a rope round him, and let him down into space. He wondered, for a moment, if his aggressors were not thus lowering him into the sea, intending to drown him quietly so that there might be no opportunity for anyone to come to his assistance. Soon, however, he reached a resting place. He struck against some hard surface. Here he was pushed along, then carried, and afterwards put down again, by persons who did not utter a word. More than once he was lifted over some obstacle to be let down again a few minutes later, and he imagined that he was in the hold. But in which hold? In which store-room? He was unable to say.

After several rough impacts—they didn't spare him, but treated him as though he were a bale of goods —they laid him on the planks, then on an iron bar, and slipped his feet and wrists into the fetters. He assumed that his enemies had decided to leave him there, in the hold, in irons, to die of hunger. A few minutes later his breathing failed him and he lost consciousness.

The story was an appalling one because though it furnished no indication as to Chéri-Bibi's hiding-place, it proved first that he was moving about the ship at will, and next that he had accomplices who were active and free, and whose numbers were unknown. It was this last consideration which was by far the most important, for it raised the question: whom could they trust in future?

The Captain remained alone with the Lieutenant and expressed to him the thoughts to which the tragic accident gave rise. But de Vilène was no longer concerned with the danger from which he had escaped. Like the Captain, he realized, above all, that they were surrounded by foes, and that their troubles were, perhaps, only beginning.

Newly embarked on an old vessel whose crew was gathered together at the last moment, with men and women passengers, clerks, and government officials, who for the most part had been sent to Cayenne because the metropolis had no further use for them, they did not know with whom they had to deal, and they had no inkling of the real mind of any of them.

Nevertheless they could trust the sailors and the chiefs of the military guard who had stood the test elsewhere, but was it not possible that some black sheep had crept into the flock unknown to them? It was much to be feared. Indeed it was certain that it was so.

De Vilène had been attacked by several men. He could vouch for it. What were those men? Anarchists perhaps, or pretended anarchists. . . . At all events they knew that under cover of the name those men were capable of anything and everything. It was they, undoubtedly, who had, for so long, helped Chéri-Bibi to evade the police, who had backed him up in his monstrous crimes, who had sworn to avenge him, and who on the very morning of his trial had blown up Ferdy's restaurant.

What might not be expected from such bandits who had declared a deadly war on society? They would stick at nothing. Some of them, doubtless, had sailed on the same vessel as Chéri-Bibi in order to rescue him, and this, too, with the assistance of the authorities who were the first to be duped, and whom these men played with at their own sweet will. Well, if this were so, it was war; it meant fighting. Barrachon and de Vilène were fighting men. They shook each other by the hand.

Cheered and strengthened by this demonstration, they stood silent for a while. A few minutes later they went on deck.

Apart from the men on duty and the military guards, who maintained an eager watch, the deck was deserted. Everyone had returned to his berth. The Toper's action and Sister St. Mary's wound, followed

by the amazing discovery of the Lieutenant in Chéri-
Bibi's irons—these things were discussed in all the
cabins with bated breath.

What was the mystery of the cell? What sort of
cell was it in which such demoniacal things could
happen? The ghostly figure of Chéri-Bibi seemed to
increase to enormous dimensions. And the general
terror was doubled by the growing feeling that anarchists were on board who were determined at any
cost to save the monster. Supposing that they fired
the ship? Supposing that they blew her up? Who
could prevent them? When the passengers heard the
least commotion behind the doors, how eager they
were to explain it away! When they heard footsteps
in the alley-way, how intensely they wished them to
move on! Two nights had passed without sleep. If
the Captain were wise he would at once return to
Europe . . . that was certain . . . quickly. . . .
What a voyage it was!

# CHAPTER V

## THE ATTACK ON THE STORE-ROOM

In the early morning of the next day, the *Bayard's* quarter-deck was swarming with women, and children huddled on their mothers' laps. The women and children had taken refuge there. They thought that there would be less fear of a surprise than in the lower decks and gangways, where they trembled with fear. Moreover, a great piece of news formed the subject of conversation. It was stated that Sister St. Mary of the Angels was working hand in glove with Chéri-Bibi. That, of course, beat everything they thought.

They knew now why and how the nun was wounded. She was acting as the convict's go-between. And it was at the moment when she was about to receive a letter from the Toper that a bullet struck her in the shoulder. If this were true, she richly deserved her fate. For, after all, she could not be a real Sister of Mercy. She was probably a girl anarchist who had assumed the dress of a nun in order to be near Chéri-Bibi, and had been entrusted by his friends with the work of rescuing him. She had "caught it." It was a case, if ever there was one, in which to say: "Serve her right."

Thus matters stood on the quarter-deck when Madame Pascaud, the wife of Sergeant Pascaud, appeared. She was out of breath, and obviously had something important to say, for, try as she might, her excitement prevented her from finding utterance. At last she quietened down and blurted out what she wished to say:

"Do you know . . . she's his sister."

At first they did not understand her. They asked her to repeat her words and to explain her meaning. Of whom was she speaking? Of Sister St. Mary of the Angels!

"Well, she is the sister of . . ."

"Chéri-Bibi!"

The amazement was general. And then doubts arose.

"Are you certain?"

"She told the Captain so herself. She thinks she's going to die. So she told the truth!"

"Oh, the poor thing!"

A deep pity was in them; and they did not doubt that she was an innocent victim whose sole offense was to have such a brother.

Madame Pascaud, conscious of the importance of the moment, entered into details.

"Of course there's nothing against her except carelessness, as the Captain told her when he freely forgave her. She came to minister to convicts because, as she said, her patron Saint Vincent de Paul used to

minister among convicts.  Pascaud heard every word.
It seems that what happened brought tears to his eyes.
She applied to be sent to Cayenne because she wanted
to convert her brother.  Convert Chéri-Bibi!  She was
a little over-confident.  She wanted him to pray to the
Almighty to pardon him for his crimes.  After that
she would die happy, she said.  The reason why she
kept secret the fact that she was his sister was because
she felt convinced that she wouldn't be allowed to stay
with him, and that the Government would forbid her
to go to Cayenne, because they'd believe that she was
there to help him to escape.  Say what you like, she's
a good girl who has the proper family instinct.  But
she's been badly repaid."

The gossips pricked up their ears to listen to Madame Pascaud, and they were about to resume their
praise of the nun with the secret hope that she might
protect them from her brother, when there was a
considerable stir on deck.

A procession was approaching consisting of the
principal officers of the ship with the Captain at their
head.  They were formed up round a stretcher carried
by four sailors, and upon the stretcher lay Chéri-
Bibi's sister, whose name, in religion, was Sister St.
Mary of the Angels.

Her transparent face was as white as the sheet
which covered her.  She held in her bloodless hands
a great crucifix which rested upon her breast and
seemed already to be keeping vigil over the dead.

Nevertheless Sister St. Mary's eyes shone with incomparable brightness and her lips were moving as if in prayer.

Behind the group, which was on its way to the cages, marched a number of sailors and a considerable portion of the staff. In a moment the quarter-deck was cleared. The women hastened to obtain the latest news, and they learnt that Sister St. Mary had expressed to the Captain the wish to be carried from hold to hold before she died, so that she might call her brother and summon him to surrender to the justice of man to which he belonged, ere he appeared before the justice of God.

The Captain promised that if Chéri-Bibi surrendered when his sister appealed to him, the life of the savage Toper should be spared.

"Well, if that's all the Captain is relying on to induce Chéri-Bibi to give in . . ." said one of the women.

"He is quite right to make the attempt," replied Madame Pascaud. "The sister considers that she was responsible for the Toper's mutiny, and she doesn't want him to be shot to-morrow, you may be sure."

"No; she would like to go straight to Paradise, poor girl, without having anything to reproach herself with. She's a saint."

The stretcher was taken down to the lower deck and the convicts could see through the bars of their cages

the white vision as it passed. When they recognized
Sister St. Mary of the Angels, they took off their caps,
and a few of them, who had not entirely lost all sense
of religion, made the sign of the Cross.

They reached the lower berth deck and opened
the hatch leading to the hold into which it was
supposed that Chéri-Bibi had escaped when he left
his cell. A great silence fell around the stretcher
illuminated by the lanterns carried by the sailors,
and Sister St. Mary of the Angels raised her voice.
It was an exceptionally powerful voice. She must
have summoned up her entire strength in this supreme
effort.

"Chéri-Bibi!" she cried. "Chéri-Bibi, it's I,
your sister, who calls you. Have pity on me, Chéri-
Bibi, I'm dying. You know how much I loved you
when you were a little child. Chéri-Bibi, I still love
you. Heaven will forgive you. In Heaven's name I
call upon you to surrender and die with me. Chéri-
Bibi! . . . Chéri-Bibi! . . ."

Her voice died away, and they listened for the least
sound to ascend from the silence of the hold. But
there was no movement and no answer in the darkness.

At the end of a few moments the nun cried:

"If I die before you, Chéri-Bibi, you know that
I forgive you."

And as there was still no response she motioned to
them to take her away. The hatches were opened in

succession—the magazine, the cordage, the cargo, the baggage holds—all of them. They visited every part of the ship, and the nun's voice was raised above the dark cavities calling her brother, but her brother did not answer. And the procession returned to the sick-bay, and Sister St. Mary went back to bed in the operating room.

She asked that no operation should be performed on her because she wanted to die, and then she realized that since the doctor maintained that he could save her life, it was her duty to allow him to have his way. She was destined still to suffer here on earth. She submitted to the inevitable.

Nevertheless it was with the Captain's support, but in spite of the doctor's warning, that she had attempted to appeal to the memories of a brother whom she had tenderly loved, but to no purpose. She was now in a burning fever, and the extraction of the bullet had to be postponed.

The Captain held her hand and she wept. Above the little iron bedstead was hung the placard which she took with her wherever she went, and which was her only article of personal property. It contained these words:

*"For a convent they have the houses of the sick, for a cell the room that charity lends them, for a chapel their parish church, for a cloister the poor house, for seclusion the duty of obedience, for iron bars the fear of God, and for a veil a saintly modesty."*

Although she was forbidden to speak she murmured in her tears:

"He did not answer me, he did not come to me, he has forgotten the sound of my voice. It was I who gave him the name of Chéri-Bibi when he was quite young. It was the name which I chose out of my love for him. Alas! What has he made of it? . . ."

Her grief seemed to know no bounds. Her eyes, raised to heaven, were bedewed with tears.

"Oh God, I am the cause of his misfortune. . . . Forgive me. . . . Forgive him."

A few moments later she said in a still fainter tone:

"Oh, I did think that when he heard my voice he would come. . . ."

At that moment a great commotion arose in the alley-way.

"Captain. . . . Captain. . . . It's Chéri-Bibi! . . . It's Chéri-Bibi!"

"Oh, I knew he would come," she cried, and she clasped her hands, transfixed.

The Captain made a dash outside. A terrible tragedy was being enacted near the galleys. Chéri-Bibi had, indeed, appeared in an alley-way for the space of a second, and a sentry fired on him. Of course he missed him. With one bound Chéri-Bibi took refuge in the mess store-room, and was firing on everyone who attempted to come near him. The fight had all the appearance of a regular siege.

The sound of firing could be heard from the upper deck and from the direction of the galleys.

The mess store-room, as it was called on the *Bayard,* was a somewhat roomy pantry, between the two galleys, in which the provisions intended for the daily consumption of crew, passengers and convicts were stored. The main store-room was in the fore part below the third deck. The mess store-room led into one of the galleys only, but it was the largest and used for the convicts, and it contained hardly anything but three immense boilers, which were, in fact, receptacles, as deep as vats and large enough to hold an entire regiment's washing, in which the convicts' soup was made. This "bare" galley was managed by the Dodger, a journeyman baker who had been promoted in an emergency to the rank of cook, while the real chief cook lorded it in the officers' galley. The galleys were situated nearly amidships between the two funnels. They could be reached almost direct from the upper deck by stairways called "ladders," and one could go up to them very quickly by iron steps which led from the deck where the Captain and his little group were standing.

When the Captain arrived at the bottom of the ladder men shouted to him to get out of the way quickly for the ladder faced the outer door of the mess store-room. It was wide open, and

Chéri-Bibi, who was right at the back and could not be seen, was shooting straight down into the lower deck.

De Kerrosgouët, revolver in hand, and de Vilène stood on the upper side ladders conducting the attack which, up to then, presented great difficulties.

Two military overseers who went too near the galley door were shot; one man in the leg and the other in the hand.

Thus Chéri-Bibi was rushing from one room to the other according to the necessities of his defense, and was ready to fire even before there was time to take aim at him, for he did not allow anyone to set foot in the hatchway in front of him.

How did he get there? How was he discovered? The story went that it was the Dodger who raised the alarm. The Lieutenant was on the point of entering the mess store-room when he stumbled against the Dodger, who was coming out, shouting:

"Don't go in! I've seen something move under the vegetables."

By an extraordinary chance the Lieutenant was unarmed. He called the two guards who were passing and they opened the store-room door without encountering any resistance; but as soon as the door was opened, the ruffian inside fired two revolvers simultaneously, and both guards had to make for the ladders.

De Vilène was in time to catch a glimpse of a

demoniacal figure which sprang from the mess store-room to the galley. He recognized it. It was Chéri-Bibi.

"Now we've got him!" he shouted with delight. "Fetch the Captain."

As a matter of fact it seemed impossible for Chéri-Bibi to escape. The cook's mates had slipped out of the galleys and fled, leaving the field entirely in the scoundrel's possession; but what could he do? The guards came hurrying up from all quarters. Doubtless a great deal of damage would be caused, but he was trapped! . . . he was trapped! Passengers and even women showed themselves on the companion-ways which were not under the enemy's fire and shouted: "Shoot him! . . . Shoot him!"

Chéri-Bibi, feeling at that moment that the guards would risk everything to effect an entrance into one of the two rooms, galley or store-room, and thus take him between two fires, managed swiftly to close the galley door and to get back to the store-room when the Captain, leading half a dozen men, rushed in.

He fired.

Three men fell to the ground, impeding the onrush of the others.

The remarkable thing was that although a hot fire was directed against the convict, he did not seem in the slightest degree inconvenienced by it. True, they were firing at haphazard at a shadow which appeared and disappeared with amazing rapidity.

The Captain ordered de Vilène and de Kerrosgouët to remain in their positions, and to guard the ladders against any desperate attempt at flight in that direction.

A deafening clamor surged up from every part of the ship. The convicts below sang and shouted:

"Cheerily, Chéri-Bibi! . . . Cheerily!"
*Who blows the blooming lot UP?*
*Sing ho for Chéri-Bibi. . . . Chéri-Bibi.*

And the warders behind the Captain wavered.

Barrachon determined to bring matters to a climax whatever happened. He dashed ahead, exposing himself to the enemy's fire, and he would inevitably have been laid low if a form, all white, like a wan ghost, had not come between and shielded him.

Sister St. Mary! . . .

Yes, it was she who had risen from her bed in spite of her weakness, and hurried to meet the shouts and the shot. Had she not called Chéri-Bibi? Well, he had answered the appeal. But his hand was still dealing out death. . . . And blood was being shed in streams around him.

She walked in front of the Captain, but with so light a tread that it looked as if her feet under her long drapery scarcely touched the deck. . . . She was a saint. . . . But she said in her gentle voice, which was growing still weaker:

"Here I am, Chéri-Bibi. . . . Don't you recognize

me? . . . Here I am. . . . If you must kill someone, kill me. . . . Kill me, my brother in Jesus Christ. . . ."

But no shot was fired, and as she moved forward, followed by the Captain and his men, they all entered the store-room.

Chéri-Bibi was no longer there!

He had closed the door between the two rooms, and was now in the convicts' galley.

It was his last resource.

The men were already trying the door. It was here that the quarry would be found. Sister St. Mary implored the wretch to give himself up and not to make any more victims.

"You've done enough killing," she cried. "Chéri-Bibi, have pity on us. Have pity on me. I've come to die with you. . . ."

They had to take her away before they could break down the door. There was a whirlwind rush into the galley. . . .

It was empty.

Smoke was escaping from the three great soup boilers, and he, too, like smoke, had escaped.

Once more the question arose how did he get away? The galley did not lead into any room—except the store-room from which they had just come. There were no scuttles looking on to the sea. Light penetrated from the great upper-deck skylights, which were riddled with bullets, and it was impossible for a man to force his way through them owing to the iron sashes. And, moreover, guards were on the lookout for him on deck.

Where was he?

Suddenly the Dodger's voice was heard shouting:

"This way! . . . This way! . . . There he is! . . . There he is!"

In a twinkling galley and store-room were cleared, and everyone followed the Dodger, who ran like one possessed along the alley-ways, rushed into a stair-way, scrambled down, fell his length on the deck, and looking up exclaimed to those who were around him:

"I saw him. . . . Oh, I saw him. . . . Look, he vanished through there. . . . Sure enough, he's the very devil."

# CHAPTER VI

## CHÉRI-BIBI

THE signalman had struck the eight bells of midnight when Captain Barrachon returned to his cabin. He sat down at his desk, and prepared to resume, at the point at which he had left off, the special report of the exceptional incidents which had occurred during a remarkable voyage. He had come from the sick-bay, where he had been visiting the guards disabled by Chéri-Bibi's shots, and he had stayed for a space by the bedside of Sister St. Mary of the Angels, who had become delirious. He was anxious to put in writing, in a detailed form, the events of that disastrous day. The weather was fine and the sea quite smooth. The *Bayard*, oppressed by its cargo of convicts, continued its course in "peace and quietness" towards the Iles du Salut. After the recent storms—the storms of heaven as well as those on board ship—this interval of calm was so unexpected and so greatly appreciated that the Captain, who was already bending over a table to write, raised his head with a sigh of relief as though he were coming to himself after a bad dream.

115

But he sat stock still, open-mouthed, wide-eyed, for he suddenly saw standing before him a gloomy figure which was smiling at him.

"Chéri-Bibi!"

He sprang to his feet.

But he at once fell back in his chair. The gloomy figure leant over the desk and leveled the muzzle of a revolver between his eyes. And it was no longer smiling. He felt his pocket. He was unarmed. Someone had stolen his weapon from him. Someone had foreseen everything. And the figure standing between him and the door was smiling once more.

"Be sensible. . . . Not a word. . . . *Fatalitas!*"

Having said which the ominous visitor took a seat without being invited and went on:

"Monsieur, I am an honest man!"

He was silent after making this declaration as if he were weighing deliberately in his mind what he had said, so that it seemed after a few moments as if he must add:

"Or, I have been."

The statement seemed to plunge him anew into an abyss of cogitation from which he emerged to say:

"Oh, I might have been. . . . *Fatalitas!*"

The Captain, observing that his visitor was so self-possessed, was infected by this air of placidity. He listened and looked at him. He had seen that frightful face before, but he did not recognize it. So far he had regarded him with disgust and dismay. Now

he took stock of him with curiosity. He saw before
him a man with a big square head, wide mouth and
thick lips, short, squat nose, immense ears, small,
round, extremely piercing eyes, always on the alert
underneath the arch of their harsh and bushy eyebrows; hair closely cropped in accordance with the
regulations, revealing the exact outline of the skull
in which Gall or Lavater would easily have discerned
bumps of amativeness, combativeness, and destruc-
tiveness which might pertain alike to a ragamuffin who
would defend his mistress to the death, or to a soldier
who would die for his country.

Every instinct was expressed in that face. The
broad, lined forehead showed that Chéri-Bibi was
capable of great things, but the perpendicular
wrinkles at the base of the nose denoted the capacity
for hatred and revenge. Small, round, piercing eyes,
we know, indicate shrewdness and cunning, and a
mischievous and sarcastic disposition. Next, the
wide, squat nose was that of a person of simple
nature, easily deceived. The jaw was formidable,
but the mouth with its thick, fleshy lips, slightly
apart, expressed good nature and candor. And the
impression as a whole which the vision of this man
produced was enormously disturbing inasmuch as it
was impossible to obtain an impression of the face
as a whole.

One could not tell what to trust in that face. It
might be that, at one time, it possessed some har-

mony which the barber, by depriving him of his natural covering, had got rid of. If Chéri-Bibi had had a forked beard and long hair he would have resembled a somewhat countrified preacher, and if he had worn side whiskers he would have looked like a valet in a great household who had murdered his master.

He might once have been handsome. Satan before the fall was the most beautiful of the angels.

And over and above all this he loved a joke and to seem to be laughing. When he did laugh he looked awful.

*"Fatalitas,"* he said, "there you have my enemy. If you knew what a run of ill-luck I've had in my life, you'd scarcely credit it. My fellow-prisoners complain of their failures. But I, what shall I say about mine? By the way, I am considered an anarchist. I should like to say positively at the beginning of this talk that I am anything but an anarchist. I, Monsieur, find society, such as it is at present, extremely well constituted. And I have always had the desire to make for myself a humble but honorable place in it. The unfortunate part is that I have never been able to succeed in doing so.

*"Fatalitas!* I have read Kropotkine. His theory of society hasn't a leg to stand on; and as for Karl Marx, I must tell you at once that I should regret all my life the efforts that I have made to secure for myself other people's property if I were forced to

share that property with persons whom I don't know.
. . . I like to do charitable deeds, of course, but I
shouldn't like to be compelled to do them with a knife
at my throat. . . . The boot should be on the other
leg! . . . I am neither an anarchist nor a socialist.
. . . You must understand that once for all. And if
you want to know what I am, well, I myself will tell
you, Monsieur. I am a capitalist. At any rate, you
understand, all that I ask is to become one!

"The most surprising thing in my career is the
obstinacy with which the anarchists who defend me
and the judges who prosecute me are at one in hurting
my feelings! I am not an anarchist. I will go a
step further—I am certain that if you knew me better,
my dear Captain, you would agree with me—I am not
at all an ill-disposed person. It would never have
occurred to me, for instance, to write a book, like
Little Buddha's, on the 'Reform of the Magistrature.' Judges do their best, and it would not
be right to forget that they are men like ourselves!
I grant you that, every now and then, one of them
goes wrong. It's a pity, but it can't be helped, and
of a certainty it's not because one glazier murders
his mother-in-law that we should regard all glaziers
as rascals.

"Look here, as we're talking of judges I will admit
that I bear them no ill-will for their mistakes, seeing
that to err is human. And yet, Monsieur, the man

who is talking to you like this, and is entered on the convicts' register as No. 3216, is innocent.

"You seem to be astonished, and I will admit that you have good reason to be. But it is God's truth, as my sister says . . ."

"Will you have a glass of water?" asked the Captain.

"No, thank you. You're too kind. Don't disturb anyone on my account."

The Captain bowed in assent. What was the object of the peculiar and remarkable farce that was being played by these two men? The Captain, in so far as Chéri-Bibi was concerned, wondered. "He must have some reason for wanting to gain time," he said to himself, "and as he is a criminal of the most impudent type, he's trying to stagger me."

As a matter of fact Chéri-Bibi was showing off, and the sight of Chéri-Bibi showing off was a monstrous one. It was only necessary to hear him say: "I am innocent. . . . That's God's truth as my sister says." The phrase "as my sister says" added to the words "God's truth" were uttered in a tone that seemed to set the whole world at defiance.

• He went on with his explanation:

"When I say 'as my sister says' I don't want you to think that my sister believes in my innocence, but that she believes in God. I, Monsieur, I do not believe in God. Brought up from infancy in principles which enabled me to do without any such

belief, I shall not have the final satisfaction of knowing exactly on whom to lay the blame for all my misfortunes. Well, Monsieur, if the Supreme Being,
as we say at school, existed he would have a devilish
bad time of it with me, please believe. There is only
one thing which can explain my case, and which it
is really worth while to dwell on, only one thing,
and that thing is a confounded *she:* I've called her
Fatality. Monsieur, you see before you a victim by
decree of fate: *Fatalitas!* I was good, I am bad. I
was gentle, I am violent. I used to love, I now hate.
Monsieur, I will tell you the story of my first offense,
and you will at once pity me. As a stroke of bad
luck, my first offense goes beyond anything that you
can imagine. And yet it was very ordinary. Here
it is . . .

"I was born at Dieppe of poor but honest parents.
My parents were servants in an old and honorable
family. My father was the gardener, and my mother
the lodge-keeper. We lived in a small cottage at the
park gates. I have nothing to hide from you. I
will mention names. My name is Jean Mascart.
Our master's name was Bourrelier, and the Bourreliers belong to an old middle-class family of
extremely wealthy shipowners who, however, were
greatly worried by having such a common name.

"The family consisted of Monsieur and Madame
Bourrelier, a daughter and a son. The son was
enjoying himself in Paris. During the summer

months they lived on their big estate at Puys, a mile at most from Dieppe, on the main road. The daughter was called Cécile, but everyone called her by the sweet name of Cecily and everyone loved her. For that matter, it was impossible to see her and not to love her. I was only fifteen at that time and she was seventeen, and I was very struck on her. Oh, in the most innocent and respectful manner in the world, for I was then as good as gold, and I had a level mind which enabled me to see things in their proper proportion; and the position that Cecily occupied was so much above my humble station that I did not allow myself to indulge in any ridiculous hopes. I loved her, that was all.

"My only happiness consisted in watching Cecily. I never lost an opportunity. I gave up my calling, which was, it seems, to be a surveyor, in order to see her every day. Yes, my schoolmaster had discovered that I had an inclination for geometry. Then my father, a simple soul who did not make difficulties where there were none, said:

" 'Very well, we'll make a surveyor of him.'

"But I should have had to go to a boarding school in Rouen. I should never have agreed to that. Leave Cecily! Why, I would rather die. Nevertheless I had reached an age when I had to make up my mind. Something had to be done. So one day I said to my father: 'Dad, do you know what I should like to be? I should like to be a butcher. Yes, I feel that I have a taste for the slaughter-house!'

"I was not talking at random. More than once I had stopped outside butchers' shops with no sort of intention of buying anything, but simply to look on and to understand. The sight of all that red meat, quite fresh, attracted me. I envied one of my young friends who was a butcher's boy and could handle it every day.

"Sometimes he took me to the slaughter-house, and it was a joy to see how he cut a calf's throat with a single stroke of his knife called 'the bleeder.' I felt a shudder, which was not wholly unpleasant, when he manipulated this big knife, which was double the size of a carver, and when he explained to me how to unsinew the animal. The knife must not, he said, be used with a 'double movement'; in other words, you had to avoid working backwards in the cut, as was done by persons who did not understand their job. Otherwise the meat would be hacked, and it was work that should be neatly done!

"Afterwards he showed me how to 'decorate' the skin of the calf's stomach with a small sharp knife. I, who had an inclination for geometry, would have liked to draw on the calf's skin, circles, squares, parallelograms, just as he drew hearts, arrows, flowers. Let it not be said that the butcher is a materialist, for, after all, nothing compels him—does it?—to draw flowers on the stomachs of calves.

"And so I acquired the taste for this very safe and respectable business which, in most cases, brings in considerable profits.  My father did not stand in my way, and indeed he was at once satisfied when I told him that I was about to become an apprentice to a butcher in Le Pollet, a suburb of Dieppe near Puys; a butcher who, as it happened, supplied the Bour-reliers with their meat.

"I had thought out the whole scheme.  I knew that I should have to take the meat to Puys, and I was certain to see Cecily every day, because her mother had made a good housewife of her, and it was she who nearly always interviewed the tradesmen. Matters turned out as I expected, and, believe me, I did not rob her in any transaction.   I always managed things in such a way as to supply her with the best cuts, and I was not the one to try to palm off on her an upper-cut as an under-cut, or a cut from the leg as rump steak.   Moreover, I took good care when I delivered veal, to do the 'decorations' myself, and I assure you that Monsieur Bouguereau, the famous painter, could not have shown off a calf more beautifully with his brush than I did with my small knife.

"I am entering into these particulars, Monsieur, because I'm very glad to spread myself a little over a time which was the most delightful in my life.  I can see myself now, my spotlessly clean apron tucked up carefully above the knee and taken in at the waist,

my steel at my side, the veal in my basket, hasten-
ing on my bicycle to meet Cecily. I left my machine
at the door of the cottage in which my parents lived,
and after kissing my dear mother and my charming
sister who, in those days, was called Jacqueline, like
anybody else, I turned my steps with a beating heart
to the park. If sometimes I stopped out of breath,
gasping, it was because I had heard Cecily's fairy
footsteps gliding over the grassy slope. How beautiful she was! What grace of movement! What
simplicity of manner!

"And then she was as fresh as a daisy and as gay
as a lark on a summer's day. To see her was all I
asked. To die for her was all I wanted. And no
one ever knew the secret of my heart. You see,
Monsieur, my voice trembles now when I recall those
exquisite moments. She had a way of asking:
'Well, young man, is the meat really spotty
today?' Was it really spotty indeed! . . . I used
to blush, and when she observed it, she would smile
and say:

" 'You are still a little bit of a muff, my poor
boy.'

"And she took the joints from me with her own
beautiful fragrant hands.

"And now, Monsieur, this is how the crime was
committed, and how I was arrested and convicted.
Believe it if you can. True, I committed the murder,
but I was not to blame. Even now, after the lapse

of so many years, I haven't got over it. I must tell
you at once that Cecily's father, an immensely
wealthy shipowner, was an old rake. He had been
taking notice of my sister. Poor Jacqueline, who
was as pious as a child's prayer, was certainly the
most virtuous girl in the district. Mothers held her
up as an example to their daughters, and the rector
would have chosen her as the winner of the rose if
the custom of crowning the best girl in the parish had
survived, in our country, the destruction of ancient
customs.

"I have nothing to keep secret in this doleful
story, which is known throughout Dieppe, where my
sister lived again quite recently amid universal
respect and the devoted friendship of the nuns in the
hospital, who welcomed her with open arms.

"How and by what piece of trickery did Jacqueline fall a victim to the old ruffian Bourrelier? For
my part, I've always believed the youngster's story.
She declared that Bourrelier enticed her into his office
in Dieppe and drugged her one Sunday, after evening
service, when no one was there. The result was that
my sister nearly died, and there were terrible scenes
between my father and Bourrelier, who, of course, got
rid of us. Even I was sacked by my master, who was
anxious to keep his customer. But I found a place
elsewhere, and my sister became a nun.

"Meanwhile, I continued to see Cecily because I
delivered meat for my new firm to the Château des

Roches-Blanches, in Puys, where the Marquis du Touchais and his family, friends of the Bourreliers, lived during the season. The Marchioness was a very fine lady who, when she went out, was invariably escorted by old Rose, her lady-companion. I know that both of them are still living, for, as you may readily believe, although the case was tried fifteen years ago, the affair will never be finished with as long as my head is on my shoulders.

"The Marquis had a son, Count Maxime, a young man who was gadding about in Paris with Bourrelier's son. Both of them used to return to their families in the season, and they often brought a friend with them who stayed at Bourrelier's house. This friend was the Viscount Georges de Pont-Marie. The sons continued to visit each other in Puys, and very close relations existed between the château and the villa. Cecily often went with her mother to the château, and, therefore, I was able to behold her as the fancy took me.

"I no longer recognized her. She had a wistful expression which was painful for me to see, even if I assumed that this air of sadness had its origin in the terrible accident which had befallen my sister whom she loved so well. The three young men endeavored to cheer her up. Her father himself, the rascally Bourrelier, did not succeed in rousing her from her dejection even when he resorted to threats.

"One day I heard him bullying her rather

severely. I walked away at once for I felt that I might not be able to control myself. Moreover, I always got out of the way of old Bourrelier, lest I should do something rash. And this was the one thing, above everything else, which I tried to avoid because of my love for his daughter. Now I learnt, some time after, the cause of these scenes. Old Bourrelier wanted his daughter to become a Countess and one day a Marchioness. . . . Yes, in spite of her opposition, he wanted her to marry Maxime du Touchais.

"The old Marquis du Touchais, of course, backed him up, for he was a poor man, and the Roches-Blanches estate, as well as everything that remained to the du Touchais's of their old Norman property, was mortgaged up to the hilt and beyond. All their schemes for my poor Cecily were nicely faked! I felt sick at heart, especially as I knew that the poor girl always hoped to marry one of her cousins, young Marcel Garacan, who was then making a trial trip prior to attaining Captain's rank in the merchant service.

"I saw Cecily every day for a fortnight, and every day she was in tears. It made me quite ill. She told her father, moreover, that she would rather die than marry Maxime du Touchais; and all the countryside was aware of it. The people pitied her, for they knew Bourrelier, and were quite sure that he would never allow her to have her own way.

"One evening, in mid-September, I was coming back from Roches-Blanches, on my bicycle, when I caught sight of two men fighting on the top of the cliff. They held each other round the body, and their struggles were such that I marveled how it was that they hadn't fallen into the sea.

"I got off my bicycle, for in order to reach them I had to run across country, and then I distinctly heard one of them shouting in a choking voice: 'Help! . . . Help! . . . Murder!' I recognized the voice. It was Bourrelier's.

"Notwithstanding that it was nightfall and growing dark, I was at once able to grasp the position. Bourrelier had his back to the sea, and was nearing the edge of the cliff; the other man, who had managed to release himself, gave him a push while clutching, with one hand, a telegraph pole. Consequently, this man had his back turned to me, and I could not see his face.

"It was not the moment to hesitate. I rushed forward and seized my man, shouting: 'Let go, murderer!' For answer he gave me a tremendous kick on the calf without turning round. I uttered a cry of pain, and grasping the knife which was hanging from my belt that evening, I aimed a terrible blow at his back. Monsieur, I must tell you that I had come from the slaughterhouse, and had on me the 'bleeder' which I was taking to Le Pollet to be sharpened. You may imagine the sort of blow that I dealt him with that knife.

"Unfortunately, at that very moment old Bourrelier, who had succeeded in again seizing his opponent by the body, whisked him round in a flash towards the edge of the cliff, compelling him to leave go his hold of the telegraph pole, with the result . . . with the result, listen to this carefully, that it was now old Bourrelier whose back was turned to me, and my knife went through old Bourrelier's back as if it were butter, my dear Monsieur.

"He did not give even a groan. He sank to the ground at my feet. He was dead.

"I had killed the man whom I wanted to save.

"What do you say to that? Don't you think that it was a stroke of ill-luck? And when I declare that it was fatality, that fate was against me, am I lying? Am I claiming too much?

"I had killed Cecily's father. I ran off like a madman towards Dieppe, while the other man ran off like a madman, too, towards Puys. The body lay on the cliff with the knife still plunged in its back.

"Before I reached the top of the hill at Le Pollet, I worked out in my mind that if I left the knife in his back, people would soon find out that it was I who struck the blow. So I wandered back again, but I could not find the body. It had already gone! Had some passer-by discovered it? Had the alarm been given? I did not think so, for in that case there would have been a crowd of people on the cliff and considerable excitement along the coast at Puys.

"So what was I to do? The other man must have returned and, doubtless, thrown the body over the rocks. But what had he done with the knife? The knife, like the body, had disappeared. It was a terrible position for me to be in.

"At that very moment I noticed that I had lost my apron. . . . But where had I lost it? . . . I hunted high and low for it without finding it. Night had fallen. I was clean off my head.

"Only one hope was left to me: to find the man with whom Bourrelier had been fighting. I went down to Puys, taking care to keep out of the way, drawing back into the fields, or hiding myself behind a hedge when I heard the sound of footsteps.

"I had noticed one thing only about the man: his large gray hat, which was rammed over his brow and the brim of which was turned down over his eyes. Moreover, the ups and downs of the struggle and the darkening night prevented me from seeing anything more. I might recognize him by his hat and perhaps, too, by his build. He was tall and slim of figure, and he had shown by running away that he was pretty wide awake.

"I wandered round the château, the taverns, the villas during the greater part of the night, on the watch for the occasional shadows that rose up before me. At length I reached Dieppe, a prey to despair, as may easily be understood, but I dared not return to the shop nor to my own home. I spent the night in the open near the railway. Early next morning I turned my steps towards Le Pollet. Outside my new employer's shop a crowd was assembled, and I caught a glimpse of a couple of policemen in the doorway. I at once took to my heels, and hid myself in a cave in the cliff which had once served as hiding-place for Georges Cadoudal.[1] He was a grave man if you like! Honor to his memory! I stayed there all day, convinced that the police were looking for me, and, worse luck, it was only too true.

"In the evening I left the cave, for I was ravenously hungry. I managed to steal, from a haberdasher's shop-front in Beville, a piece of Gruyère cheese which lay there, wrapped up in a newspaper. An accident had made me a murderer, and the circumstances of my new life made me a thief. It was the finishing stroke; and I was under sixteen!

"It was a nice beginning, but wait a bit, the story is not yet over. I am keeping the tit-bit for the end.

"The newspaper in which the cheese was wrapped was a Dieppe paper of that very day. When I finished eating, I read it seated under a porch at the back of a poor, lonely farm up to which I had crept hoping to find something that might stay my

[1] Georges Cadoudal, leader of the Vendeans, executed for conspiracy against Napoleon, as First Consul, in 1804.—TRANSLATOR'S NOTE.

hunger, for the Gruyère cheese had by no means satisfied it. A flickering light disclosed the headline of an article which I shall remember all my life:

'TERRIBLE REVENGE BY A BOY OF
FIFTEEN.'

Now I knew all about it. It concerned me. There was no possible mistake!

"The story seemed obvious. The evening before, M. Bourrelier's family had vainly waited dinner for him. As it was growing late Madame Bourrelier, in a state of great anxiety, sent her son Robert to make inquiries. He went to Roches-Blanches, where he was informed by the astonished Marquis that Bourrelier had left the place in good time to return home for dinner by way of the cliff. Fearing that some accident had happened, the Marquis, his son Maxime, their friend Georges de Pont-Marie and Bourrelier's son, set out along the cliff, and there, with better luck than I had, they found a butcher-boy's apron; but there was no Bourrelier.

"They returned to the spot with lanterns, and finally they discovered traces of a struggle on the ground and in the grass. Feeling convinced that Bourrelier had been thrown over the cliff, they went to the village and along the beach, and the tide, as it happened, was low and there was no difficulty. It was not long before they saw in front of them the shipowner's body.

"They carried the dead man to his house after the Marquis, who went on ahead, had broken the dreadful news to the family. You can imagine Cecily and her mother's grief. The young girl was taken ill there and then and had to be put to bed. Meanwhile they telephoned to Dieppe; and the Commissary of Police appeared, accompanied by his secretary. The investigation was soon made. . . . A stab in the back and a butcher-boy's apron. . . . That very evening my apron was identified by my employer. Besides, the Marquis remembered having seen me start off from Roches-Blanches a few minutes after Bourrelier, and declared that I had taken the same road.

"In the eyes of everyone, my connection with the matter was as clear as spring water. I had determined to avenge my sister whom the shipowner had, to use the expression of the newspaper, 'treated badly.' Moreover, I had benefited personally by the act of vengeance inasmuch as I had plundered the man whom I had murdered. Bourrelier's pocket-book was not found on him, and, it seems, it contained several thousand franc notes. I was rich!

"The thing that astonished me, however, was the fact that the knife was nowhere to be found. Oh, they knew exactly what it was like! In a special edition of the newspaper, which was issued at ten o'clock in the morning, the knife was fully described. How was it that at ten o'clock in the morning they had not found the knife, the 'bleeder,' with which such splendid cuts could be made that there was no need to strike a second blow! The newspaper explained furthermore that the stab could only have been inflicted by someone who was an adept at that sort of thing, by a young butcher.

"Now that very night I myself found the precious knife in circumstances which were by no means ordinary, I can tell you.

"I folded up the newspaper, which foretold my early arrest, and went back to my cave in a somewhat dispirited frame of mind, believing that it was all up with me. What, indeed, could I do? What could I say to get myself acquitted? Tell the story of the man in the gray hat? The judge would shrug his shoulders, and no one would believe me. I could do nothing and say nothing unless I brought the man in the gray hat before the judge.

"There was no getting away from that. The man in the gray hat must be found. It struck me that his general appearance was not unfamiliar to me, and that I had had occasion to meet that particular form in Puys during the season. I ought not to despair, but to return every evening, every night, to Puys so as to spy upon all the shadows that passed in the dark.

"I still had my bicycle with me. I brought it out of my cave, and off I went to Puys. When I heard the sound of approaching footsteps, or caught sight of a light, I retreated into the open country and lay

on the ground. Now, that night, I had given up all
hope of meeting the man for whom I was searching,
and after stealthily hunting throughout the village,
I went off to the beach and was about to lie down on
the sand under the cliff when a figure passed in front
of me. It was my man!

"Oh, there was no mistake about it. It was he
right enough. . . . Please believe that my heart
throbbed wildly. At first I lay motionless. I was
watching him. What was he doing on the beach at
that hour? It was past two o'clock in the morning.
I saw him make for a small, extremely narrow flight
of steps, hewn in the solid rock, which led directly
to the garden of Roches-Blanches, whose heavy and
lofty outline towered above the sea.

"I did not want to alarm my man! I did not
want him to run away as he did the night before,
and I followed him on all fours. He mounted the
steps. I stayed below and waited, intending to go
up in my turn when he reached the top. Every now
and then he stopped short and gazed around him,
with ears on the alert for the least noise. I swear
that I didn't make a sound. Then he dived into his
pocket, took out a key, and opened the little door
which led to the Roches-Blanches garden.

"He closed the door, leaving it slightly ajar. The
moon illuminated the entire scene. But I could only
see the man from a somewhat restricted angle of the
beach because there was a set-back in the cliff; and

as he failed to observe anyone on that part of the beach, he might well believe that his presence was undetected.

"I clambered up the steps. When I reached the top, I pushed the door and slipped into the garden. A great calm reigned over the château. Everyone seemed to be asleep. Not a light gleamed in any of the windows. Which way had my man taken? I carefully closed the door behind me and bolted it lest he should escape me; and I hid myself in a pathway close by, ready to jump out upon him, and to call for help when he returned, for there was no doubt that he would come back that way. I had no idea what he came to the house for, but the fact that he left the door ajar suggested that, in all likelihood, he was relying on getting quietly away by the same means.

"Before he could unbolt the door I should be on him! And we should see what would happen. I was a match for him. I wasn't afraid of him.

"Nearly a quarter of an hour passed.

"Nothing seemed to have stirred in the house when suddenly I heard a hollow cry, like a cry of fear and pain, followed by the heavy impact of a body falling to the ground. I darted forward. A window was open on the ground floor of the château. A figure hastily revealed itself at the window and seemed on the point of jumping out. It was he. It was the man in the gray hat.

"I sprang forward and found myself in a large dark room.

"At that moment a door opened and someone cried: 'Who's there? If you move a step you're a dead man!'

"The light of a lantern was thrown on me, and I saw a short, stout man in night attire who threatened me with his revolver. 'Don't fire,' I said, 'I won't move. There's a man in the house!'

"'I can see that well enough,' was the reply.

"And he straightway kicked up the devil's own row and shouted for help.

"The household came rushing in from all quarters; all of them in their night attire. Lights were brought, and I was recognized, and they exclaimed: 'It's Chéri-Bibi!'—I was known throughout the countryside by the náme which my sister had given me—'It's Chéri-Bibi! We've got him!'

"'He's up to more mischief here,' interposed a voice.

"And suddenly they raised a great outcry, for they had just discovered the Marquis du Touchais stretched at full length on the floor, in a pool of blood, in front of his safe. . . . He was dead with a big knife driven in his back. . . . I recognized the knife. It was mine.

"Well, Monsieur, what do you think of that, eh? Something out of the common in the way of chance! Have you ever heard of such a run of bad luck?

If you have, say so. But I know that you've never heard of anything like it before, have you? *Fatalitas.* I am not, you understand, a disciple of Kropotkine or Tolstoy. I am not the product of anarchism or dubious reading. Nor am I the victim of evil instincts; that's humbug. The circumvolution of the brain, as the Kanaka would say, is, as far as I am concerned, humbug also. When you're born, you have all the bumps and none of the bumps . . . a disposition for everything and nothing. At the beginning, take it from me, our instincts and our bumps mean nothing to us. They represent energies which demand to be utilized. That's all. . . . That's my theory of life. It's not a complicated one. But, of course, these energies will flow into whatever channel they may be directed, that's a certainty. But who manipulates the lever? . . . That's what we want to find out. . . . That's what we must take into consideration. . . . That's where we must fix the responsibility. . . .

"Sometimes the parents are at fault and sometimes society. It is never the child. . . . The poor kid himself is only too willing to go ahead—straight or crooked. . . . Well, who pulled the lever in my own particular case? It was neither my parents nor society. It was *Fatality*, that was all. The fact hits you in the eye. I can see it. I've faced it all my life. It was Fatality that pointed the way. When, by chance, I did not see the way, it drove me from behind. *Fatalitas!* Oh, the jade!

"You understand me, I hope. . . . It's all the better if you do. It shows that you have your wits about you. . . .

"So it was my knife that they found! . . . You can imagine how they laid hands on me, and how they treated me. And how they settled me. . . . What was the good of my telling them that I was after a man in a gray hat? They disbelieved me all the more after they had searched the house from top to bottom so as to discover whether I had an accomplice, and found no trace of anyone. A couple of months later I appeared before the Assize Court, and as I was too young to be guillotined, I was sent to Cayenne to finish my education.

"I didn't care one way or the other once I knew that I shouldn't see Cecily again. What happened to her young life? I learnt the facts after my escape and return to France. Three days after her father's death, and consequently two days after the Marquis's death, Cecily sent word for Maxime du Touchais to come and see her. The young man had lost a great deal by Bourrelier's death; for it seemed as if the man who had killed the shipowner had killed the marriage. He knew that Cecily would only marry him if she were compelled to do so by force. And even so, she had given him to understand that she would never yield to her father's entreaties.

"So you can picture the young Marquis's amazement when immediately after Bourrelier's funeral, Cecily, in Bourrelier's study and under Bourrelier's portrait, gave him her hand saying: 'Monsieur du Touchais, I regard you as my affianced husband. I give you my promise. A terrible misfortune has afflicted both of us, and in marrying you I am fulfilling my father's last wishes.' So saying she bowed to him and left him in a state bordering on stupor.

"This young 'nut,' as we should say in these days, could not understand from the beginning how a girl who had rejected the wishes of her father when he was alive should conform to them when he was dead. The idea of sacrifice over her father's grave, which arose in that young girl's heart, was far beyond his limited comprehension, and he could not rise to such heights for a moment; and if he had been told that old Bourrelier had threatened to curse his refractory daughter on the day of his death, it would not have sufficed to account for Cecily's conduct. In his eyes, a father's curse was one of those conventional phrases which have come down to us from a somewhat old-fashioned literature, and which have now ceased to pass for currency. He accepted his happiness, therefore, without understanding it, and when the period of mourning was over, Cecily and he called in the services of the mayor and the rector, not forgetting, of course, the solicitor."

"How well you express yourself," observed the Captain, who took care not to interrupt the speaker, but wished to convey to him from time to time that he was following him with attention. As a matter of fact, while listening to the engrossing story, Barra-chon kept wondering: "How shall I set about laying hold of Chéri-Bibi without doing too much harm?"

Chéri-Bibi continued:

"It so happens that I have often been astonished like you, Monsieur, by the good form and lucidity which my language reveals at times, but apart from my considerable reading during the hours that I wasted at the convict settlement, my only explanation is that at those particular moments my thoughts are centered wholly in Cecily, and are expressed in elevated language because Cecily elevated everyone who came in contact with her.

"Nevertheless we must make an exception in the case of the loathsome Maxime du Touchais, who encountered perfection on earth and did not perceive it. He was too busy looking after the money bags. The fortune that he acquired through his marriage left him no time to trouble himself about Cecily, whom he entirely neglected after she became a mother. He built a splendid yacht for himself in which he sails in the holiday season with his boon companions of both sexes. These extravagant parties and scandal-ous cruises take place while the young wife mourns at home in the château."

Chéri-Bibi stopped, heaved a deep sigh, and went on:

"At this point, Monsieur, this part of the story

finishes. My first thought on returning to France, after my escape from the convict settlement, was naturally to see Cecily. I made my way to Dieppe, but I was still pursued by incredible misfortune, for I no sooner reached St. Valery en Caux than I learnt that Cecily, taking advantage of her husband's absence, had gone with her son to England so as to improve his knowledge of a language which I cannot too strongly recommend young people to learn. If I had known English, I should never have been caught when I slipped away from the lock-up. But I didn't know the language. *Fatalitas!*

"And now, Monsieur, I will make only a slight further demand upon your patience, and you will know at last why it is that I have thought it my duty to inflict upon you this long confession. Fate still continued to persecute me. I was anxious to be reinstated in an honest and respectable life, for I was young still and in no way corrupted by the 'old offenders,' and moreover the thought of Cecily had always obsessed me, and I was, I venture to say, filled with eagerness to do good. After performing veritable marvels on the outskirts of society in the art of good-natured burglary, and of swindles that did no harm to anyone—because it's the law of nature that whatever happens one must live—I had the good fortune to glimpse a harbor of refuge. At last I should live a quiet life. . . . I should be honest like other people. . . . I became a porter in the office of a millionaire banker.

"Well, will you believe me, Monsieur, I was fixed up with an anarchist. The fellow associated with none but anarchists, whom he entertained every day at his table. He read only anarchist newspapers which he subsidized, and thus considered, apparently that he had done his duty by humanity, for he was not over-generous with his servants. It was he who gave me Kropotkine to read; it was his New Year's present to me. . . . The whole thing disgusted me. Here with this pot-bellied person—I mean my employer —keeping his millions for himself, and trying to convince other people that they had no right to possess anything at all. It was sickening, upon my word, and I gave him notice to leave. Oh, I didn't hang about very long over it.

"Now, as if by chance, fatality was on the watch, determined that the day after my departure the bank should be robbed by a few smart lads who adopted the literary theories of my ex-governor and unhesitatingly shot down the unfortunate staff who mounted guard over the cash. From the start of the investigation the banker spoke of me. I had left too opportunely not to be aware of what was going to happen. From that assumption to the conclusion that I entered his employ solely to give my confederates the requisite information was but one step.

"In order to get over that one step they wanted to know exactly who I was. And they might not, perhaps, have succeeded but for a man called Costaud.

Who was Costaud? Have you ever read 'Les Miserables?' . . . Yes, you have read the book. Very well, Costaud played the same part as Javert did in Victor Hugo's story. That is the long and the short of it.

"Costaud got to know me in Dieppe at the time when I committed what we agree to call my first offense. He was the secretary to the Commissary of Police. Ever since my escape from penal servitude he had been after me. He and Fatality were in collusion.

"One chilly, misty evening in January I met them both in an omnibus shelter, and he proceeded to lay hands on me, when I remembered in time that I had a small pocket knife with me, and I made Costaud a present of it. That settled him, and he swooned in the arms of his companion. He did not die from his wound and I don't bear him any malice. For all that, Costaud, while looking for the office-boy of the looted bank, found Chéri-Bibi.

"They were all agreed from that moment that it was Chéri-Bibi who did the trick, and one heard of nothing but Chéri-Bibi and his gang. I was obliged to run to earth like a rabbit. Now I never committed so many crimes as when, like a wise man, I lay in my hole and didn't stir a foot. That infernal Chéri-Bibi's gang were up to their old games again. They stole motor-cars, robbed bank messengers, frightened the ordinary public out of their wits, and finally worked wonders which covered me with glory. At times when the newsboys' shouts brought me details of Chéri-Bibi's latest crime I longed to come out of my retreat and cry: 'That'll do. . . . That'll do. . . . You are choking me with cream!' . . . Monsieur, I must bring my story to a close. I will pass over a few insignificant details, such as, for instance, my arrests and escapes, to come to the young servant girl. You remember Marguerite Berger, the girl who was cut into I don't know how many pieces?"

"Seventeen," interposed the Captain.

"Look here, I thought there were only sixteen! But after all, perhaps you're right."

"At the sixteenth the effect was so great on you that you were obliged to take a mustard foot bath," added Barrachon, becoming more and more self-possessed and master of himself, for, taking everything into consideration, he reckoned that it was impossible for the wretch to escape him. When Chéri-Bibi went to open the door he would hang on to him whatever happened and shout to the sentry on guard, whose movements to and fro he could hear in the passage, to fire even if he himself were the first to fall. "And now my man, go ahead!" he thought to himself.

"Oh yes, the mustard foot bath," returned Chéri-Bibi. "You haven't forgotten it! I suppose you thought it was a bad joke. Well, it wasn't; it was the truth. Poor little serving-wench! Poor child! It occurred after my last escape. I hadn't a penny in the world, and was wandering round the slaughter-houses at La Villette, feeling very depressed, and thinking to myself that if ever I managed to get back to respectability again, it would be in the meat trade for which I had an inclination, and which was my real trade as a respectable man. I had stolen a butcher's smock, and put it on; and I tried to open up a conversation with men in the trade who had finished their day's work. One of them passed me arm in arm with a young servant girl. He was treating her so roughly that I felt compelled to interfere, and ask him to behave himself a little better, seeing he had a girl with him, for the honor of the trade.

"I spoke quite politely, not intending any harm. He tried to give me a dressing; but he got one instead, and the servant girl, fearing for herself, in her turn, begged me to see her home. Her name, she told me, was Marguerite Berger, and she lived in the Avenue de Saint Ouen. It was some distance away, but I escorted her there like a gentleman.

"When we reached her place she asked me, as she was still in fear of her lover, not to leave her before the morning. But I went off at once, considering that I had done enough in the way of rescuing beauty in distress, preferring not to prolong my stay, in the circumstances, in a neighborhood the geography of which I had had no opportunity of studying.

"The next morning Marguerite Berger was found

in her room cut into pieces. Well, I had nothing to
do with it. When I left her the night before she
was in one piece! Her lover, the butcher, had
undoubtedly done the deed after a violent outburst
of jealousy. Of course Costaud arrived on the scene,
and on observing the pieces, exclaimed: 'That . . .
that's Chéri-Bibi's handiwork.'

"The door-keeper who saw me go upstairs to the
girl's room the day before gave a description of me.
The thing was at once settled!  I always learnt of
my murders from the newspapers.  The same thing
happened on this occasion, and I nearly had an attack
of apoplexy.  And that's why I took a mustard foot-
bath.  There's no witchcraft about it.  It was then,
Monsieur, that, disgusted with life, and thinking that
it was impossible for me to do any good in this world,
I put myself in Costaud's way.  He arrested me and
received the Legion of Honor.

"In the meantime the anarchists considered that I
was a champion, for they found that I had taken away
the body of an old marchioness and robbed her of her
jewelry in order to buy food for a large family who
were starving; they believed no end of things to my
honor, I can tell you.  For my part, I didn't mind.
I no longer denied anything, for I saw that such an
attitude gratified the judge.  I asked him if he wanted
any more.  He could have as much as he liked!  I
only required one thing: a quick finish.  Well, you
see, there again I had no luck.  The jury were in a
funk, and found that I was partly irresponsible on the

grounds of insanity, and instead of sending me to the
guillotine, a room was provided for me at the convict
settlement. I was to go back to Cayenne. It was
this decision which rendered me desperate.

"I've sworn that I will never set foot in Cayenne
again. Do you understand me, Captain? If you
refuse to understand me, there is sure to be a row. My
sister who joined the ship to try to influence me, my
sister herself can't prevent it. You can take that from
me . . . I may have been a little long-winded in my
story, but I think I have shown you that I am a good
man, a good man down on his luck. I have it in me
to become a tiger; not a tiger in a menagerie, but a
regular tiger who will destroy the lot of you.

"There are over eight hundred men here, who will
blindly let themselves be guided by me. You haven't
half that number. Your men would hardly be
a mouthful for us. We are armed. We have weapons.
So, be assured, they are only waiting for me to give
them the signal to begin the fight. It would have
been given before but that I caught sight of my
sister's cornette. That sight inspired me with a kindly
thought. Once more I felt a sort of pity for my
fellow-men, and this is what I've come to you
to propose: Monsieur, society was wrong to close its
doors against me. Society would be incomplete without me." Chéri-Bibi gave vent to a tremendous
sneer. "But I have my self-respect, and it's I, now,
who don't want to have anything more to do with
society." He was speaking seriously. "You may,

therefore, be easy in your mind. I promise you, on my conscience, not to return and make myself a nuisance to my fellow-countrymen.

"What do I want? We are not far from Africa. A sharp turn of the wheel and the trick's done. Lower a boat, and there I am landed in a new country. It will be said once again that Chéri-Bibi got clear away, and no one will think any the worse of you for that. And I, Monsieur, I can start life afresh among the savages. Does the plan appeal to you? What will it cost you? A little salt beef, some biscuits, a cask of brandy—I must be able to sustain .my strength when I take to the bush—and a cask of water. If it's a bargain, say so. You'll have nothing more to fear from Chéri-Bibi. Neither you nor any one else.

"With Chéri-Bibi away, everything will settle down quietly here, because the prisoners can do nothing without me. If you refuse to accept my offer, look out for yourself! I am not a bad sort of man, but I have already proved to you, in the store-room, that when I am attacked I know how to defend myself."

There was a pause.

The Captain was silent and seemed to be reflecting deep down within himself. Chéri-Bibi began to lose patience.

"Well, you'd better say something. Is it to be yes or no?"

"No," replied the Captain.

"*Fatalitas!*"

# CHAPTER VII

## THE REVOLT OF THE CONVICTS

THE two men were on their feet with the table between them. For some little time, the Captain had not heard the sentry's step in the passage, and he felt a certain anxiety. How was it that the sentry had allowed the ruffian to pass? By what piece of strategy had he succeeded in reaching the cabin? By what means did he hope to escape? Chéri-Bibi was nearing the door by imperceptible movements, his revolver leveled at Barrachon. He was on the point of reaching the door when Barrachon suddenly leapt aside. Chéri-Bibi thrust the revolver between his eyes.

"If you stir before I've opened the door," he said, "I'll shoot you as I would a dog."

Then the Captain grasped the significance of Chéri-Bibi's coolness during his story. He had the key of the cabin in his pocket. The Captain did not move a muscle until the door was opened slightly, for imprisoned with the convict and unarmed as he was, he had not the slightest chance of getting the better of him. Chéri-Bibi cast a glance outside. Then it

was that Barrachon resolved to act.  Suddenly stooping he rushed at him, shouting for help.

Chéri-Bibi in a flash seized him by the throat and
held him under him while he gasped for breath.

"I won't kill you," he said, "because I've no
liking for useless crimes.  But if you get out of this
business alive, I swear that I myself will land you
on the coast, as naked as a savage, as a punishment
for refusing my last request."

He hurriedly left the cabin and the door closed
behind him.

The Captain picked himself up and flung himself
at the door, but Chéri-Bibi had turned the key.
Barrachon was a prisoner on board his own ship.
He shouted and yelled and stamped his feet so as to
attract attention in the ward-room, which, as it
happened, was just underneath his cabin.  And at
that very moment the *Bayard* was filled with an
indescribable tumult, amidst which the sound of
firing could be heard from all sides.

A number of men rushed up in answer to the
Captain's calls for help.  De Vilène himself opened
the door, the key of which was in the lock.

"The convicts are in revolt," exclaimed the
Lieutenant.

"Chéri-Bibi has just left me," returned the
Captain, who was foaming with rage.

They wasted no time in explanations.  Over their
heads and under their feet the noise of continuous

firing could be heard. The fight seemed to be taking place without any definite plan. By the officers' orders the sailors whose watch it was, and the military overseers who were on guard, were hurriedly warning their comrades, who got out of their beds in dismay. Every man in the ship on foot and armed was the order. As they passed near a companion-way they heard young de Kerrosgouët shouting commands from the deck near the entrance to the cages.

At the companion-way leading to the upper deck, they came up against a crowd of persons shouting and gesticulating and apparently in a state of mad excitement. They were held up by some obstacle the nature of which they could not at first distinguish. At length they perceived that the companion-way had been taken away. Yes, the iron ladder was no longer in its place. It had been removed. And throughout the length of the alley-way the same thing had happened to the other ladders; with the result that all the men hurrying up from the lower decks were struggling there, while near the cages the fusillade continued to the accompaniment of howls and shrieks.

The overseers' wives hastened up also, crying out as though they were being flayed alive. In the presence of this inconceivable confusion the Captain resumed his usual self-possession and ordered the men to go into the store-room and look for a few boxes with which to make a temporary stairway.

Some sailors and a dozen convict guards by standing on the shoulders of their comrades had already
managed to gain the upper deck. But valuable time
had been lost. What exactly was happening up
there?

The Captain leapt on deck and joined de Kerrosgouët, who, with the assistance of a few sailors, was
dragging the 37 mm. Hotchkiss gun to the hatchway which ran down to the cages. Fortunately the
naval constructors whose business it was to transform
the old cruiser, as they called her, into a transport
for Guiana, had permanently closed every other
entrance in order to render the supervision of the
convicts less difficult. They would find themselves,
as it were, bottled up. The hatchway was already
surrounded by a cordon of military overseers who
kept up a continuous fire, at random, into this dark
cavity from which also a mortal fire was issuing.

It was a fine night, with a touch of tropical
splendor in it, and the moon threw sufficient light
over the scene of carnage to enable the Captain, as
he drew near, to perceive a number of bodies lying on
the deck. As soon as the first alarm was given, the
Sub-Lieutenant gathered together the men under his
command and attempted, at all costs, to go down to
the cages. His efforts were fruitless. His men were
obliged to fall back, and de Kerrosgouët himself
received a shot in the forehead from which the blood
streamed over his face. He informed the Captain

that here, likewise, the ladder was no longer in position. How and from whom had the convicts obtained their arms? The fire which came from them was most deadly. Not one of the thirty convict guards whose duty it was that night to keep watch over the cages had been seen.

The unfortunate men, it was certain, had been massacred, and it was equally certain that it was with their rifles and revolvers that the convicts had so vigorously returned the fire which was being directed against them from the hatchway.

At this juncture de Vilène rushed up to the Captain with an appalling piece of news. The men who were not on guard and were wakened in haste, had made a dash for their arms, but they discovered that the rifles were no longer in the arms-rack. They were bound to conclude, therefore, that these rifles had passed into the possession of the convicts owing to treachery which they did not suspect, and which constituted a fresh danger, the more to be dreaded inasmuch as it was unknown. The Captain turned pale.

The ruffians, who were now well armed, and doubtless possessed no lack of munitions, had a considerable advantage in point of numbers. They were obviously determined to stick at nothing, for they had nothing to lose, and the life that awaited them in the penal settlement had no attraction for them. The game would be lost to the officers and

crew if they did not succeed in massacring the convicts to the last man, by turning the cages into a
bleeding mass. From this infernal pit, riddled with
shot just as the crater of a volcano is riddled with
shafts of light, thick wreaths of smoke from the firing
ascended, and at the same time the outlaws' Song of
Death floated up:

> *Who blows the blooming lot U P?*
> *Sing ho for Chéri-Bibi.*

Fortunately for Barrachon he had at his disposal
two Hotchkiss guns, one of 37 mm. and the other of
47 mm., with which he would be able to shoot down
the rabble.

It was a stroke of luck that at the last moment he
had requested the authorities to supply him with
this additional means of defense. In ordinary circumstances they would have laughed in his face. But
they knew that Chéri-Bibi was on board, and they
regarded the precaution as a· legitimate one. The
two small guns were shipped at the eleventh hour,
and were hoisted on the *Bayard* at night. The
Captain ordered them to be stowed temporarily in
the flag-locker until he was ready to fix them in their
regular places. Then he overlooked them, which in
itself was another piece of luck, for if the mysterious
confederates had known that those powerful weapons
were on board, they would have been in the convicts'
hands, in all probability, at that moment.

After his first failure, it occurred to young Kerrosgouët, who knew where the guns were, that in the terrible position which had arisen he should use them. The sailors were already placing the second gun by the side of the first when Barrachon, who had an eye for the future, stopped the men in their work.

One gun was all that was needed at the hatchway if they were to be the victors. In view of certain eventualities which they must provide for, such as a rush of convicts in other parts of the ship, or on the deck itself, it would be well to hold back one of those formidable weapons. Thus he had the 47 mm. Hotchkiss hoisted on to the bridge, on the very roof of the chart-room. From that position he could dominate the ship's upper works and sweep them from end to end.

Meanwhile at the gaping mouth leading to the cages, firing continued on both sides. De Vilène and de Kerrosgouët had set up their Hotchkiss on an improvised platform whence they could shoot down into this infernal hole. As soon as this hole was cleared they would jump down into it; and there would be a pitiless slaughter. Reassured for the time being, Barrachon went below to the lower decks. He ordered the women and children to be locked in their quarters; and the women wept and cried out in terror for their husbands.

Accompanied by a squad of military overseers he went still further below.

His chief fear was lest he should be attacked from the rear.  He had to remember that Chéri-Bibi had escaped from the lower deck through a cavity in the cell, the old ammunition magazine, and some opening which still remained to be discovered.  Chéri-Bibi must have returned by the same way, and his assumption was at once confirmed when he came upon two convict guards writhing in their death agony.  The way which was afterwards taken by the ruffian was a mystery, impossible to divine. Barrachon came across bulkheads which were uninjured.  He had some fifty men under his command, spread around the old ammunition magazine, into which seemingly no one could enter, except by way of the cages, owing to the alterations effected by the naval constructors.

His rear and his passage below having been secured, he made his way to the upper deck.

The Captain was filled with a new hope.  The revolt was localized, and the convicts were surrounded and besieged.  Though they might not succeed in penetrating into the very center of the rebellion, they would end by stifling it.  It would die a natural death for lack of munitions and food.  The ruffians would be vanquished by hunger and thirst.  Nevertheless there was an increasing tumult.  Wherever he went, however far he might venture in the hidden recesses of the ship, convicts could be heard around him singing their terrible song.  And those fateful syllables which might have sounded so pleasant, reached his ears like a violent and perpetual menace: "Chéri-Bibi . . . Chéri-Bibi."

What was the secret of this power of crime over crime? . . . How all those wretched beings submitted to the scoundrel who maintained that he was the victim of Fate! And how he lured them on to follow him to the death, for they were marching towards death! What slaughter there would be! What bloodshed! Streams of blood were about to flow from deck to deck, from gangway to gangway, from bilge to bilge to the main bilge, which the Captain saw would not be emptied, but would one day pour out through the pumps naught but blood.

Shots behind the bulkheads, cries of fury and of men in their death throes, singing by those dregs of humanity. Yes, the rebellion had broken out at the call of Chéri-Bibi. But how was it that it had taken place? Once more the question arose, how had the convicts obtained arms? How had they escaped from their cages, with a double guard watching them unceasingly? Those were mysteries which the Captain, whose heart was filled with a desperate anger, was unable to fathom.

And this is what had occurred: That night after eating their dinner from the tubs suspended on the chain, Little Buddha asked Carrots to search carefully in his kit-bag. To the no small astonishment of the men, he revealed to view half a dozen revolvers fully loaded which "asked only to be allowed to go off."

"Fine shooters!" exclaimed the convict in a stifled voice, while his comrades around him nudged each other and could scarcely restrain their joy. So it was planned for that night! During the last forty-eight hours they were gasping for the moment to come. And now they could scarcely bring themselves to believe in it. And yet it was high time if they meant to save the Toper from execution in the morning for attempting to strangle a warder.

The revolt, then, was a reality. With the Toper out of the way and Chéri-Bibi out of sight, they had no longer believed in it. Little Buddha alone, who was in the Toper's confidence, had maintained a slightly mysterious air which puzzled and reassured them.

And now by some inconceivable miracle they were in possession of revolvers, of weapons that would set them free. Without a doubt it would put renewed heart into them. The moment had come to turn in, and there was a great commotion as they unrolled their hammocks and hung them up for the night.

Little Buddha made the most of the uproar to explain to the others who were expecting the watchword what was about to happen.

To begin with, nothing was to be done until Chéri-Bibi gave the signal for a general uprising; and this signal was to be a shrill whistle which would come

from the lower deck during the night, but at what
hour exactly he was unable to say. They had to bide
their time. Little Buddha thought he could vouch
for the fact that arms had been introduced into three
other cages. In any case they were agreed to strike
together. They would go ahead in unison. They
had sworn it. Only they must not "have a funk"
because blood would be shed.

The other cages would not enter the struggle when
they heard the whistle, which was a signal intended
only for Little Buddha, but would wait for a revolver
shot from Little Buddha. But he would not fire until
the cage was opened.

The Kanaka answered that the cages were never
opened at night time, whereupon Little Buddha
divulged the entire plot in order to inspire confidence.
One of his pals would "give him the hold"; in other
words, while he pretended to be asleep, this man
would unhook his hammock as if he were playing a
practical joke on him; and he would fall violently to
the deck uttering cries and moans. He would not
rise, but pretend that he had broken a limb. Thus the
guards would be bound to come to his assistance. As
soon as the door opened, before the guards knew what
was going on they would kill them. And one hundred
and fifty pals would hurl themselves into the alley-
way.

In each alley-way and deck were ten guards, and
it would not take long to tackle them and do for them.

Afterwards to take the keys from them and open the cages and cells would be simplicity itself. They would release the Toper, the African and all their mates. They would constitute an army. And Chéri-Bibi would be with them! He would appear from they knew not where like a good omen, and bring with him rifles and munitions and anything else that might be needed to complete the feast. Everything had been thought out from the beginning of the voyage, and success was a certainty. As for the military overseers who would make for the upper deck, there was nothing to fear from them for the companion-way at the main hatch had been loosened. To take it down would be Little Buddha's job. Nothing had been overlooked. They would be masters of the ship and do just as they pleased. Only, he repeated, they must understand that those who backed out of it would be killed. Every man's skin was at stake, and it would be a battle for life or death.

The plot seemed splendid to some, problematical to others, and impossible to others again, who, however, kept their opinions to themselves; but they all agreed that they had to go ahead for all they were worth; even the Lamb was in it.

Convicts have a method of communicating among themselves, of talking, of arranging the minute details of a plan of escape, under the very eyes of the guards, who do not know how it is done. No sooner were the hammocks slung up in the cages and the men lying in their swinging beds, than the whole plot was understood and settled. Each man knew what part he had to play in it.

And yet the "turning in" that night was like the "turning in" on any other night, and the same sound of men snoring, the same hoarse gurgling from brutish throats arose between decks, while the warders on guard, revolver in hand, or rifle on shoulder, paced up and down before the cages.

Ten o'clock, eleven o'clock, midnight. . . . Nothing as yet had occurred. The men, growing a little impatient, turned over in their hammocks, straining their ears for the least sound, counting the bells as they were struck, during the watch, by the signalman on the upper deck. They had endured too many hours of sleeplessness in the past not to know exactly the meaning of the bells as they were struck. At one o'clock, five o'clock and nine o'clock the signalman struck twice; at half-past one, half-past five, and half-past nine he struck twice, followed by one slightly softer note; at two o'clock, six o'clock, and ten o'clock he struck two double bells; at half-past two, half-past six, and half-past ten he struck double bells twice and a half bell, or four sharp notes and a softer one; at three o'clock, seven o'clock, and twelve o'clock he struck three double notes; and at the half-hours a small note extra. Finally, at four o'clock, eight o'clock, and twelve o'clock he struck four double notes with a half note extra to denote the half-hours.

The eight and a half bells of half-past twelve had struck when a shrill whistle rang through the lower decks. It came from the hold, and the guards wondered what the meaning of it was. They put the question from deck to deck, and some of them in order to find out leant over the companion-ways. Then at the back of the alley-way in which the cells were situated, some one shouted that the Toper or the African must have whistled, for both of them were locked in the same cell, the other cells being occupied or not sufficiently secure. Nothing further was heard, and quietness was soon restored among the guards, who resumed once more their accustomed beat.

Suddenly there was a crash in Chéri-Bibi's old cell. It was Little Buddha, who had been "given the hold" and was rolling on the deck near the bars, cursing and moaning in a most pitiful manner.

The guard who was nearest the cage went up to the bars and ordered the convict to hold his noise unless he wanted to be sent to the cells in the morning. . . . Little Buddha groaned still louder.

"I've broken my leg, I'm certain. . . . I've broken my leg."

"Well, it will be set to rights to-morrow," growled the guard. "Stop your row, or I'll blow your brains out. . . . Shut your jaw, damn it!"

And as though the threat had frightened him, Little Buddha, crouching in the dusk of the cage, became silent. The men in their hammocks and in the adjoining cages wondered what he was waiting for. Soon they were reassured, for Little Buddha again set up his moaning. He was suffering more than he could bear, and wanted to go to the sick-bay at once. His leg was broken. He would kill the man who had played him such a dirty trick, he declared. Finally nothing could be heard but his clamor. There was a general protest. It was impossible to sleep in such a din. And the convicts advised the warders, in surly tones, to take the "flabby legged" person to the sick-bay. It was the hour for having a snooze, what!

The warders once more ordered him in threatening language to be quiet.

"I can't bear it . . . I can't bear it.  My poor leg. . . . Let me go to the sick-bay. . . . Besides, my head's broken.  I don't know what's the matter with me.  I'm covered with blood.  I'm done for, I know I am."

The guards went up to the bars to which he had dragged himself, and threw the light of a lantern over his face.  It was bleeding.  To hasten the climax Little Buddha had cut his forehead with a knife.

It was then that Pascaud, who was going his rounds, stopped and decided what was to be done.

"He is bleeding.  He says he's broken a leg.  Look sharp, and take him to the sick-bay."

"Yes . . . yes . . . take him away," snarled the other men, who seemed to have exhausted their patience.

The sound of Pascaud fumbling with his keys could be heard. He was looking for the one which opened the cage. A great silence fell; the decisive struggle was at hand. The success of the revolt depended upon the next moment.

Little Buddha, with one hand in his trousers pocket, clutched his revolver.

The men above in their hammocks held themselves in readiness to jump out; but their seeming sleepiness deceived Pascaud, who little suspected what was about to happen to him.

He opened the door, followed by a guard who stood at the entrance and unconsciously helped the plotters by preventing the door from closing with a slam. As a further precaution one of the convicts stretched out his leg, above his hammock, to keep the grille open.

Pascaud bent over Little Buddha.

"Come, what's the matter with you? Let's have a look."

At that moment Little Buddha, rising to his feet, fired his revolver point blank at him. At once pandemonium reigned, more shots were fired, the convicts leapt on to the deck, and made a rush at the guards.

Pascaud sank to the floor, killed, it seemed, on the spot. His fellow-guard on the doorstep had not time to move a limb, for a bullet struck him down almost at the same time, and he fell head foremost into the alley-way.

In the other cages the convicts armed with revolvers

fired on the guards through the bars, and a general fusillade blazed out from the three cages.

Terror stricken, unable to understand what was happening to them, nor, in particular, how the convicts had secured revolvers, the guards fired into the cages as they fled like madmen, throwing themselves flat on the deck and shouting for help.

On the upper gun deck the plot which Little Buddha had revealed to the convicts was carried out in every particular. His cage, near the ship's prow, was quickly cleared, and its hundred and fifty convicts, after breaking down the companion-way at the main hatchway, threw themselves upon the guards and overwhelmed them by weight of numbers.

Some fifteen of these hapless men lay on the deck mortally wounded, while the other half at length darted from the upper gun deck to the lower gun deck, and thence to the lower deck, where the cells stood, and here they defended themselves with the courage of despair; but at that moment they were caught between two fires. And a frightful cry of victory signalized their destruction: "Chéri-Bibi! The Countess!" No one knew whence they came, but they both plunged into the fray like fiends. The awful woman was as dreadful a sight as Chéri-Bibi himself under the rays of the lanterns which cast a sinister light upon the appalling carnage.

Now the few survivors begged for mercy.

Chéri-Bibi stopped the slaughter.

"We must have hostages. Stop fighting," he commanded his men on the lower gun deck. And in a voice which drowned all other cries:

"Let these men be dragged into one of the cages and locked in!"

The cages were opened with the keys which were taken from Pascaud and the guards, and the convicts swarmed into the alley-way in a regular crush. They were seeking their prey. Half of them whom Chéri-Bibi drove from behind had to mount to the upper gun deck, where the struggle with the men under de Kerrosgouët's command had become more desperate than ever.

The Toper himself, standing behind Chéri-Bibi, saw that the dead and dying, both overseers and convicts, and the few guards whose lives had been spared, were dragged to the "financiers' cage." And in a trice they were crammed into it helter-skelter and the door locked on them.

Suddenly a voice cried: "Shooters!" And, indeed, rifles were being distributed to the men who were on their way to the upper gun deck; next supplies of cartridges were passed from hand to hand. And the men who had no arms hurried to the place where they were being given out. The distribution was taking place in the Countess's late cell.

Unseen hands were passing up arms and munitions through the gap by which the Kanaka's wife had escaped, and men were eagerly laying hold of them.

The guards whose duty it was to watch this darksome corner of the ship, this part of the hold in which the first battle against the shadowy figure of Chéri-Bibi had been fought at random, had made for the ladder when they heard the report of firing in the cages, and were massacred with most of their comrades in sight of the cells.

The distribution was effected at this spot because there was no fighting and no danger. When it was completed, two hands were outstretched from the cavity, and a voice begged some one to pull him through to the deck. Then an odd pale little figure appeared with the ingenuous look and the smiling face of a boy who had succeeded in playing a smart trick. On his head was the white cap of a cook's mate, and the body which followed showed the poor, trembling, timid body of the Dodger. The convicts grasped the meaning of many things when they saw this little scamp among them. They shouted "Hurrah!" while the journeyman baker ran up to the deck yelling:

"Chéri-Bibi . . . Chéri-Bibi for ever!"

The fight round the hatchway now simmered down. The men on deck ceased their fire, and in the thick smoke of battle could no longer sight the besiegers at the infernal opening.

The convicts wondered what new plan was in preparation on deck. Obviously it was one that boded them no good.

Chéri-Bibi satisfied himself that the convicts were

ready to follow him now that they were well armed. He explained in a few peremptory words that the moment had come to conquer or die. They must dash like a whirlwind on deck, and make short work of the warders. . . . No quarter in this fight. . . . Nothing could resist them, and if they had any stomach for the fight the *Bayard* would be theirs.

While he was speaking in this strain, the ladder was put up in its old place. Then he led them forward. The Countess, intoxicated with the fight, rushed headlong behind him, and then came the Toper, the African, Little Buddha and the rest. The Dodger joined them at the moment when Chéri-Bibi shouted "Up, rebels!"

The great mass of men holding their rifles above their heads bundled themselves into the hatchway. To clamber up the ladder was the work of a moment, but at that very moment a terrible whizzing noise, an amazing quick succession of shots re-echoed, and howls of fury and pain went up from the convicts, who for the most part fell and rolled to the feet of their comrades.

It was the Hotchkiss gun which had entered the struggle. Its small shrapnel, its gleaming glittering bullets, its "little pills" penetrated the flesh, tore the convicts' ranks, struck the steel plates of the bulkheads and the lower decks, and disseminated death on every hand.

The few men who were uninjured among the first

group of convicts fell back, leaving a pile of corpses at the entrance to the cages. Chéri-Bibi was obliged to retreat with the rest. He was not wounded, though, to all appearance, he sought death in this sanguinary encounter in which he seemed to be playing the return match with fate. The Countess pressed one hand against the bulkhead for support, while with the other she wiped with an unconscious gesture the blood from her face. A splinter from a shot had ripped open her forehead. The madness of defeat and death dwelt in her infuriated eyes and screaming mouth.

"We are done for!" growled Chéri-Bibi, while his forces behind him, crowded within the narrow channel of the cages and the ladders, yelled their determination not to die "down there" but "on deck . . . on deck."

The men behind pushed forward the men in front into the radius covered by the Hotchkiss gun, which, fortunately for the convicts, was rather narrow. Nevertheless, more men were killed.

Chéri-Bibi had reckoned without the gun.

Nothing remained but to die in their retreat unless they could succeed in getting out . . . and to get out of it. . . .

Suddenly an idea occurred to Chéri-Bibi.

"Bring the kit bags," he shouted, "all the blooming lot, and the deputy-warders' mattresses. We'll set 'em on fire; a fire as hot as a furnace! They won't stand it, and we'll get through. It's a poor look-out for those who funk scorching their paws. Who's got a light?"

"I have," said the Dodger, handing him his automatic match-box.

They heaped up the straw mattresses and canvas bags in front of the hatchway, and soon a great and acrid cloud of smoke ascended, and was succeeded by long tongues of flame, and then by a denser mass of smoke, forcing the men on deck to draw back. The Captain and his men had to move away with their Hotchkiss gun to prevent themselves from being suffocated.

Oaths and shouts abounded: "Get at the warders! . . . Fire! Fire! . . . To the pumps! Fire! They've tricked us by firing the ship. . . Ship on fire! . . . To the pumps, damn and blast it!"

And from this miniature volcano, for such the hatchway became, from this smoking chasm whence issued a clamor of pitiable or savage cries, from amid the smoke as it swept upwards, fiends in human form leapt into view. Some possessed, as it were, wings of flame and flung themselves at the overseers to set them on fire in their turn; others who had divested themselves of all clothing the better to plunge through this furnace, brandished their rifles on high as though they were clubs. . . . That was how Chéri-Bibi labored with the butt end of his terrible rifle, swooping down on many a head and creating round him a wide reddening circle.

"Forward! . . . Forward! . . . rebels, . . ." he shouted, foaming at the mouth. "Forward! . . . They can't kill the dead!"

Standing at his side was a veritable fury. It was the Countess, who waved her blood-stained hands while her abundant tresses played round her livid temples like serpents. She fought with a cutlass. Then came the Dodger, whose head had been injured by his own rifle, and who had abandoned fighting in order to act as "scout" to Chéri-Bibi and to defend him from an unlucky blow. Like King John's son at Poitiers, he cried out to Chéri-Bibi during the combat:

"Look to your left! . . . Look to your right!"

The smoke died down when the mattresses and kit bags blazed up, and from the hatchway, which was now clear, an innumerable and hideous band of men with a thousand heads crept in an unceasing stream. . . . The inferno was vomiting forth its devils. . . . The fight was no longer anything but a hand-to-hand struggle in which it was impossible to distinguish one man from another. The Hotchkiss gun was of no service in this indescribable mêlée. The Captain and de Vilène, covered with wounds, continued to fight, yielding their ground by inches and heartening their men by the force of their heroic example.

With his own hand the Captain struck down half a dozen convicts, and he strove to come face to face with Chéri-Bibi, but that elusive individual seemed invulnerable.

Overwhelmed by weight of numbers, half of his men unarmed, Barrachon was forced to give way, and he ordered the retreat when young Sub-Lieutenant de Kerrosgouët fell gloriously beside the Hotchkiss gun which was under his charge. It was necessary to save the gun, to retire to the protection of the second Hotchkiss, and to run out both guns against the rabble who had mastered the entire forecastle deck. That was their only chance of safety.

Suddenly a terrible hail of shot took the sailors and military overseers in the rear. Barrachon and de Vilène turned round, and a simultaneous exclamation of despair escaped from their lips. Above them, on the roof of the chart-room, they sighted three fiends all black and a little man all white. Three coal-trimmers and the journeyman baker, the Dodger, had seized the 47 mm. Hotchkiss, and were turning it on the men on deck, not hesitating, in their frenzy for destruction, to mow down their own men.

Nothing was left to the Captain but to get away with the last of his men to the quarter-deck and there to entrench himself with the other gun.

The Captain ordered the retreat. He could depend on some hundred and fifty unwounded men who would sell their lives dearly.

Drunk with victory, some of them black with powder, others red with blood, Chéri-Bibi's men were getting ready to rush forward and finish off the remainder of the crew and warders, when a dense smoke issued from the hatchways, and the sinister cry "Ship on fire" caused them to waver.

The conflagration made a barrier between the two forces.  And the necessity to arrest the scourge before it could destroy the ship which had cost them so much to conquer, seized the entire mass of insurgents. Under the direction of the Dodger, who knew how to man the pumps, the convicts set to work to extinguish the fire.

At the same time this strange figure who understood more about the ship than any one else, ordered all the entrances which led to the heart of the conflagration to be closed, and the hatches covered with wet tarpaulins.  The convicts fell foul of each other, like men possessed, in this great and frightful confusion of dead and dying.  Cries and oaths went up in the fast closing night.  From the depths below, where the women and children were incarcerated, came heartrending shrieks as though they were being burnt alive. In the after part of the *Bayard,* on the quarter-deck, spasmodic firing still continued.  And then it died into silence, for Barrachon and his men had fired their last shot.  Every man thought that the end was in sight.

To the unparalleled evils of fire and sword was added yet another: tempest. The roaring of the fire, and the hissing of the water as it evaporated amidships, were succeeded by the howling of the wind which once again had veered to the north-west and was blowing a gale. In the sky, above those figures covered with blood, clouds were gathering from the pale distant horizon, with the coming of an ominous dawn. Tremendous waves already swept the seas and played with the wretched vessel which could not maneuver now that she was without a chief to control her.

With no sort of guidance she could neither keep her head nor sail before the wind nor avoid the violent buffeting of the waves on her quarter.

The demons who came out of the inferno returned to the inferno. Standing on the Captain's bridge, at the post to which pride and rebellion had raised him, and where he could do nothing for himself or others, nothing but rejoice at the disaster which had befallen them and take the lead in it, Chéri-Bibi was like an evil spirit, with head once more upraised—in defiance —to the God who afflicted him, his own particular God, whom he called *Fatalitas*.

On the deck in the midst of this confused medley of men and sea and skies, a young girl was on her knees praying to the God whom she called "Our Father which art in Heaven," and beseeching His mercy for all the souls on the ship without exception —convicts, convict guards and Chéri-Bibi.

# CHAPTER VIII

## BROTHER AND SISTER

TAKING advantage of the leisure which first the return
of calmer weather, second the successful handling of
the fire, and finally the "restoration of order" on
board, had left him during the last twenty-four hours,
Chéri-Bibi was trying on, before the wardrobe, his
new clothes. It must be admitted that the uniform
fitted him like a glove, and he turned round and round
with an expression of ingenuousness on his face that
would have disarmed his judges.

"For that matter," he said to himself, "I don't see
why this uniform should not suit me, seeing that my
own suits the Captain so well."

At this juncture the Dodger came in. He had been
appointed Sub-Lieutenant. His pierrot-like face, or-
namented with strips of court plaster from temple
to chin, bore witness to a scar of which he was so
proud that he would not have exchanged it for a king-
dom.

"Captain," he said, "the Lieutenant has just been
taking the ship's bearings."

"I see," said Chéri-Bibi in a tone which indicated an
indifference to anything but stripes and brass buttons,

the fascinating effect of which he was examining and admiring in the glass.

"It seems that we turned a few degrees too far to the south."

"Quite possible. . . . Tell me, Dodger, what do you think of my uniform?"

"First rate, Captain. . . . It looks as if it had been made for you."

"All the same," sighed Chéri-Bibi, twirling an imaginary moustache, "it was unfortunate that we had a Minister of Marine who abolished full dress. I once saw full dress when I rowed in the Admiral's boat, on the first of January, in Cayenne. Think of the cocked hat!"

"The epaulets."

"The trousers with gold braid."

"The dress-coat," sighed the Dodger. "Oh, at La Rochelle whenever there was a ball at the Prefecture the military came from Lorient in full fig. In my opinion the Minister was jealous . . . and you may depend upon it, he was a civilian."

"A socialist minister," said Chéri-Bibi with a contemptuous grimace. "There's no hope with such people. They are the enemies of government and of all discipline. Now, bear this in mind, Dodger, without discipline, which emanates directly from government, and which can only be respected if it is adorned with distinctive badges, everything goes. There's an end of civilized society."

"How well you put it, Captain. You ought to repeat that to Little Buddha, who turns up his nose
when I ask him to do anything, twiddles his thumbs,
and passes his time in getting as drunk as a lord.
. . . He is under my orders and he ought to do what
I say. He tells me he doesn't care a damn. But it's
not my fault if he hasn't found a non-commissioned
officer's uniform that'll fit him."

"What about the Top? Has he found a uniform
that suits him?"

"Yes, he's managed to unearth one."

"What is his rank?" asked the Captain.

"Well, he's yeoman of signals."

"That's right, it's just as well," returned Chéri-
Bibi as he crammed his fingers into a fine pair of
white gloves. "That's a bit of luck. We haven't got
a yeoman of signals, have we?"

At that point the Toper showed his face at the door.
He was attired in a lieutenant's full dress which was
much too tight for him, but he did not complain lest
they should find him a petty officer's cast-off uniform
which would not have satisfied his ambition. His
right arm was in a sling.

"The Kanaka has just found the ship's position,"
he said.

"Yes, I know that," returned Chéri-Bibi with an
astonishingly easy bearing. "Will you have a cig-
arette?"

"A stinker. I don't mind if I do, Captain."

"Damn it all, I'll put you under arrest if I hear you use such language again. Do you understand, Toper? A stinker! Get it into your nut once for all, my lad, that you are my second lieutenant. Well, speak like a gentleman or give up your gold stripes."

"Very good, Captain," replied the unfortunate Toper, lowering his head with an abashed air.

There was a knock at the door and Little Buddha came in, as round as a top and as red as a turkey-cock. Dressed as an ordinary seaman, but wearing the distinctive marks of an orderly—jacket, trousers with wide ends, large turned back collar, oilskin cap —he wore a white bandage over his forehead almost completely hiding the traces of the late fight. He gave the regulation salute.

"Captain, I've come to tell you that the Lieutenant, who was able to determine the hour-angle this morning and was on the point of finding the meridian altitude, has just taken an accurate observation . . ."

"You, my dear fellow," interrupted Chéri-Bibi, "are trying to show off on the plea that you've been longer at school than we have. And perhaps you'd like to make us believe that you know something of navigation. You've got a swollen head, Little Buddha. What good is it going to do me that he's taken the ship's position? I don't care one way or the other as long as the fine weather lasts."

"All the same, Captain, we must know where we're going and what we're going to do," they objected.

"I'll tell you when it suits my fancy, you understand, you fellows. I am the only person to give orders here. If you are not satisfied with your positions you'd better say so. Isn't the program for the day good enough for you? Stroll in the Zoological Gardens, ball, banquet, junketing. . . . Serious business to-morrow. Hold your jaw until the yeoman of signals enters your cabin and says: 'Gentlemen of the Staff are expected to report themselves to the Captain.' Then I will tell you what I intend to do. Do you follow me? Well, right about turn, march!"

"Captain, I want a word with you on behalf of the Countess," ventured Little Buddha diffidently, turning back when he reached the door.

"Oh, rats! What does she want with me?"

"A few moments' conversation."

"What does she take me for?" exclaimed Chéri-Bibi in an indignant voice. "Every moment of my time belongs to the community. I have no right to waste a single second, particularly in listening to a woman's chatter."

"I say, Captain, she's been very useful to us. . . ."

"She's in love with you, Captain," cried the Toper. "You can see that from the fiery glances which she casts at you . . ."

But the Toper stopped short when he saw the look which Chéri-Bibi shot at him. The Captain went up to the Lieutenant as if he intended to annihilate him.

"Be quiet!" he snarled. . . . "You may as well understand one thing: Chéri-Bibi has always been a moral man, and it is not at this moment when you see him wearing a Captain's uniform that he'll begin to go to the bad. The Kanaka is a friend of mine. A friend's wife is sacred. Besides, I want the women on board to be respected. The reason why you, Toper, are not dead at this moment is because Sister St. Mary of the Angels saved your life. Don't forget that. And if you say another word which is not strictly proper you'll have her to deal with, I can tell you."

"Very good, Captain," said the Lieutenant, standing to attention.

"How is the saintly girl getting on?" he inquired.

"Much better," replied Chéri-Bibi. "The Kanaka and I passed the night at her bedside. She is now out of danger. She was suffering from a little fever. As to the bullet, that's a mere trifle. It can stay where it is in the shoulder blade, and be extracted later on. Nothing is the matter with her lungs, which is the important point. And now go, all of you, where duty calls you."

They went out after the Captain. A number of men on the lower decks were washing, cleaning, rubbing and polishing, and endeavoring, as far as possible to remove the traces of the frightful agony which had convulsed the *Bayard*. The men wore convicts' garb and they bore a number on their arms. They were closely watched by convict guards, revolver in hand.

The Sergeant on duty saluted the Captain as he passed.

"Anything fresh, Carrots?"

"Nothing fresh, Captain."

"How about the ward . . . ?"

"Captain!" the Toper had the courage to interject.

"Oh, yes, I was forgetting," said Chéri-Bibi, smiling at his slip. "And Messieurs the late military overseers," he went on, bending over and examining the convicts' work, "are they getting used to their new positions?"

"Daren't grumble, Captain. Besides, the first who kicked would have his brains blown out."

"That's the standing order, Sergeant," said Chéri-Bibi approvingly. "By the way, stock-jobber, what's been done with my standing orders?"

"We've read them to the men and to the prisoners in the cages, and in addition I've posted them on deck."

"Good," complimented Chéri-Bibi. "Authority and system, those are the twin masters on board represented by myself. Before those two precious forces— listen to this, you fellows—every man on board must bow, officers and ship's company alike. If we want to do any good, we must have an iron discipline. There must be no exceptions. Every man must perfectly understand that he is the master of nothing on my ship but the air he breathes, and then only when he is actually breathing it. . . ."

He strode on, drawing himself up to his full height

and followed by his staff, who were turned to stone while the military overseers—the convicts of yesterday—presented arms.

He stopped for a moment, gazed at the deck, and addressed a few short sharp words to a petty officer who was lazily directing the cleaning of a ladder.

"There are bloodstains here. . . . Have them scraped off."

He entered the sick-bay, which was crowded with the wounded and re-echoing with their sufferings. For twenty-four hours the Kanaka and the hospital orderlies had been amputating legs and arms amidst shrieking men. Chéri-Bibi's appearance was greeted with shouts of mingled enthusiasm and hostility. And suddenly the man who had come with the intention of making a little speech of encouragement to them, felt suffocated in the oppressive odor of iodoform, and he turned his back and went away unashamed, declaring that "war was a horrible thing," and that he wondered at those generals who, after a victory, could ride over the battle-field amid the dead and dying with a smile on their lips, such as he had seen when he was a schoolboy in pictures in his "History of France." For himself, it made him feel rather inclined to weep.

He was under the influence of this impression when, having sent a message that he was coming, he opened the door of Sister St. Mary's cabin. She lay in bed under the assiduous care of two nurses. A look of unspeakable sadness was on her pale face, and she did not return her brother's greeting. Her eyes were lifted to heaven as if in prayer. Indeed her glance avoided the terrible man. After he had dismissed her nurses she murmured, still without looking at him:

"Is that you, Monsieur? What do you want with me? I cannot help you now that God has forsaken you. I prayed that He would bring you to repentance. But your fresh crimes surpass in horror those which you committed before. . . . Heavens, what a number of slain!" and she covered her face with her hands as though to shut out the awful spectacle of mutiny and massacre of which, sick unto death, she had been a witness towards the end.

Chéri-Bibi regarded her for some time without speaking, filled with a new emotion which he vainly strove to conceal. At length he took a chair and sat down by her bedside. Then he grasped her hand, which shook and trembled in his. For a moment she tried to withdraw it, but finally it remained passive under his dominating pressure.

"My little Jacqueline," he gasped in a hoarse voice. "My little Jacqueline."

The unhappy girl shook her head gently, mournfully, for there was now no little Jacqueline . . . had not been for a long time, a very long time. There was no little Jacqueline since men had made her suffer so greatly. Not since there happened to be one man —the father of her best friend, of her young mistress,

of her good Cecily—who had dared to run foul of
that innocence which, until then, had been untouched
save "by the wing of prayer," to use the language of
Chéri-Bibi, which at times was singularly poetic.
There was no longer a little Jacqueline since her
Chéri-Bibi had . . . Oh, Chéri-Bibi, Chéri-Bibi!
She had loved him so!

She saw him once more quite a little boy, joining
in innocent games with her in the fragrant garden
in the break of the cliff in those happy spring days in
Normandy. He was a very ugly little boy, slightly
capricious, slightly odd, but entirely gentle and good,
and obedient in whatever she told him to do.

In turn they sought each other at school in Dieppe,
and went back home like sensible children, saying
"How do you do," to the good wives of Le Pollet
mending their nets, on the doorsteps, with long wooden
needles. And then she saw again the hill at Puys
with the flowers and butterflies all along the way.

Sometimes, though it was forbidden, they returned
home by way of the cliff so as to have sight of the
white sails on the sea, and to throw pebbles from the
top onto the beach. They played and rolled about in
the grass, or else, while eating their bread and butter,
watched with curiosity the waving arms of the sema-
phore. He was even then strong and brave and stood
in front of her when the cows drew near and stared
too closely at them. How very fond they were of
each other! . . . Chéri-Bibi! Chéri-Bibi! Her lips

could not hold back the four dear syllables; they slipped out, softly, musically, as of yore. Chéri-Bibi!

Chéri-Bibi burst into tears. He sank with his head on the bed and wept in his fine Captain's uniform as he had never wept in his cast-off convict's clothes.

She too cried; and at length she said, gently withdrawing her hand from his despairing clasp:

"I ask God to forgive me for it, but, you see, in spite of your crimes I have not forgotten those days . . . that blessed time of our childhood . . . and if I still think of you without execrating you like other people, it is because I cannot forget that you committed your first crime for my sake. Oh, why did you set your mind on avenging me, Chéri-Bibi?"

As he heard those words the monster raised his head, instantly dry-eyed. He was consumed with a fury that burnt up his tears.

He rose with a wild gesture, stood erect above the poor nun's bed, and lacerated the skin on his face with his nails to still the need in him to tear something to pieces.

"Oh, you too . . . you too! You believed the Judge, and you always thought that I was lying. And yet you knew what I was. You saw me every day. You kissed me every day. You read my heart as you read a book. I've never lied to you . . . to you. Yet you were like every one else, you believed that I was guilty of that crime. I wrote you fifty times explaining how it all happened. I swore to you that I was innocent. And now this is what you tell me. If it is for this that you came so far you might have stayed at home, Sister St. Mary of the Angels."

"I came about another crime," she said, laying her hand on her breast, for she felt as if she were stifling, and Chéri-Bibi's anger had appalled her.

"For another what?"

"For another crime of which I know that you are innocent."

"Oh, really, there are many of that sort," he said in a thick voice. "But the first one means more to me than all the others. It is a load on my mind. It was the cause of everything . . . the starting point of everything. . . . The others have passed from my memory. . . . But that one . . . that one made me what I am. . . . Oh, I swear to you that I did not commit that crime as people believe. Why did you not have faith in what I wrote to you; what I once said to you in the Assize Court? Is it worth while to worship the Almighty if He makes you as blind as other people are? You were the first to condemn me. . . .

"There you have the justice of your God, which does not see more clearly than any other justice. Oh, Jacqueline . . . I'll tell you something. I expected you to come to the Assize Court, and to cry aloud: 'What he says is true. . . . On my soul my brother is innocent!' But you didn't come, and you still believe that it was I who faked up the whole story."

"Yes, I believed that you did it, Chéri-Bibi," said Sister St. Mary, sinking her voice. "But I say again that I have nothing against you for that. I have taken upon myself, before God, the burden of that particular crime, because you cared for me sufficiently to commit it for me."

"Perhaps you're right. . . . And it might well have happened. But if it had happened, believe me, Jacqueline . . . if it had happened, well, I wouldn't have made a mystery of it. I would have told you. I would have told all the world. I would have boasted about it in the country. That is the point which you haven't realized, Jacqueline. That is the point which you must realize. . . . If you had understood it in that way, why, I shouldn't be looking to-day for the man in the gray hat, the man who was the cause of all my troubles. You would have played your part. You would have remained in the country. . . . You would have kept your eyes and ears open. . . . You would, perhaps, have discovered him. You would have won back your brother's honor before he had become what he is. Now it's too late; there's nothing to be done. I am looked upon as a terror in the world from what I can gather. Every murder that is perpetrated is put down to Chéri-Bibi. Well, it was bound to come true in the end, for here I am at the head of a notorious gang. And since they would have it so, I must employ them. . . .

"I am accursed, Jacqueline. It's no use praying

for me. . . . Well, while I'm on this point, I may
tell you that no trouble of any sort would have occurred but for the Captain, whose obstinacy is the
cause of it all.  He is a pig-headed fellow is the
Captain, I can tell you. . . . I offered him a way out
of the difficulty which was highly original.  Do you
know what I suggested?  That he should land me
quietly on some deserted and uninhabited shore . . .
far from the society which sickens me.  And it may
be that there I should have become a saint.  Upon my
word, when I think of it I feel myself capable of
being one!  He refused to hear of it.  He wanted
war.  I said to him: 'Since it is war between us, I'll
fight you.'  Then the fighting broke out, and there
you are!"

"No, no, it wasn't fighting, wretched men that you
are, cursed of God," faltered Sister St. Mary, whose
eyes were filled anew with the awful vision of the
slaughter.  "You murdered them."

"What do you mean?  What do you mean?  Look
here, have you lost your senses?  Come, tell me this:
What did they do when they fired upon us?"

"They did their duty."

"And I tell you that you know absolutely nothing
about it.  You are a girl who can't see the difference
between one kind of death and another."  He went
past the glass and caught sight of himself in uniform.
"Many more men were killed at the Battle of Tra-
falgar!"

He sincerely believed that his sister was quite unjust in comparing his "naval battle," as he called it, with the criminal incidents in his extraordinary career.

As she did not answer his sharp retort he turned round and observed that her head had fallen on to the pillow. Her face was so white that he was greatly alarmed, and thought of calling in the Kanaka, who had taken the place, in the sick-bay, of the chief surgeon killed on the field of honor. But she opened her eyes again and said with a sigh:

"Chéri-Bibi, I hope that God, in His mercy is going to take me to Him. I will pray for you, but before I die you must promise me one thing, that you will respect the lives of the people who are left, and will not touch a hair of the heads of the women and children here."

"I can promise you, my sister, that we will land them uninjured on the coast as soon as we can do so without danger," said Chéri-Bibi, almost forcing her to take a few drops of a draught which gave her renewed life. "The women and children are in their own quarters. I will see that they want for nothing. I am having them guarded, and there is nothing to fear on that score."

In spite of his promise Sister St. Mary betrayed a certain anxiety.

"The poor things," she complained. "I fear the worst from such ruffians."

"You can be easy in your mind, I assure you,"

he replied with a knowing air. "The ruffians have everything they want."

"What do you mean? . . . You frighten me."

"Weren't there women prisoners in the cages?"

"Oh," she muttered with a blush.

"There's no 'Oh' about it. . . . Both parties are made to understand each other. And then don't think that my men are heartless. Some of them even burst into poetry. They used to write each other love letters, and the unfortunate thing was that they were kept apart. Well, now they are together. They are satisfied; they don't want any wrong-doing, and they are as meek as lambs in my hands. Listen to this as an example: Yesterday, when we were clearing the ship of the dead bodies, throwing them into the sea, two men from the old financiers' cage took advantage of our saying a *De Profundis* to fight like a couple of bruisers on the lower deck, for a woman, an old offender, uglier, upon my word, than the seven deadly sins. I broke the heads of both of them with my revolver.

"Oh, but I intend to have some regard for morality on board. The men have grasped the position, and, please believe me, are now civil to women. For that matter I promised the Captain that it should be so, for he feared lest they might behave badly to the fair sex. Forgive me for speaking of these things, but you brought it on yourself."

"Where is the Captain?"

"He insisted on joining his crew and the military

overseers who were already in the cages. I promised that their lives should be spared in return for their assistance, which we forced them to render us, in weathering the storm."

"How do you work the ship now?"

"By our own resources," replied Chéri-Bibi, "and with the assistance of the old crew. We've kept two helmsmen and the chief engineer, and such other men as are required for the ship's working. They continue to help us, under pain of death, and subject to the authority of the Kanaka, the doctor who looks after you with so much devotion. He was a bit of a jack of all trades before he found himself among us. He was once at the naval school at Brest, then he studied medicine, afterwards he became a ship's surgeon, and he's been round the world several times. He knows a thing or two, and has been very useful to us."

"In what way has he been useful? You are convicts and madmen. The day is not far distant when you will be hunted out and punished. Have you considered that an adventure like this can lead to absolutely no good?"

"My dear girl, people will think that the ship was lost with all hands in the storm. He shall know how to manage that. And afterwards, we shall take our chances like so many other people in the world. But, first of all, I promise you that all the men who are left over from the old crew shall be landed in a safe place. Furthermore, I hope that you will soon be well again. And you too, my dear Jacqueline, you shall be delivered from this hell."

"In which you are Satan, Chéri-Bibi. Oh, may the Lord lead you to think things over before you add new crimes to the old ones. Just now, you spoke of the desert. You wanted to become a hermit. If you wish it, Chéri-Bibi, I will go with you."

"Too late! I can't leave my friends in the lurch. After getting them in such a fix, it would be cowardice, take that from Chéri-Bibi."

"Your friends?"

"Of course," said Chéri-Bibi, "they are detestable rascals. But I didn't choose their company. . . . It was the judges who wrongly condemned me. It was society which put me in a cage as if I were a wild beast. It was Fatality which, as I know full well, one cannot fight against."

"I, too, Chéri-Bibi, have had my troubles. I, too, have been pursued by Fatality. But I took refuge in religion, not in crime."

"You! That's a very different thing," said Chéri-Bibi in a dogmatic tone. "You are a girl and I am a man. . . . There are certain things that a man will not take lying down if he has any grit in him. He begins to kick . . . particularly if he's a butcher's boy! You see, Jacqueline, they were too unjust to me. It was bound to lead to disaster. . . . But, tell

me, what did you mean just now? . . . You spoke
of another murder."

Sister St. Mary of the Angels once more raised her
eyes to heaven.

"One drop of blood," she said, " a tiny drop of
blood which was not shed by you in the red sea in
which you are sailing."

"Out with it. It doesn't often happen that any
one says to me: 'You are not guilty of this crime.'
To what crime are you referring?"

"To the murder of the Marquis du Touchais,
Cecily's father-in-law."

"Cecily! . . . Tell me about her. . . . Tell me
about her. . . . Now that my poor parents are dead
I'm not interested in what may happen at Dieppe.
. . . But Cecily . . . Just now when you recalled
our walks on the cliff I was thinking of her. . . . I
saw her as she was when sometimes she came among
the corn with her mother. . . . She made herself
garlands of corn and corn-poppies . . . and then
afterwards when I delivered the meat she weighed
the joints, and always ordered calves' bones for the
gravy. . . . She asked for them in so soft a voice.
. . . She liked both of us. . . . Does she still believe that I murdered her father on purpose?"

"Yes, she still believes it."

"Oh! . . . Does she still believe that I murdered
her husband's father as well?"

"Yes, she still believes it."

The monster clenched his fists and wrung his fingers.

"That, you see, is the most awful thing of all. . . . Because I can tell you, and perhaps you have guessed it . . . I was in love with Cecily. I idolized her. . . . Oh, of course, it was from such a distance that it couldn't do her any harm. Well, I shall never forgive your God, you understand, Jacqueline, for allowing fate to sully my reputation in her eyes. . . . You may say so on my behalf."

"God knows that you are innocent of the Marquis du Touchais's murder."

"God is not sufficient. Is there any one else who knows it? Tell me, Jacqueline."

"I know it."

"Any one else?"

"Some woman whom you know very well, Chéri-Bibi."

"What's her name? . . . You must tell me. . . . You must tell me everything. . . . As you may well believe, this is something more than a piece of childish nonsense. I am not asking you at random as though it were a date in French history. I insist on your telling me. If I said that it was to demand justice you would laugh. Is there any justice for Chéri-Bibi? No! But I want justice done to me. Because the person who knows that I am innocent equally knows who is guilty. She knows the man in the gray hat. She might perhaps give me his name. Oh, pray to your God, Sister St. Mary of the Angels, for if

it is true I may be able to lay hands on him. . . .
Afterwards I will ask nothing better than to enter a
Trappist monastery."

"Chéri-Bibi, I haven't told you all this so that you
may be revenged on him.  Besides, I can't help you
to wreak your vengeance, for I do not know who the
guilty one is."

"No, but there are people who do know.  Come,
my little sister, my little Jacqueline . . . tell me how
it all happened . . . tell me what I ought to know.
You say that you're going to die.  I tell you that it's
not true, but if you think so, you can't wish to carry
a secret like that to the grave with you. I'm listening."

"It's not I who ought to speak, but some one else.
. . . Some one who will reveal everything at the
proper time."

"But suppose she dies, what would happen then?"

"She has made arrangements for everything to be
known when the time comes."

"When the time comes!  A lot of good that will
do me!  But look here, is there no way of putting the
clock on a bit?  Tell me what you know about it."

He spoke to her, the better to persuade her, in the
slightly sing-song schoolboy tone and in the rough
phrases which were characteristic of the country round
about Le Pollet.

Sister St. Mary of the Angels passed her hand over
her forehead, and seemed for a moment to be taking
counsel with herself.

"Yes," she said, "you ought at least to know who it is that possesses the secret. Listen then, Chéri-Bibi. It occurred some days before Christmas. I was going round the country collecting subscriptions for the poor children in the public nursery. I called on the Marchioness du Touchais."

"Cecily."

"Yes, Cecily. She was still very friendly with me, often confiding her troubles to me, and never losing an opportunity of alleviating want when I brought a case under her notice, if it was in her power. . . ."

"What do you mean, if it was in her power? Hadn't she always the power to do so? I thought those people were millionaires."

"They're getting richer and richer every day, Chéri-Bibi. Old Bourrelier . . ."

"The man I murdered," he jeered in a dismal voice.

Sister St. Mary went on as if she had not heard him.

"Old Bourrelier invested his money well. After his death it was discovered that he had bought, for next to nothing, a considerable amount of property in Rouen, in the old St. Julien quarter, and an immense number of old tumble-down houses which, at that time, brought in very little, but which since the municipality transformed that locality have become one of the finest properties in Rouen. It all belonged to old Bourrelier, and it now belongs to the du Touchais's.

People say that they cleared more than twenty million francs out of this affair alone."

"Twenty million francs!" sighed Chéri-Bibi with eyes upturned as if he could discern the promised land.

"Oh, the du Touchais's are immensely rich now. Madame Bourrelier is dead, and her death brought more grist to the mill."

"Not altogether," said Chéri-Bibi. "Cecily Bourrelier had a brother."

"Yes, Robert. . . . She still has him, but I don't think she'll have him very long. Cecily's husband will see to that."

"What do you mean?"

"Oh, it's simple enough. The two young men were scarcely out of each other's sight before Maxime was married. It is the same thing now. They lead very dissipated lives, you understand. Maxime is killing him by degrees with drink . . . and other things. He arranges for his brother-in-law always to be surrounded by a certain class of women who play his game for him. . . . For many years it's been a great scandal in Dieppe. They carry on in a way which arouses comment in the entire district, particularly in the summer during the racing season. Robert Bourrelier is only the shadow of his former self. When he dies, his money, like the rest, will go to the Marquis."

"You always say the Marquis's money," returned

Chéri-Bibi, who was listening to his sister with absorbed interest, "but I suppose it belongs in part to Cecily. . . . And with a fortune which exceeds thirty million francs, she can certainly help the poor and buy Christmas trees for the public nurseries," he added dogmatically.

"That's exactly where you make a mistake. . . . There's something that I haven't explained. The Marquis keeps a tight hold of the purse strings in his wife's house. She has nothing at her command. He controls everything. Sometimes she has to ask him for money as if she were a beggar woman."

"That's too thick. But she's only got to say the word. Everything belongs to her."

"I dare say; but she is forced to give way to her husband's every wish because of their son, Bernard, whom his father is continually threatening to send to a boarding school in Paris to be brought up as he pleases. Remember that the only consolation the unhappy woman has is this son whom she worships, and trains and educates herself. She would rather die than be parted from him, and the thought that he might be taken from her and placed in a school, some distance away, is enough to make her submit to anything. Besides, she never opposes the arbitrary decisions of her husband, and her life is entirely bound up in Bernard. She knows that a part of the fortune, whatever her husband may do, must revert to her child. Consequently the Marquis can go his own way. For that matter he doesn't worry himself, as I've explained. There are many things that I could tell you on that subject, things of an unheard-of cruelty to poor Cecily, but it does not behoove me to enter into those horrors."

"Yes, yes, please, Jacqueline, my little Jacqueline, tell me everything . . . everything that can make me still further loathe and detest the monster who took Cecily from me."

He spoke in such tones, alike of entreaty and fury, and the language seemed so extravagant coming from his lips that his sister paused in alarm.

"When I say 'took Cecily from me,'" muttered Chéri-Bibi, "I know what I mean, and I am certainly the only one who does know, seeing that she was never mine. But, after all, he robbed her of happiness. Well, it is as though he had robbed me of my happiness, assuming that I ever had any. Do you realize something of what I feel now? Go on, my little Jacqueline . . . what else has he done, the scoundrel?"

"Many other things like those which I have just told you. . . . You will be able to grasp the position. The young Marchioness lived after her marriage at the Château du Touchais on the cliff which you know so well. She settled down there with the Dowager Marchioness, Maxime's mother. Her own mother, I must tell you, died almost immediately after old Bourrelier."

"Yes, yes, you needn't dwell on that," said Chéri-Bibi.

"You will remember what a princely domain the Château du Touchais was," went on Sister St. Mary, "and how Maxime was as proud as Punch of it. Well, one day he made his wife and his mother give up the place, and do you know why? To establish there under the nose of the poor things a . . . a woman . . . his . . . exactly . . . you've guessed it."

Chéri-Bibi, incensed, gave a start.

"That was too awful, you know, Jacqueline. I have done many things in my life," he said in a tone of sincerity, "but I would never have hurt my mother's feelings or put my wife to shame. . . . Where did the poor women go to live?"

"They had no wish to leave the country in which they were both born. Cecily went back to the Bourréliers' house, and the Dowager Marchioness rented a small cottage close by."

"I can imagine that there was a great deal of tittle-tattle in the country."

"You cannot conceive what a life the Marquis led her. Not a day passed without the other woman managing to inflict some affront upon her. . . . As you know, Puys is a small place; it's almost like living in the same street. The odious woman had only to turn round to belittle the Marchioness with her show, to splash her with her carriages and motor-cars. In short, as we say at home, she was the only one in it.

. . . Throughout the district, within a certain radius, although she did not belong to the place, people called her the 'Belle of Dieppe.' That was the name which the Parisians who stay at Dieppe during the summer christened her, because the Marquis's yacht was called the *Belle of Dieppe*."

"But what's her real name? I don't suppose she's any better than she should be," growled Chéri-Bibi, making a wry face. "Some woman who hangs about Paris, some chorus girl!"

"No, no; she's a lady, moving in fashionable Parisian society. She comes from Poland, and she has a name, a real name, and lives at her husband's place during the summer. He is the Baron de Proskof."

"Well, and what does the husband say about it?"

"He doesn't say anything, and the story goes that he has no say in the matter. . . . It seems that the Marquis du Touchais took over the Baron's wife, who is very beautiful, and paid the Baron a million francs."

"What a delightful world to live in!" exclaimed Chéri-Bibi, with a gesture of disgust, and tears in his eyes as he thought of Cecily. "Oh, I fancy I see her now. . . . She must suffer greatly with such carrion round her; she who is so fastidious and sensitive. I can't help pitying her. . . . It's all very fine to say that the creature is 'the only one in it.' It's not fair to allow respectable women to be crushed by a thing

like that. . . . Oh, if I had the power I'd make her
sit up. So you say that poor Cecily . . ."

"Well, yes. . . . All this has led me away from
the subject, but you now realize that Cecily is not
her own mistress and is very unhappy. Every one at
Dieppe sympathizes with her . . . she is so kind.
. . . As I was saying, I called on her one evening
before Christmas. It was last winter. I went to see
her at her house, but I was told that she had 'returned'
with her son, the Dowager Marchioness, and Rose,
the lady-companion, to Puys, to the Bourreliers' villa,
where they were intending to spend quietly the Christmas holidays. I had to see her at once since I wanted
to make up a certain sum to buy a Christmas tree for
the poor children. In spite of the snow and the rough
weather I did not hesitate to climb the hill, and behold
me ringing the bell at the Bourreliers' house. I never
go where we lived so happily with our parents, my
poor Chéri-Bibi, without a feeling of emotion which
you will readily understand."

"Do I understand! . . ."

"I rang the bell more than once. Some one in the
distance called out in a voice which I did not recognize, 'Who's there?' for of course the keeper's lodge
was unoccupied. I replied that it was Sister St. Mary
of the Angels. A lantern and a shadow appeared and
the door was opened. Who opened it? It was Rose,
the lady-companion, to whom I had never had the
opportunity of speaking, because though the old lady
was pleasant enough with her mistress, she was quite

surly with other people. . . . She never stopped to
chat with any one. Apart from her association with
the old Marchioness there was something mysterious
about her. On that evening, however, she received
me quite amiably, though it seemed to me that when
she took my hand to lead me through the garden her
fingers trembled. I thanked her, telling her that I
knew the house perfectly well, for I had lived in it
when I was a child. . . . With that she coughed in an
odd manner and changed the subject . I already had
a vague feeling that a trifling something had happened
that was not entirely natural. When all is said, it may
have been usual for the old lady's hand to shake like
that. She showed me into the drawing-room, where
I found the two marchionesses and the little boy."

"How old is Cecily's child?" asked Chéri-Bibi in
a low voice.

"Young Bernard must be six years old now," answered the nun, who had not failed to observe the
emotion which seized her convict brother whenever
she mentioned Cecily's name. "The child is very
fond of me because I've rather spoilt him when I've
had the opportunity."

"He's like his mother, I suppose?" questioned
Chéri-Bibi fiercely.

"No, he is not a bit like his mother; he is almost
dark, while she is fair."

"Hang it all, he's like his father," snarled Chéri-
Bibi, clenching his fists.

"Well, no; he isn't like his father either. He hasn't got his father's heavy and rough manner or anything that resembles him in the slightest degree."

"Come, that's a good thing. It would have been a pity had he taken after his father. It was the color of his hair which made you say he wasn't like his mother, but he will be like her later on, you'll see. . . . At all events; I hope the poor little chap will be like her. . . . Go on. I'm listening."

"Old Rose sat down with us in the drawing-room, busying herself with her needlework and not saying a word. Nevertheless I felt that she was looking at me all the while. Why was she staring at me like that? We talked about the poor children, about Christmas, about the treat that we were preparing at the hospital, and, of course, the ladies promised me their assistance, and slipped a little money into my hand. I wanted to take my leave, but they would not allow me to go owing to the weather, for the snow was falling in great flakes. The wind, too, had risen. You can imagine the battle of the elements on the cliff. I saw that I must be sensible, and I stayed to dinner with the ladies, hoping that after dinner I might get back to Dieppe. But nothing of the sort. There was a regular storm. They had no conveyance at the villa at that time. They kept me for the night after sending their manservant, Jacquart, whom you knew, to inform the hospital that they need not expect me. After dinner we returned to the drawing-room, and the Dowager Marchioness, thinking to please me, recalled the days when as a child I lived in the villa with our parents. She spoke of me, but she took care not to speak of you."

"Of course," agreed Chéri-Bibi with a gloomy look. "Go on."

"And yet for a moment she let herself go over the recollection of a fishing party, on the beach, when you were quite a kid, and saved from drowning a child who was bathing. Do you remember?"

"No . . . I've forgotten my good deeds . . . they would embarrass me," growled Chéri-Bibi with a still more gloomy air.

"The Dowager Marchioness allowed herself to mention your name. . . . And then a silence fell. . . . We remained there, the four of us, without uttering a word."

"Yes, my name created a slight sensation. Incidentally, the Marchioness was a blunderer. . . . What then?"

"I . . . I felt as though I were choking . . . and I had nothing to say. . . . I could not speak a word. . . . The two others . . ."

"Yes, the two others were thinking: one of them that I had murdered her husband, and the other that I had murdered her father. What a delightful party! And you, Jacqueline, for your part, were entitled to consider that Cecily's father was the worst of blackguards. It was difficult to carry on a conversation in such circumstances. . . . You all three felt that you were the victims of the monster man. . . . Go on."

"I seemed to be about to choke, and I began to cry wildly, unable to keep back great sobs. Then they were on their feet, the two Marchionesses who were also weeping, and kissed me affectionately, and little Bernard, who did not know what to make of it all, came over and kissed me too."

"What was Rose doing during that time?" asked Chéri-Bibi bluntly.

"She did not kiss me, but she shook my hand in a very queer manner. She herself was trembling more than ever. She semed to be shivering with the cold; her face was exceedingly white; and she stared at me with an extraordinary look in her eyes. Her lips, too, were bloodless as she said: 'Poor Sister St. Mary of the Angels. Poor little Jacqueline!' That was the most peculiar thing of all, for we did not know each other. At least we scarcely ever met in the old days. Then why did she say, 'Poor little Jacqueline!' What did it mean? There was almost a haggard look about her. Besides, she wanted to leave us at once, on the pretense that she was feeling cold and not quite well. Cecily said to her:

" 'Would you like me to send anything up to you? Shall I go with you?'

" 'No, no,' she replied hastily. 'I don't want anything. I'll go and lie down. Good night, Mesdames.' And she left the room, closing the door quickly behind her. It was as though she had fled.

" 'She's down in the dumps again,' said the Dowager Marchioness. 'She didn't used to be like that, so odd and silent all of a sudden that one can't get two words out of her in the twenty-four hours. At one time she was liveliness itself and loved to make me laugh. One would imagine that she suffered from some nervous complaint which comes and goes without our knowing the reason why.'

" 'I have often noticed that Rose was not quite natural,' said Cecily. 'How long has she been like that?'

" 'Oh, for many years,' replied the Marchioness evasively.

"They were silent before me. Obviously my presence prevented them from continuing the conversation. As a matter of fact Rose's curious mannerism must have dated back to the time when troubles fell on the country."

"Say rather from the time when I began my crimes; it would be simpler," said Chéri-Bibi. . . . "Afterwards? . . ."

"Afterwards we said good night, and they gave me a room next to Rose's. I heard her moving about during the night. She was walking up and down, and occasionally talking to herself, but I could not catch what she said. I also heard her heave deep sighs. I was greatly perplexed, as you may readily imagine. Nevertheless, worn out by fatigue, I fell asleep about two o'clock in the morning, and suddenly I was roused by my door being carefully opened.

" 'Who's there?' I cried.

" 'Hush. . . . Don't make a noise, it's I,' said

Rose. And she appeared before me whiter than a ghost.

"After closing the door she stepped up to me like a shadow, knelt at the foot of the bed, and shaking in the peculiar manner that had perturbed me before, took my hand in hers as she had done in the garden and drawing-room, and repeated:

" 'Poor little Jacqueline!' And this time she added: 'Poor Chéri-Bibi!' "

"What! She said that. . . . She really said that? 'Poor Chéri-Bibi!' "

"Yes, that's what she said. . . . She spoke as one in a dream."

"Anyway, she said it. Therefore she had good' reasons for saying it," declared the convict with a catch in his breath. "Rose must know everything; that's a certainty. Go ahead, be quick."

Chéri-Bibi placed another spoonful of the draught between his sister's lips in order to give her renewed strength. The spoon shook in his hand.

"Yes, she knows everything. She confessed as much. She said, 'Poor Jacqueline, your brother was innocent. . . . 'Twas not he who killed the Marquis. It was some one else . . . some one else . . .'

"Thereupon, as she repeated in increasingly stronger and even frenzied tones 'it was some one else,' her eyes dilated as though she saw that other person. . . . And she had a fit of hysteria. The ladies hastened in. We thought it was all over with her. But then she grew silent, and clenched her teeth to prevent a word from escaping her."

"It is very unfortunate that she had that attack," muttered Chéri-Bibi.

"Yes, it was indeed unfortunate, for I've always believed that she came to me that night to tell me the truth; at least the truth as she knew it; whereas next day she was herself again, and nothing more was said. In fact she affected not to understand me when I tried to reopen the conversation. But as you may well believe, I did not let her off. I endeavored several times to see her. Once when I met her in church and begged her, before God, to explain herself, she asked me 'to be patient; the time would come, but the time was in God's hands; she would do nothing to hasten it, and it would be wicked for me, as well as for her, even to wish for that time to come immediately.' Then she said: 'Don't speak to me of such things; forget what I said if you wish to avoid a terrible catastrophe.' "

"Yes, but meanwhile I was hunted like a wild beast and taken back to penal servitude."

"That's exactly what I told her. She replied that you would probably be the first to wish her to keep silent."

"It's a bit too thick," exclaimed Chéri-Bibi. "What can the whole thing mean? Rose no longer knew what she was talking about, that's evident."

"It was the last conversation I had with her. We were in the church square. Suddenly I saw her turn

pale as she had done on the first night. She bowed
to two persons who went past whom I did not at first
notice. She left me abruptly. I have never seen her
since. In the street I met the two persons who had
passed us; they were Cecily and M. Georges de Pont-
Marie.

" 'Rose is still a little strange in her manner,' said
the young Marchioness.

" 'Yes, a little,' I replied, somewhat vaguely.

"Then M. de Pont-Marie added: 'Personally, I've
always had the impression that she was cracked.'

"You see, Chéri-Bibi, I am telling you everything
that can interest you, and everything that I know. I
declare before God, who hears us, that I know nothing
more, not a scrap more."

"How is it that Cecily and M. de Pont-Marie were
out together?   Are they on friendly terms?"

"As you are aware, M. de Pont-Marie has been her
brother's and the Marquis's friend for a long time.
He knew Cecily when she was a child.  He was taking
her out for a little change.  Besides, M. de Pont-
Marie has much improved during the last few years.
He is a reformed character.  He has given the go-by
to the Marquis, who at the present time is cruising in
his yacht, the *Belle of Dieppe*, in South American
waters."

At that moment a knock came at the cabin door,
and Little Buddha's voice was heard.

"Captain, the look-out man signals castaways on
our starboard bow."

# CHAPTER IX

## FATALITAS

Chéri-Bibi went on deck at the moment when the Top, promoted to the rank of chief helmsman, was receiving instructions from one of the old crew who had been forced to serve as helmsman, and was shouting to the man at the wheel:

"Hard a starboard. . . . Give way. . . ."

The chief engineer at the same time gave orders in the engine room:

"Ease her. . . . Three-quarter speed."

A number of inquisitive persons had already crowded on deck. Chéri-Bibi burst through them with scant ceremony and in three bounds was on the bridge yelling:

"What do I care about shipwrecked sailors? Aren't there enough people in the cages?"

He asked for a telescope and levelled it on a white object, a long-boat which could now be seen very distinctly on the calm blue sea. The weather was superb and was rendered all the more perfect by a hot sun which was pouring down on the poor survivors in the frail boat, perhaps stricken with thirst. The boat was at most three cable-lengths away, less than a third of

213

a mile ahead, and the *Bayard* was rapidly nearing her.

Chéri-Bibi had his eye fixed to the telescope.

"*Fatalitas.*" The word suddenly slipped out, to the astonishment of his officers, who were standing by. What had the Captain discovered through the glass?

Chéri-Bibi was no longer using it. He looked up quite pale, muttering incoherent words.

Then he placed the telescope in the field of vision again, glued his eye to it, kept it there for a while, and this time looked up with glowing cheeks. There was no mistake about it. Chéri-Bibi was in a state of high glee.

"*Fatalitas,*" he repeated, "but it is all to the good." Fate, it was obvious, was continuing to play tricks with him, but it would appear that on this occasion he was by no means dissatisfied.

"Gentlemen," he said, "we are going to the assistance of those poor shipwrecked sailors."

Standing around him were the Toper, his lieutenant, the Dodger, his sub-lieutenant, the Top, Little Buddha and the "principal" erstwhile members of his cage.

"Get your men together," he said, "all of them, and tell them that fortune favors us by sending us shipwrecked persons whom, I hope, we may turn to good account. It's a matter that concerns me. But for the time being my order is for each one of you to remember his rank and new position. Let there be no blunders. No change has occurred on board the *Bayard* since she left the Ile de Ré, nothing except a grave mutiny among the convicts, who were eventually brought to book and are again in their cages. I am more than ever Captain Barrachon. As to Captain Barrachon, he is Chéri-Bibi."

The staff burst into a fit of laughter.

"Laugh to your heart's content," said Chéri-Bibi, "for presently you will have to be serious. Do you follow me? Well, let every one bear this in mind: I will hang, with short shrift, the first man who doesn't behave himself properly. You can take my word for it."

They needed no second warning. They quickly left the bridge, and soon the bugle rang out on deck. When the crew received the word of command there was an indescribable feeling of elation. It was an unexpected interlude which the convicts greatly enjoyed. Only fancy, women were in the boat, and they would show them how they bore themselves in uniform, and that convicts could be smart enough when the occasion offered. They were immensely grateful to Chéri-Bibi for devising this new farce which promised to afford them a delightful entertainment. The ascendancy which the new Captain exercised over this confraternity of thieves was enormously enhanced by it.

At all events here was a chief who knew how to

laugh, and understood life. No one was likely to be dull with him in command.

Matters were arranged in accordance with Chéri-Bibi's instructions. The *Bayard* gradually drew near the boat, whence could be heard exclamations of joy, shouts of "bravo," and enthusiastic salutations. It was noticed that ten persons were in her: seven passengers and three sailors. A piece of linen fastened to one end of an oar was used as a signal.

The convicts were particularly delighted that three women passengers were in the boat, and, indeed, they appeared to be very attractive women.

"Oh, lovely women!" exclaimed Little Buddha, whose enthusiasm received a check when the Toper gave him a sound kick to remind him that he must be on his best behavior.

Oddly enough the survivors seemed by no means to be starving or unduly exhausted. Nor did they have the haggard look of persons who have just escaped a watery grave.

The women, for instance, were well and full of spirits, and dressed in good taste, their heads elegantly covered with wraps; and they looked just as they might have looked after a pleasant row on a lake.

Standing upright among the survivors was a tall, powerful, broad-shouldered man; one of those persons who, as it were, displace a considerable amount of atmosphere when they move. His full face and ruddy complexion, which was not devoid of a suggestion of aristocracy owing to the shape of his nose, which was the Bourbon nose, seemed to be that of a country squire and sportsman. Above his blue eyes were bushy brows, auburn in color, which lent some degree of hardness to a countenance whose heavy outline might otherwise have indicated good-nature.

Chéri-Bibi, leaning on the bridge, kept his eyes fixed on him. And if the entire crew of bandits had not likewise been watching the boat, they would have been astonished to see the singularly fierce look which overspread Chéri-Bibi's face while the *Bayard* crept nearer the survivors. His jaws were thrust out in menace, and he hissed between his clenched teeth the name "Maxime du Touchais!"

Chéri-Bibi drew himself up, mastering the excitement which impelled him straightway to rush at the throat of the man who had been, and who still was, the torturer of her whom he loved best in the world; of Cecily, the ideal being who had never ceased to shine through the blood-stained mystery of his life. . . . And he repressed the emotion which moved him to cry aloud with joy at the thought of the revenge that was so near . . . Cecily's husband!

"It's my sister's God who has sent this man to me for punishment as he might have sent him to the devil."

How he hated him, this handsome gentleman, who had the right to go near his idol while he had never dared look at her but from afar, nor speak to her

in the glad days of his youth but with lowered head
and trembling voice. . . .

How he hated him when he thought that this man
had held her in his arms and made her suffer. . . .

Chéri-Bibi grinned as the demons in the depths of
Dante's Inferno grinned. . . . And he strode towards
the guests whose arrival was so opportune.

He was completely himself now in his new part as
Captain of the ship. He ordered the accommodation
ladder to be set up, and here he waited for his guests
who were climbing out of the boat with the assistance
of his men. The first man to step on to the accommodation ladder wrested from Chéri-Bibi the muffled
exclamation: "Robert Bourrelier!"

So Fate had delivered the entire family into his
hands!

He started back.

He seemed less satisfied this time. Not only had
he no cause of quarrel with Cecily's brother, but the
fact that he was her brother would, in itself, prevent
him from entertaining any evil intentions towards him.
His chief fear now was lest he should be recognized by
him.

He had no cause for apprehension as far as Maxime
du Touchais was concerned, for it was certain that
the Marquis had never cast a glance at the humble
butcher's boy from Le Pollet. Robert Bourrelier, on
the other hand, used to spend some weeks of his holidays in Puys with his parents, and might well have

retained some recollection of the "gardener's young-ster."

Chéri-Bibi took courage again when, not without reason, he reflected that he had greatly changed since those days, and that the amazing ups and downs of his anything but commonplace life had endowed him with a different physiognomy. In any event the experiment was one which he ought to make.

He had to reckon on the publicity which the great daily papers had thrust upon his alarming personality during his crimes; but in that regard he had been assisted by the poor quality of the photographs, and the indifferent character of the reproductions used by the newspapers to make his image known to a terrified world. Moreover, the newspapers had pictured a very ugly person, a sort of composite photograph of ugliness, and they had grossly exaggerated, for the purpose of selling their papers, the general brutality of his appearance. It was he and yet it was not quite he. There were moments, moments of crises and moments of violent passion, when it was perhaps he, but it was not he at moments of happiness such as he experienced then when, with the rank of Captain in the navy, he was preparing to extend hospitality to the person whom he hated most in the world after the man in the gray hat.

But the die was cast. Robert Bourrelier appeared in the gangway.

Chéri-Bibi played his game with perfect assurance.

"Ladies and gentlemen," he said, with a pomposity which was slightly ludicrous, "I am very pleased to see you on board my ship." And he held out his hand to Cecily's brother, who shook it with an unmistakable expression of gratitude.

Robert Bourrelier seemed to have suffered from the strain more than any of the others. The health of this tall, gawky young man was obviously precarious, and the dissipated life which he had led from the days of his early manhood clearly marked him down for an early grave.

"Anyway," thought Chéri-Bibi, "the Marquis won't have to wait very long for his inheritance."

He was quite content with the experiment. Robert had not started in surprise. And then, of course, how could he possibly dream of meeting the terrible Chéri-Bibi in the uniform of this friendly Captain in the French navy?

Next the ladies came on deck, and then Maxime du Touchais, followed by the rest of the survivors.

Before the Captain could say another word of welcome the Marquis, waiving aside all offers of help of which the newcomers did not appear to be in any urgent need, placed the officers of the *Bayard* in possession of the facts of the disaster.

They were the victims of the recent storm which had wellnigh proved fatal to the *Bayard*. The Marquis and his guests were returning from Buenos Ayres to France in the *Belle of Dieppe* when at two o'clock in the morning, during a tremendous gale, the yacht, which answered her helm only with great difficulty, came into collision with a ship which she must have seriously damaged. The storm, which continued to increase, tore asunder the two ships as swiftly as it had caused them to collide, and in the darkness they soon lost sight of the other vessel.

The *Belle of Dieppe* was in evil case for there was a large rent in the bows and an inrush of water against which it was impossible to battle. The forward part was already sinking slowly beneath the waves. Maxime ordered the boats to be lowered. Fortunately these were numerous enough to carry all the crew and the few passengers who leapt into them in spite of the raging sea.

But death seemed as certain and as near in those frail craft as on the yacht. The Marquis, seeing things as they were, refused at the last moment to leave the vessel, stating that if it came to a choice of deaths he preferred to die comfortably in one of the *Belle of Dieppe's* cabin. Several of his friends, the women especially, agreed with him, observing, moreover, that during the last few minutes the vessel had ceased its downward course into the abyss. Perhaps the water-tight bulkheads would hold. . . . Thus he and a few others remained behind while the boats disappeared into the murky night.

The bulkheads did, in fact, hold. They held for three days, which was long enough for the great storm to subside, for the demoralized sea to become like an azure lake, for the sky to sweep away its dark clouds, and for the passengers who remained on board to prepare the two boats for the moment when they would of necessity have to abandon the *Belle of Dieppe;* an event which occurred scarcely two hours earlier in a perfectly calm sea and without the shadow of anxiety, for the Marquis knew that they were near the route followed by the great liners sailing to the Antilles or South America.

The *Belle of Dieppe* vanished beneath the waves, strewing the sea with wreckage which before long they saw. There was no trace of the other boats, whose fate must have already been sealed, for either they had perished or been picked up as the long-boat was picked up with Maxime du Touchais and his companions. That was all.

Thereupon the Marquis introduced them.

He began with the ladies. First came Mlle. Nadège de Valrieu, a tall, handsome, but rather stout blonde who must have been known by hearsay to the Captain and his officers because her talents as an actress, although she was still young, had brought her fame oth hemispheres. Then came Mlle. Carmen de nebleau, who was young and dark and lively, was already addressing her smiles to the crew. e was the celebrated æsthetique dancer who had achieved renown in her "love waltzes." The third lady was of elegant and distinguished appearance, though her manner of gazing at people and things through her lorgnette had more than a suggestion of haughtiness about it. She was Madame d'Artigues, a literary star, and was accompanied by her husband, a brilliant society journalist and dramatic critic, well known in the Paris press under the pseudonym of Charles des Premières. Then came M. Robert Bourrelier, and finally Baron Proskof, a Polish nobleman, who was married to "the most beautiful woman in Paris," but who could no longer boast of that distinction inasmuch as the dear Baroness had insisted on embarking in one of the small boats, too frail to fight against the tumultuous seas.

"The Baron is very much upset and so am I," concluded Maxime du Touchais.

The freedom with which the Marquis spoke of the poor Baroness, who was certainly no more, and to whom he had paid considerable court, if gossip in Dieppe could be believed, was repugnant to Chéri-Bibi, who always had a sense of family life.

Chéri-Bibi did not take long, on his side, in his introductions. He pointed to the officers and crew as a whole and declared in a rasping voice that they on board the *Bayard* were glad to show hospitality to such agreeable guests. He did not for the time being enter into any further particulars.

Du Touchais and Bourrelier imagined, from a first glance, that they had been picked up by a troopship, the Captain of which was a worthy man somewhat lacking in polish. As a matter of fact the sight of Chéri-Bibi trying his hand at politeness was a remark-able one. The word "agreeable" coming from him contrasted strangely with the ugly grimace of his mouth and the amazing smile which he assumed for the benefit of the ladies.

His manner of being amiable, or of wishing to appear so, was so brusque that the ladies could not refrain from smiling. Chéri-Bibi noticed the smile, and it wounded him in his innermost self, for he was not without a considerable amount of self-esteem as the phrase goes.

The Marquis, observing that he turned scarlet and made a wry face, realized that he had to deal with a "touchy sea-dog." He determined to put him at ease, and he gave him a friendly tap on the shoulder.

"Captain," he said with a great affectation of cor-diality, "we are sworn friends to the death. You were our last hope. . . . The Marquis du Touchais never forgets!" And he shook him warmly by the hand.

Chéri-Bibi remained passive while he rolled his small eyes in which there was a look that boded no good, and murmured aside: "Yes, old bluffer, to the death, as you say!"

He determined to conduct the ladies to the best cabins, the occupants of which had been ordered to pack up and begone in five seconds; and overcoming his feelings of antipathy and hatred he was particularly friendly towards Robert Bourrelier and Maxime du Touchais.

As they crossed the deck the ladies were greatly surprised to perceive so many disabled sailors and soldiers, with such rough and resolute faces under their tam-o'-shanters and *képis,* staring at them as they went past with an eager and fiery gaze.

"Have you been fighting, Captain?" inquired the beautiful Madame d'Artigues.

"You couldn't have made a better guess, dear lady," returned Chéri-Bibi. "We have been fighting. We've had a mutiny on board."

"Mutiny on board!" they exclaimed in one breath. . . . "Oh, tell us about it. . . . But how awful!"

"Mutiny on board a troopship!" exclaimed the Marquis. "You don't mean to say so. Isn't there such a thing as discipline in our navy? . . . Obviously everything's going to the dogs. I hope, Captain, you had no great difficulty in getting the better of the mutineers."

"Ugh! We had to shoot and hang a good few of them," replied the Captain rather vaguely.

"But what you tell us is very funny," cried the charming Mlle. Carmen de Fontainebleau. "A shipwreck . . . a mutiny on boardship. . . . What a succession of adventures!"

"Well, we shall have plenty to talk about when we get back to France," said Mlle. Nadège de Valrieu.

The entire French nobility would seem to have met on board the *Bayard*.

"We shan't be in France yet a while," Chéri-Bibi thought it well to observe.

"Where are we making for then?"

"Yes, by the way, where are you landing us, Captain?"

"In Cayenne, ladies and gentlemen, at your service."

"Cayenne?    Are you bound for Cayenne?"

"Why, yes, Marquis, with a shipload of criminals, scamps of convicts, and we've had our work cut out with them, I assure you."

"Convicts!  Oh, good gracious!" exclaimed the ladies, more and more interested.  "Where are they? They can't do us any harm, can they?"

"Don't be alarmed.  We've got a tight hold of them now.  They're not allowed out of their cages.  The first one who budged . . . we'd smash his jaw . . . I beg your pardon . . . saving your presence."

"Well done, Captain. . . . We're too easy going with that sort of game.  Ought we to be saddled with such villains?   I bet you that half the men in the cages would be guillotined under a proper government."

"Half of them at least," said Chéri-Bibi, "to say nothing of Chéri-Bibi, who is here."

"What do you say? . . . Chéri-Bibi . . . Chéri-Bibi on board! . . . Is it a fact, Captain, that you have Chéri-Bibi with you? Oh, what a piece of luck! Let's have a look at him at once."

At that moment the men were bringing up the baggage belonging to the survivors, and Chéri-Bibi turned round. He felt as though he were being scorched by a look, and he saw the Countess standing in front of him. At first he did not recognize this refined, elegant and graceful looking woman who was attired in a perfectly fashionable traveling costume made by a first-rate ladies' tailor. It was a present which he himself had given her that very morning as an acknowledgment of her services in helping him to escape, and, later, during the stress of the fight.

In his wanderings through the holds Chéri-Bibi had ripped open a large case intended for society ladies in Cayenne, the wives of the officials, and he found in it a great selection of finery—costumes, dresses, underlinen. He gave the whole of the contents to the Countess there and then. "Now we are quits," he thought. "She won't worry me any more." He was mistaken, for the Countess appreciated the gift only in so far as those adornments could make her more beautiful in Chéri-Bibi's eyes.

She was another person who was in love with him, excited by his fame; and he had been forced to repulse her in the darkness of the store-rooms. . . . The Countess had not lost sight of him since the long-boat was signaled; and she was a witness of his agitation, his restlessness, and finally of the malicious delight which inwardly possessed him.

It was obvious that he knew the survivors. At first she imagined that he was interested in the ladies, and she showed her claws as if she would tear their eyes out. But she soon realized that his main concern was with the Marquis du Touchais. What was the connection between those two men? She made up her mind to know the truth before long.

"My dear Captain," said the Countess in a voice of peculiar sweetness which was new to him, "I am told that you have given my cabin to these ladies. Allow me to say that I am very pleased to hear it. It's the best cabin in the ship."

The ladies uttered a general protest. Was it true? They wouldn't hear of it. How could they think of such a thing. . . . They had no wish to disturb any one. And so on and so forth.

"Let me introduce you to the Countess," said Chéri-Bibi, playing the gentleman.

The ladies flocked round to press her hand. The Countess! So there was a countess on board. The Countess of what? They dared not put the question. They regarded the introduction as somewhat lacking in detail, and Maxime du Touchais and Robert Bourrelier turned away from Chéri-Bibi to hide a smile. Oh, these old sea-dogs did not waste overmuch time in polite phrases, nor care a rap for forms and ceremonies. . . . Here's the Countess. Good morning.

. . . Good evening. Would that do? And, in truth, it was enough for them. Besides, she seemed very ladylike did the Countess. Nevertheless, Chéri-Bibi, after a moment's reflection, thought it well to add that she was going out to her husband in Brazil.

"Did you see the mutiny, Countess?" asked Mlle. Carmen de Fontainebleau.

"As plainly I see you now," replied the Countess in her best society manner.

It was she who wished to proceed with the accommodation of her new friends. She proved so gracious and charming and kind that they were captivated by her on the spot. She placed her entire wardrobe at their disposal; and they did not conceal their satisfaction, for they had been able to bring with them in the long-boat only the strictest necessities. They were filled with admiration for the luxurious manner in which the Countess was equipped.

They dressed themselves for lunch, which was delayed an hour at their request, and entered the Captain's dining-room "arrayed in all their glory."

Meanwhile the men had strolled round the deck. They came back in a state of astonishment, having observed a number of things that would help them to keep the conversation alive. Lunch, which was presided over by Chéri-Bibi, was transformed into a great banquet to which the officers were invited, and at which room had to be found for the "principal persons who distinguished themselves in the recent fighting." They had begged the Captain to grant them that honor for once. They were not all wearing officers' uniform, but men, like Little Buddha, who were dressed as ordinary seamen or petty officers, were placed at small tables—"to reward them for their good conduct," as Chéri-Bibi explained. They were satisfied as long as they could see and hear and admire the ladies.

The Captain, who was fully aware of the dangerous frame of mind into which the crew had been thrown by the arrival of these society ladies on board, had succeeded, for the time being, in calming their excitement by letting them know that the ladies would be present at the festivity which was in preparation for that evening, and that if they behaved themselves he would allow the ladies to dance with them. He took the opportunity of informing them that if they failed to conduct themselves properly they would have him to reckon with.

The Dodger himself kept an eye on the various dishes, and looked after, in particular, the cod with tomato sauce flavored with herbs of which Chéri-Bibi was very fond. The Top, who had an excellent hand, wrote out several copies of the menu. The entire company were in good humor and exceedingly hungry. Accordingly, to begin with, they did full justice to a savory and appetizing joint of beef.

Chéri-Bibi ate very little, taking care that each man should have his share, and that the wines should flow

without stint. Moreover, he was not a little impressed
by his new part as the host receiving his guests, and
he had no wish to "put his foot in it" before his men,
who were watching him with curiosity. Seated on one
side of him was Madame d'Artigues and on the other
Mlle. Nadège de Valrieu, while facing him was the
Countess. Maxime du Touchais was placed a little
to the left, next to Mlle. Carmen de Fontainebleau, so
that he had to lean forward to see him, for he had
no wish to be embarrassed while he was eating. In
this way he seemed to have postponed for the present
any serious encounter with him.

The meal had passed off quite well up to then. The
Top, from the financiers' cage, who knew something
about the sort of people present, having robbed them
to the advantage of high-class restaurants and night
taverns, kept watch over the general arrangements of
the lunch; that is to say, over its proper service.

"This food is really delicious," declared Mlle.
Nadège de Valrieu.

"It's a tip-top cut of chump of beef," explained
Chéri-Bibi. "Please do have some more."

She accepted another helping with such gusto that
Chéri-Bibi, repelled by the young lady's greediness,
ended by observing to her that "no one was waiting
for the table." And he turned his attention to Madame
d'Artigues, who was a perfect woman of the world
and must have suffered greatly during the voyage
from the presence of the younger ladies forced upon

her by the Marquis's whim.   The Captain perceived
that Madame d'Artigues was casting sheep's eyes at
the Marquis, while her husband was pretending not
to be aware of the fact.   Chéri-Bibi assumed that
Madame d'Artigues was striving to take the place in
the Marquis du Touchais's heart, left vacant by the
recent loss of the Baroness de Proskof, and that her
husband would not be sorry to hand over his wife to
this rich man if the latter were disposed to pay the
price that he had paid for the Baroness.

These mercenary calculations into the scene of
which Chéri-Bibi's fantastic destiny had thrown him,
induced a feeling of small respect for "the privileged
classes," for whom, for that matter, he had always
felt but scant admiration.   He wanted, with the help
of champagne, to forget present intrigues; to fly beyond the seas and to dream of Cecily's angelic face,
of the virtuous wife and perfect mother devoted to
the duties of her home.   What would he not have given
to see her seated by his side in preference to those
perfumed dolls who had never known the meaning
of the word virtue.

"In the meantime, old chap, your wife is carrying
on with some other . . ."

The words burst like a thunderclap on Chéri-Bibi's
reverie.   They were flung at the Marquis, in a burst
of laughter, by the mistress of the lanky Robert, who
at once requested Mlle. Nadège de Valrieu to moder-
ate her language.

Chéri-Bibi became as pale as a ghost.

"It's not true," he cried.

At once every eye was turned on him, and the guests exchanged glances; and then there was an outburst of gayety.

The Countess took up the running.

"What did you say?"

"I?" exclaimed Chéri-Bibi in a blank voice. "I . . . I didn't say anything."

It seemed to him, in fact, that he had not spoken, but that it was some one else . . . some one else who uttered those words which he, like the rest of them, had caught. . . . He did not enter into any further explanation. He was fiercely silent, feeling intensely that he could not be too silent successfully to master the rage which consumed him against the wretched creatures who had dared to insult his idol; against the baseness of the Marquis who had expressed no indignation, nor uttered even a protest, fully occupied as he was, doubtless, with the airs and graces of Madame d'Artigues; against the brother who had not struck down the hussy for speaking in such terms of his sister.

The Countess interposed with wonderful cleverness and tact, and with the grace of a great lady whom nothing can disconcert and who utters the exact word that is needed in the most difficult situations. She paid a great compliment to Chéri-Bibi, to his rough exterior and his golden heart, his fine conscience and the many qualities which made of him a "veritable French knight-errant."

Never had she heard him speak ill of women, and he strained points of honor to such an extent that he would not allow others to speak ill of them in his presence. In truth the Countess was astonishing. She had amazed her fellow-prisoners by her command of the lowest form of speech, and now she was expressing herself "in society" with the utmost elegance. . . . Unfortunately her charming intervention on his behalf had no other effect than to turn the conversation on poor Cecily.

"Well, be careful, for it won't be long before she is carrying on with . . ."

Nadège de Valrieu and Carmen de Fontainebleau were at one in hinting that M. de Pont-Marie's assiduities in regard to the Marchioness du Touchais were self-interested. They knew him of old, that particular bird; and he would never have remained behind unless he had found something to interest him.

"Well, between ourselves, he isn't difficult to please," ended Mlle. Nadège de Valrieu, who, as the mistress of Cecily's brother, could not endure the Bourrelier family. "The last time I saw her in Dieppe was when I was coming back from the races. She was wearing a hat! . . . I fancy I see myself wearing one like it. . . ."

Carmen added her quota.

"Look here, she's not so very plain."

"You're too funny when you talk like that," said the Marquis, and he burst into laughter.

Chéri-Bibi was suffering like a soul in pain, and such he was, but never from his earliest days had he borne such torment. His punishments as a convict were caresses on his thick skin compared with the searing of his soul at that moment, the soul of Chéri-Bibi. The Countess was startled by the sight of him. She feared for a while lest he should fall stone dead in the middle of the banquet. And then by slow degrees his color returned . . . returned with a smile.

"Very soon," thought Chéri-Bibi, "very soon, Mlles. Nadège and Carmen, I will hand you . . . you who are not so very plain . . . over to my men. And as to you, Maxime du Touchais, as to you, I shall have to think of something . . . think of something."

His eyes encountered the gaze of the Kanaka, who had not hitherto uttered a word, and he recalled the ugly story which ran through the cages about that peculiar individual.

"Very soon I'll hand you over to the tender mercies of the Kanaka."

That was the reason why Chéri-Bibi was now smiling.

# CHAPTER X

FROM that moment Chéri-Bibi took the lead in the conversation and gave it a singularly sprightly turn. He entered with dash and spirit into a burlesque version of the mutiny of the convicts, and of the extraordinary adventures through which the crew had passed after Chéri-Bibi's daring escape. He described the incidents in detail so well, in fact, that Chéri-Bibi himself could not have told the story with greater effect. Now he was expatiating on scenes of horror which sent a thrill through the ladies, and anon on scenes of comedy which were tremendously emphasized by the boisterous laughter of his officers and crew who had "particularly distinguished themselves in the recent affair"; so that what the tragic vision conjured up by the Captain, and the disquieting merriment of most of the persons p esent, the shipwrecked guests felt an indefinable dread steal over them which hampered their enjoyment.

The champagne flowed like water, and the gaiety, which was almost general, increased in consequence until it became somewhat coarse. The officers especially began to forget the reserve which is the tradition with Frenchmen in uniform, and, above all, in the presence of ladies.

A certain lieutenant was at the table who alone made a considerable noise, and it was impossible to keep him quiet.

"Will you hold your tongue, Toper?"

So all those gentlemen had odd surnames—Little Buddha, the Top, and so forth—and flung them from one end of the table to the other with a familiarity which difference in rank in no way deterred.

Baron Proskof, whose mind had been depressed by the loss of his beloved wife, roused himself from his lethargy to express to his friends by a bewildered look the astonishment that filled him on observing such laxity of manners in the French navy.

Robert Bourrelier shook his head, and Maxime du Touchais coughed in a way that was understood by M. d'Artigues, who, as a journalist accustomed to move in official circles, could not refrain from whispering:

"They've no idea of such things at the Ministry of the Navy."

These various movements were not lost on Chéri-Bibi, who accounted for the tone at the banquet by a good-humored sentence which secured the approval of the ladies.

"We belong to one and the same family on board the *Bayard.*"

"It's extraordinary," said Madame d'Artigues, "what a resemblance there is between you all."

"No doubt that comes from the fact that you have as little hair on your heads as mushrooms," said Mlle. Nadège de Valrieu.

"Or as convicts," added Mlle. Carmen de Fontaine-bleau, laughing heartily at what she considered to be an excellent joke.

The last remark threw, as it were, a "wet blanket" over the company. A silence fell, during which the men looked at each other askance, and then Little Buddha slapped his thigh and exclaimed, "What a good joke!" whereupon a tremendous burst of laughter resounded through the Captain's cabin.

Chéri-Bibi, with his usual presence of mind, replied that if the officers and men had had their hair cut so short it was entirely because they wished "to show the convicts a good example."

"However many rings the Captain has," exclaimed Carrots, "that doesn't prevent him from being a jolly good fellow."

"Yes, yes," they shouted, "a jolly good fellow."

"He certainly looks one," agreed Carmen de Fontainebleau.

"You are a jolly good fellow," said Madame d'Artigues, "but what are 'rings'?"

"Rings," replied Chéri-Bibi, without turning a hair, "are, in service slang, gold stripes. Don't imagine, ladies and gentlemen, though I allow my men to treat me as the father of the family," he thought it well to add, "that discipline is any the worst for it. I know my duty, and I can be terrible if needs be. Of course," he went on in the most natural manner, "if I did not combine firmness with friendliness where should I be with a shipload like this? I put the question to you. And if you will allow me, I will answer it myself. After the revolt the other day it is we who would be in the cages at the present time!"

A great outburst of cheering and shouts of hurrah greeted the Captain's daring supposition.

"Yes, that's true," agreed Mlle. Carmen de Fontainebleau, "you can't be joking all day long when you have convicts in your charge."

"But I say, the villains had to be in agreement in order to mutiny. They were in their cages and guarded. How was it possible for them to come to an understanding?" asked Madame d'Artigues.

All eyes were fixed on Chéri-Bibi, who experienced a certain satisfaction as he observed the interest which seemed to be attached to his least word, and he took advantage of the opportunity to deliver to his guests a short dissertation on prison life. Moreover, the importance of the subject inspired him not a little, and the turn of his phrases, without his suspecting it, partook slightly of the professional air characteristic of lecturers.

"You do not know these men," he said, laying

stress upon his words, "or you would not be astonished at anything from that point of view. Nothing betrays the intimacy which exists between them. They may be lying on the same bench, but no movement or sign reveals that they know each other if, by chance, they have already met outside or in prison. They have a language of their own which it is impossible for others to understand.

"In the position of their feet, in the natural gesture of their arms, in the direction of their look, there is a word, a dictionary, a complete language. This mute conversation escapes the observation, and the long experience, of the convict guard, the military overseer, and the cleverest chief himself; in a word, it escapes me. Nevertheless, some of my men and I have been able to discover a few words of this secret language.

"We will make an experiment. Step forward, Little Buddha, and place yourself here. You, Carrots, go to the other end of the room. . . . We have sailed together for so long that I don't hesitate to call them by their nicknames. . . . There! . . . Now begin. . . . Good. . . . Very good. . . . That'll do. . . . Be quiet, you naughty boys!"

"But they didn't move," exclaimed Madame d'Artigues.

"You think so, Madame, but you are mistaken. From the manner in which Carrots raised his eyebrows and put his hands in his pocket, and by the position of his lower lip, and, on the other hand, by the position of Little Buddha's feet, and the three changes in the direction of his glance, a complete conversation took place between the two men, but I won't venture to repeat it."

"Oh, yes, please do, dear Captain, tell us what they said."

"Do you mean it?" said Chéri-Bibi to Madame d'Artigues, who was the most eager of them all. "You shall have your wish. In speaking of you in their own particular slang they said: 'She is very sweet is the little lady; the big man, the Marquis, is making eyes at her, but the thin man, the husband, is watching them. We must take advantage of the quarrel presently to tell her that we've fallen in love with her.'"

"Well done, well done. It's marvelous," exclaimed Mlle. de Valrieu.

"Yes, and it's true," declared Mlle. Carmen de Fontainebleau.

"Madame, I offer you my apologies," said Chéri-Bibi in his best style, turning to Madame d'Artigues; "but these gentlemen are not accustomed to the polite world, and are easily astonished by the sight of society at play."

"Not at all, it's very amusing," returned Madame d'Artigues with an affectation of pleasure. "And your conversation, my dear Captain, is most instructive."

"I've lived among convicts for so many years, Madame."

"The whole thing is excellent," said Robert Bourrelier; "the wretches understand each other. But how did they manage to get out of their cages? You told us that your Chéri-Bibi was in irons and guarded by two warders."

"Oh, Chéri-Bibi's escape!" exclaimed the Captain. "I will explain that to you presently at the exact spot. Irons, fetters—these things don't stop him. Chéri-Bibi himself, you understand, disclosed to me a dozen ways at least of breaking fetters and of hiding from sight the bites made in them by file or chisel. And the convicts have as many files and chisels as they need. Chéri-Bibi gave me as a birthday present a basket in each twig of which was buried a saw which was practically invisible."

"Oh, tell us something more about Chéri-Bibi, Captain."

"Chéri-Bibi can force any lock or padlock with an ordinary brass wire," said the Captain in a voice of pride.

"But did you not suspect anything before the mutiny broke out?" asked Maxime du Touchais. "How was it possible for the secret to be so well kept? For, after all, is it not an extraordinary thing that among eight hundred convicts not one, not a single one, gave the others away?"

The Captain swallowed a glass of champagne.

"Blacklegs and informers are rare among us."

He at once comprehended from a sign from the Kanaka that he had committed a blunder. He went on to explain himself, stumbling somewhat in his speech.

"I mean in our world, in the world that we have to guard, in the world of convicts in short. They crop up still from time to time. But the kind of brute who betrays his comrades is tending more and more to disappear.

"You may take it that vengeance is swift and terrible. If the informer lives in the cages, he is found dead one morning, and the cleverest doctor is unable to discover the cause of his sudden disease. If he lives in Cayenne, an immense pile of wood gives way, apparently from some lack of intelligence on the part of the workers, and when the ground is cleared a corpse is picked up.

"Sometimes when the sea is rough, when a large ship's boat on fatigue duty is battling with the waves, a man disappears into the deep. Was it an accident due to inexperience? No. It was a punishment inflicted upon an informer. The convict gang, ladies and gentlemen, has its bench of judges which pronounces its sentences with due regard to justice, and those judges have their scale of penalties. If the offense against a man's comrades is a light one, the verdict may discover 'extenuating circumstances,' but in any event if the finding does not entail the death penalty it implies the men's contempt. The man who is convicted loses the respect of his comrades.

"The respect of his comrades is the most valuable asset that a convict can possess. There are various degrees of respect. God knows how onerous the conditions are which have to be satisfied before he can reach the highest point. But though it is not given to everyone to attain the highest point by brilliant exploits, each prisoner does his utmost to take his place and to maintain it worthily. He knows that at the bottom of the scale, as I was saying just now, the word 'contempt' is written; and more than one convict has proved that he preferred death to that particular word."

"But it seems to me, Captain, heaven forgive me for saying so, that you have an admiration for them," interposed the beautiful Madame d'Artigues with a suggestion of alarm in her voice.

"I . . . I admire them!" protested Chéri-Bibi with an innocent look. "Say rather that I pity them. Chéri-Bibi himself is to be pitied, believe me. I have had long conversations with that curious and unfortunate individual. I can assure you that he was not born into this world to terrorize it. Circumstances and men have involved him in a sort of deadly game of chance. Oh, it's an easy matter when one's reputation is beyond the abyss of evil to lecture and give good advice to those who are unfortunate. But we must not forget that fate lies in wait ready to strike the blow. To have good luck or not to have good luck. I don't say that everything turns on that, but I do say that nearly everything turns on it. To be or not to be, that is the question. *Fatalitas, Fatalitas,*" cried the amazing Chéri-Bibi in a lyrical outburst in which English and Latin were mingled. "O Fate . . . Fate, must you associate this just man with the vilest of mortals? Nothing is more demoralizing in all things than the society of the wicked; the fruit thereof is bitterness. It is a field of misery, and the harvest is death.

"Ladies and gentlemen, I apologise to you most sincerely. I hardly know what I am saying," confessed Cecily's admirer, wiping the tears that sprang to his eyes. "I fancy that I've had a glass of champagne too much. Come, let us take the air on deck. Afterwards we will have a little stroll in the Zoological Gardens."

The entire party rose from the table in a peculiar state of mind. The Captain's agitation had impressed the company at this extraordinary banquet in different ways. The convicts remembered that many of them had always claimed Chéri-Bibi as "an innocent victim" in the first instance. As to the shipwrecked guests, they felt some difficulty in accounting for the old sea-dog's emotion when he spoke of the monster Chéri-Bibi.

"He was weeping," said Madame d'Artigues in an undertone. "Does it not look as if he liked him?"

"As a brother," exclaimed Chéri-Bibi, who overheard the remark.

"What's that? . . . What did he say?"

"Nothing, Madame," said the Toper. "Can't you see that he is soaked?"

"The worthy Captain is quite drunk," said Robert Bourrelier.

"He is not so tipsy perhaps as he looks," said Mlle. Carmen de Fontainebleau to Mlle. Nadège de Valrieu. "From what I can gather, this Chéri-Bibi is an amazing person, and in spite of his ugliness possesses an irresistible attraction. He seems to have bewitched this poor man, who does not look as if he had a very strong head on his shoulders."

"The thing that impressed me most in what he said," observed Mlle. Nadège de Valrieu, "was that the convicts have a dozen ways of escaping from their cages. That's not very comforting for us, and we're not absolutely safe here."

"You may be right," replied Mlle. Carmen de Fontainebleau. "The unfortunate part is that I don't see where we could take refuge. Say what you like, I am far from being easy in my mind. Those men alarm me with their stories of convicts. I don't say it in disparagement; I state the plain truth: they have the faces of convicts themselves. . . . So we're going to see Chéri-Bibi, my dear Captain," she said to him as he passed her, lurching slightly against the persons round him.

"Come with me," he invited.

When they reached the ladder leading to the galleys, he stopped them to point out the store-room, and the traces of the fight which Chéri-Bibi had kept up there.

"You see, we were here," he explained, "and he was over there taking pot shots at us. You should have seen it! I must admit that he's a plucky fellow. We were more than a hundred to one against him. There was no getting near him. He leapt from one room to the other as if he were made of india-rubber, and in spite of all he was bullet-proof. Finally he fled into the galley from which there was no way out. Of necessity he was caught. We made a dash for the room. It was empty. How did he get away? That was the mystery.

"After looking everywhere we went off. Well, I can let you into the secret now because he told us the story. We had no sooner departed than he rose from the .soup which was beginning to get hot, showed his head above the boiler, ascertained that he was alone, left his culinary bath, and concealed himself under the vegetables in the store-room, which we had searched just before in order to make sure that he was not hiding there. What do you think of that? We didn't dream of looking for him in the boilers. They were hot, and steam was issuing from them.

"How could we suppose that Chéri-Bibi was hiding in the soup which was cooking over a slow fire? Obviously it was not yet boiling, but he told me that it was high time for him to leave it as the poor fellow can't stand a bath above 104° although he has a pretty tough skin. Oh, he had more than one string to his bow. I must add that he was specially assisted by one of his friends who was in league with him and managed to get himself and several coal-trimmers taken on the *Bayard* at the last moment, to replace men who had failed us. They all belonged to Chéri-Bibi's gang. You can imagine how they worked for him!

"The cook's mate, who was responsible for cooking the convicts' rations, was made messenger to the cages, though most of the convicts hadn't the slightest idea of it. When the food was distributed on the chains and the men were occupied round the tubs, or when they left the cages for their exercise on deck, it was he who found means of slipping into their kit-bags the bottles of rum with which those gentlemen regaled themselves; and, later on, arms such as cutlasses and revolvers stolen from the armory or straight from the convict guards. This baker's man was as artful as a monkey and as nimble as a pickpocket."

"Shall we see him also?" asked Mlle. Nadège de Valrieu.

"No, Madame, he is dead. We've lost him.

Chéri-Bibi was exceedingly upset about it, for this youngster—he was young, not quite twenty-two, and had big blue eyes—loved Chéri-Bibi as a dog loves his master. He followed him everywhere, in all his misfortunes, and often rescued him from starvation, for he was full of generosity and imagination.

"Poor little baker's man, the victim of the feeling sacred among us all which we call friendship. Don't be alarmed, ladies, I'm not going to shed a tear on his account. He caused us too much anxiety. It was he who, with the help of the coal-trimmers, paved the way for the mutiny. Ever since we sailed from the Ile de Ré he and they worked in the holds, making a hole in a bulkhead here and in a floor there, arranging ways of getting about the ship of which we were in complete ignorance, and fixing up hiding-places for Chéri-Bibi in boxes which we thought contained goods; hiding-places which we should never have suspected; and when Chéri-Bibi escaped they lent him clothes which enabled him to roam about the decks in broad daylight. Moreover, these were the men who, when the struggle began, stole the rifles of my brave warders and handed them over to the mutineers. You see, ladies and gentlemen, we were in a fine mess!"

Having said which Chéri-Bibi beckoned his hearers to follow him on deck, in the manner of an official guide in a public building whose business it is to

exhibit and to expatiate upon the curiosities of which
he is the faithful guardian.

Arrived on deck the pilgrims were filled with
wonder. They might have been at a county fair.
Small flags and festoons of Chinese lanterns were
hung out on every hand. The Captain explained that
after the terrible tragedies which had taken place his
men required some diversion. Thus he had promised
them an entertainment in which some of them would
sing and some act in a farce such as is the custom in
the French navy; and afterwards there would be a
dance to the music of an improvised band. Then
speaking directly to Mlles. de Valrieu and Fontainebleau Chéri-Bibi said:

"If you would deign to accept the applause of
poor sailormen and be kind enough to contribute a
'number' I'm sure that my men would never forget
it."

How was it possible to refuse him? Besides, the
suggestion greatly amused the ladies; and doubtless
the entertainment would help to dissipate the strange
feeling of uneasiness which weighed upon them
though they knew not why.

"Toper," shouted the Captain, and the second-in-
command at once rushed up to him. "Is everything ready in the cages?"

"Yes, Captain."

Chéri-Bibi added in a lower tone:

"Do they know that at the first word I'll have them shot where they are?"

"That's perfectly understood, Captain, and I don't think they'll need a second warning."

"All right, off we go to the Zoological Gardens."

The ladies stood round him; they wanted to be in the front row. They descended to the main gun deck. A deathly silence reigned in the cages. The visitors, greatly impressed, dared not utter a word. And for some moments they looked at each other, standing motionless by the side of the bars.

When their eyes had grown accustomed to the semi-darkness which prevailed on this deck, they began to distinguish the details of the crude accommodation in which the wretched men were crowded.

"Poor fellows!" exclaimed Madame d'Artigues.

The others also were moved to pity. "Poor fellows!" They asked about their beds and what food they were given, and wanted to know if they were well looked after.

"Oh, of course they're well looked after. There's no mistake about that," replied Chéri-Bibi. "Aren't you well looked after, you fellows? Come, answer me. Is there a single one here who has any complaint to make? You see, ladies, they don't answer, and not a soul complains! They're quite satisfied."

Chéri-Bibi exhibited these men in the same way as

the proprietor of a menagerie shows off his wild beasts and enlarges on their good points.

"Come . . . Step out of the ranks, you Whiskers. Come here, Miser. And you, Spoon-face, over there. What are you whining about? Is it your rheumatism?"

"What's the matter with that man?" asked Madame d'Artigues.

"He's mourning for his poor wife, who met with an accident."

"Dear me, what was that?"

"He poured some molten lead over her."

"Oh, the villain! You wouldn't think it to look at him. See, Marquis, what a nice face he has."

"Yes, indeed, as if butter wouldn't melt in his mouth."

"I remember reading about the case at the time," said Robert Bourrelier.

"It's amusing to see all the notorious criminals whose trials were reported in the newspapers. Don't you think so, Marquis?"

"I do indeed, Madame."

"Say what you like, they were represented as much more brutal in appearance," said Mlle. de Valrieu. "It's very funny, but they don't look a bit vicious."

"This brute is not vicious, but when he is attacked he defends himself," growled Chéri-Bibi, hurrying his guests along towards the other cages.

He was carrying a stick, and he struck the bars with it as if he were a wild beast tamer rousing his animals from their lethargy.

"Now then, stand up in the cages. Can't you get up, you fellows? Don't you see that we're paying you a visit? Honor to the ladies! Come, Guillotine, Anarchist and Tuesday Night! . . ."

"What do you say that man's name is?"

"Tuesday Night."

"What a funny name! Why do you call him that?"

"Oh, one name is as good as another. Probably all his troubles happened on Tuesday Night. . . . You see that man over there. . . . Do you know what he's called? His name is Lace Stealer."

"What did he do?"

"Now then, answer. . . . What did you do?"

"I don't know, Captain."

"What, you don't know! With a name like that! . . . You smuggled lace; of course you did. . . . Another case of dodging the Customhouse. . . . Stand up, Cow's Tail. This one takes his name from Cow's Tail Alley, where he committed his first crime. He had a fight with a policeman and killed him. Isn't that so, Cow's Tail?"

"I don't know, Captain."

"What, you don't know!"

Chéri-Bibi turned to the sergeant of the guards, infuriated.

"It's very extraordinary, sergeant. The men in the cages know nothing whatever. How do you spend your time? You've got to make them repeat what they've done."

"How do you mean make them repeat what they've done?" asked Robert Bourrelier.

"Well, the object is to force them to remember their crimes and feel some remorse for them."

"Look, Captain, at that man over there shrugging his shoulders."

"Is there a man here who dares to shrug his shoulders!" shouted Chéri-Bibi in a voice of thunder. "I dare say it's some hot-head. I don't allow men with hot heads on them to shrug their shoulders."

And as a grin followed this slightly hazardous figure of speech Chéri-Bibi lost patience.

"What do you suppose will be the result of such conduct?" he shouted, beside himself. "You want to make me lose my temper. Devil take you all! Try to respect what is worthy of respect, and respect yourselves if possible by respecting the decent people who happen to be on board with you. If you continue to behave in this way, what do you suppose these shipwrecked ladies and gentlemen will think of you? . . . And now we've had enough of the main gun deck   Let's go below to the lower gun deck, but first of all I'll show you Chéri-Bibi's cell."

He took them to the famous alley-way in which the

cells were situated. First he went to the cell in which the Countess had been incarcerated, and he pointed out the cavity through which she had escaped with the notorious convict. In the same way the concierge at the Château d'If in "Monte Cristo" showed visitors the underground tunnel by which the Abbé Faria communicated with Edmond Dantès.

"Here was imprisoned a wretched woman whom we have since hanged," he said. "She had obtained permission to accompany her husband to Numea. You will, perhaps, recollect the story of the doctor who cut strips of flesh out of his patients, and was suspected of cannibalism."

"Oh, how horrible!" exclaimed Madame d'Artigues.

"Yes, yes," said Mlle. Nadège, "the trial was reported in the newspapers. Is the doctor here? We should like to see him."

"We hanged him."

"Good Lord, how many have you hanged?"

"As many as were necessary to secure the safety of the ship," declared Chéri-Bibi in emphatic tones. "This woman was, as I say, accompanying her husband, but she had occasion to see Chéri-Bibi, and was at once seized with a mad infatuation for him. It was she, chiefly, who helped the cook's mate, of whom I was speaking just now, in his schemes for Chéri-Bibi's escape.

"Look at this cell, and now look at the other one.

There's no passage between them, is there? Now it was in this cell that Chéri-Bibi was imprisoned in irons, and watched by two warders. How was it possible for him to pass from this cell to the woman's cell and to escape down that cavity? It was done in the simplest way imaginable. Look . . .

"The woman got herself sent below to the cell on purpose, knowing that this was the only unoccupied cell, and that as soon as she was locked in, she had only to go to work on this little contrivance." Chéri-Bibi started to unscrew the bolts which secured one of the iron plates between two cells. "Don't assume that this work was prepared by some miserable convict in his spare time. Not at all. It was done by the warders themselves—in the navy we call convict guards, warders. The unscrewing of the plate by a woman prisoner, who knew the trick and had done it before, caused no surprise to the two warders who were in the next cell guarding Chéri-Bibi and boring themselves to death.

"Listen to this carefully: One guard said to the other, 'Hullo, this is a bit of all right'' as the face of the woman appeared when the plate was removed. . . . You can guess the rest. . . . The devoted cook's mate was hiding behind the plank bed. When the first guard climbed over here to get to this spot which you see, the woman threw her beautiful arms round his neck and a bootlace as well, which the cook's mate tightened with a will.

"Astonished that the first guard did not return the second guard climbed over in the same way, and was at once furnished with the explanation which he was seeking.  He understood and died, whereupon the cook's mate, who had taken the precaution to obtain the key of the padlock from the Captain's jacket—they would have done without it if necessary, be assured—had only to set Chéri-Bibi free, lock the padlock again, put the dead warders back in the first cell, screw up the iron plate, replace the key in the Captain's pocket—I am always so absent-minded and preoccupied—and the trick was done.  What do you think of that, ladies and gentlemen?"

"Amazing! . . . Wonderful! . . . Extraordinary!"

"That ass, Captain Barrachon, hasn't got over it yet," added Chéri-Bibi.

"But don't say such things, dear Captain," laughed Mlle. Carmen de Fontainebleau in a flattering voice.  "Please don't speak ill of Captain Barrachon."

"That's true, I was forgetting," growled Chéri-Bibi.  "I mustn't run him down before the crew.  But there are times when I am very angry with myself, you know.  To be humbugged like that is enough to give one a fit, as my concierge says."

"Now take us to Chéri-Bibi. We must see Chéri-Bibi."

They left the orlop deck to mount to the lower gun deck; and here they saw more men in cages.  The ladies acknowledged that these men did have the abominable faces of convicts.

"Now look at that man over there," said Mlle. Nadège de Valrieu. "I shouldn't like to meet him alone in a wood." And she pointed to the distinguished Lieutenant de Vilène himself.

This naval officer, the chief personage in the tremendous adventure, looked in truth at that moment extremely sullen. The condition of this man was to be pitied, for he was compelled to restrain the rage which filled him against the monster Chéri-Bibi, conscious that if he did not succeed in mastering himself, or if he permitted a dubious word to escape him in regard to the peculiar circumstances which had reversed their individual parts, he might, perhaps, be giving the signal for a general massacre, and the shipwrecked persons who were visiting them would not be the last victims. But the prodigious moral effort that this condition entailed betrayed itself in his features, which by no means offered a welcome, as Mlle. Nadège de Valrieu had at once observed.

"You ought to be ashamed," Mlle. Carmen de Fontainebleau flung at him. "What did this man do?" she asked.

"He didn't do anything particularly bad, but the jury none the less brought him to book. Twenty years hard labour for attempting to murder his mother-in-law. Look at him, and believe me, it's not pride or obstinacy or scorn which keeps him silent.

He is tormented by a bitter regret, the regret that his attempt failed."

"Certainly all the men here have a wicked look."

"We are in the only spot on earth where we can really judge people from their actual appearance," declared Chéri-Bibi in sententious tones.

"Why so, Captain?"

"Because a convict's dress suits everyone perfectly," he growled fiercely. And he added with emphasis, turning to Maxime du Touchais: "Who can boast to-day that a convict's dress wouldn't suit him? A convict's dress is the only dress that makes a man look as he ought to look."

Delighted to have produced a certain effect he passed on to the next cage.

"The poor man is quite drunk," whispered the Marquis to Madame d'Artigues.

"I must confess," she returned, "that he frightens me a little. . . . Have you noticed his face and eyes when he speaks to you? Oddly enough, it seems to me that the man himself, who isn't very nice to look upon, is not a stranger to me. Of course, I may have seen his portrait in the newspapers. . . . Captain. . . . Captain. . . . Your portrait was published in the newspapers, wasn't it?"

"Yes," returned Chéri-Bibi, giving a start. "It was printed beside Chéri-Bibi's when it was announced that I was to take him to Cayenne. . . . Look, there he is, your Chéri-Bibi."

He pointed to Captain Barrachon, who was in the

financiers' cage.  Poor, brave, estimable Captain!
He would gladly have died at the head of his men.
His officers would have followed him to the death,
and preferred a hopeless massacre rather than submit
to the rule of a man like Chéri-Bibi. . . . But alas!
they were obliged to stop fighting for lack of ammunition, and to surrender in order to save the lives of
the crew.

"You conducted yourself like a brave man.  We've
nothing to complain of in you.  You did everything
that you could for us.  You can remain at liberty on
your ship."

It was the crowning insult of all—to have deserved
Chéri-Bibi's gratitude.  Barrachon reflected upon his
past weakness and reproached himself with it as a
crime; at the very least as if it had made him an
accomplice.  More than anyone else he deserved to
be put in this cage in which, in consequence, perhaps,
of his pusillanimity, the wicked had imprisoned the
good; and he had insisted on being confined with
the others.  He thought that if a brute in gold lace,
as he used to say in the time of his humanitarian
dreams, had in the early days broken the heads of a
few of these convicts or strung them up at the yard-
arm, this vessel belonging to the State would not at
that moment have been under new management!

The worthy Barrachon was floundering in the
bottomless pit of a distraught philosophy with as
many difficulties as the daring Chéri-Bibi had
floundered in when he grappled with his new duties

on deck and talked about government, discipline and the necessities of his new command; in a word, of a position for which fate, unkind until then, had not accustomed him. But, after all, one gets used to everything. And by degrees life on board had resumed its usual course. Inside the cages the whilom free men began to assume the sickly and worn-out aspect of the slave in whom pride of race vanishes and brutishness appears. In the alley-ways the ex-convicts who were now free put on the look of authority, and, as conscientious warders of the vanquished, learnt without difficulty to make themselves obeyed.

The hours slipped away between decks as they did of old, and Chéri-Bibi had cleverly made of them the last word in discipline. On the upper deck, in the cabins, in the crew's quarters, on every hand where the bright light of day penetrated, men might laugh and enjoy themselves on condition that there was nothing to fear from their enemies below.

Chéri-Bibi's men like other bodies of men who have no intention of being taken by surprise had secured their rear. The same system was carried out as before, with the same punctuality, but with greater severity, for they had learnt something by experience. The same "watches" were called by the signalmen, and Barrachon saw the "warders" going the same rounds, and guarding the "old offenders"; and it would have seemed to the Captain as if nothing had changed on board but that the "old offender" this time was himself! . . .

"So that man . . . the one in the corner who looks such an arrant fool, is Chéri-Bibi. Well, really I never pictured him to myself like that," said Mlle. Carmen de Fontainebleau.

"Nor did I," added Mlle. Nadège de Valrieu. "He looks to me regularly knocked up. Don't you give him anything to eat, Captain? . . ."

"It's impossible that he can be the terrible Chéri-Bibi! He looks like a solicitor gone to the bad."

Captain Barrachon did not even turn his head. But a man in the cage stepped forward to the bars. His face was wrapped in bloodstained bandages. Speaking in a firm voice he said:

"My name is Pascaud and I am the sergeant of the military overseers. I was put in this cage like my fellow-overseers by the convicts who seized the ship. As to that man," he added, turning to the Captain, who had risen to his feet on hearing Pascaud's voice, "he is not Chéri-Bibi; he is Captain Barrachon. And Chéri-Bibi is there! . . ."

He thrust his hand through the bars and pointed to the real Chéri-Bibi, who burst into laughter. The laugh was drowned by an explosion of curses and insults, which arose from every cage. The prisons seemed for the moment to have broken into revolution. Clusters of human beings hurled themselves against the bars, hung on to them, gesticulating, their fists driven through the grilles menacingly, yelling: "Robbers. . . . Murderers. . . . Miserable convicts. . . . Kill us. We've had enough. . . . Or land us at once. We don't want your pity," and other shouts, howls, groans and infuriated cries.

The prisoners in the lower gun deck, suspecting what had come to pass, mingled the thunder of their clamour with that of the revolt above them. Like wild beasts whose fury is let loose when they struggle against an insuperable barrier, they gasped and foamed and rolled over powerless against the bars. Barrachon himself had lost his self-command and all sense of dignity during his captivity. He was no longer anything but a wild beast like the others, like all the others, who would gladly have torn their keepers to pieces. It was an awful and tragic spectacle and was repeated in the next cage, in the cage behind, and in all the cages.

The visitors fled in dismay, and Chéri-Bibi himself followed them, stopping his ears. It was a stampede to the upper deck while the new guards, shouting as loud as their one-time jailors, besought Chéri-Bibi to give them the order for a general massacre.

Chéri-Bibi reached the deck. Here he breathed freely once more and saw with relief the light, and the brightness of sky and sea, and felt a delight in life that he had never known before.

"Poor beggars," he said. "Give them double rations."

# CHAPTER XI

THE ladies reached the deck in a state of terror, and it was some time before they recovered their equilibrium.

"Oh, it's frightful," sighed Madame d'Artigues. "Did you hear them? Did you see them? I thought they were going to devour us."

"And telling us that story," said Mlle. de Valrieu, falling into a seat, "and trying to palm themselves off as . . ."

"Yes," interrupted Mlle. de Fontainebleau, cutting her short, "that's the most amazing thing of all. . . . Suppose it were true?"

"Look here, are you taking leave of your senses, dear lady?" broke in Robert Bourrelier.

"I say, do try to be civil. Anyway, you can say what you like but I can't make out this Chéri-Bibi. . . . Did you recognize him, Mesdames? Come, his portrait was in the newspapers. . . . Was it anything like him?"

"Well," said Madame d'Artigues, "between ourselves, the Captain is much more like him."

"Exactly," agreed Mlle. de Valrieu, with a shudder. "He is the very image of Chéri-Bibi."

"You acknowledge it yourself. . . . Why, ever since lunch I've been saying to myself that it's astonishing how the Captain résembles Chéri-Bibi. . . . Heavens, if it were true . . . if it were true. . . . What would become of us?"

She was quite pale, and the three of them were trembling with apprehension. Robert Bourrelier was obliged to talk to them and make them listen to reason.

"Just like women," he said, "you're always the slaves of your imagination. To be shipwrecked is not enough, you must have a few adventures with convicts. Look here, really, have you lost your heads? Don't look so scared. When the Captain comes I shan't fail to tell him the reason of your fear so that we may have a little fun. A portrait in the newspapers!

"Come, let us consider the matter seriously. The Captain said himself that his portrait was printed beside Chéri-Bibi's. You take the one for the other. You mix up the two characters. The Captain's hair is cut short, and many sailors have their hair cut short like Chéri-Bibi's, and thereupon you fly off at a tangent. If all the men with closely cropped hair were either going or coming out of prison, Paris, in summer time, would be a branch establishment of Cayenne, and one would imagine, in the height of the season, that the doors of all the departmental prisons had been thrown open!

"Come, be sensible. Consider the splendid discipline that exists on board. How cheerful the crew are. Remember how kindly you were received. If all these people were what you fear them to be, I daren't even tell you what would have happened to you after you had set foot in this hospitable ship. Do you follow me so far?"

"Yes, that's true," said Madame d'Artigues, who in reality asked for nothing better than to be convinced. "We were silly. . . ."

"Depend upon it, convicts wouldn't mince matters."

"The day is not over yet," the nervous Carmen thought it well to observe.

"It is only beginning," came from a voice behind them.

They turned round and found themselves confronted by three officers, who bowed with every mark of politeness.

The "old offenders," now at liberty, had sent them the pick of the basket, which consisted of a forger of legal documents, a notorious poisoner, and a swindler who had misappropiated the funds of a religious society.

The ladies were agreeably impressed by the cut of the clothes, the white gloves, and the society manners of the three rascals.

The man who spoke first and possessed a pleasant voice went on:

"Yes, Mesdames, the day is only just beginning for us, seeing that the entertainment is to be graced with your charming presence. The Countess is waiting for you to open the ball. May we have the pleasure of dancing the first quadrille with you?"

The Countess! They had forgotten her. Yes, indeed, they must have been crazy. Had they for a moment remembered the charm and distinction of this great lady, who had taken them under her protection, they would certainly not have given such rein to their imagination. And they laughed at themselves, and Robert Bourrelier laughed with them. What could they have been thinking about? And then these young officers, such excellent fellows, so polite, so correct, expressing themselves with such good form. The ladies rose to their feet with a simper.

"The entertainment! Oh, please forgive us. We had forgotten it. . . . We hardly know if we dare come. . . . The Countess has doubtless dressed specially for it," lamented the delightful Carmen de Fontainebleau.

"Not at all, not at all. The Countess, like all great ladies, loves simplicity. She came just as she was. And then, you know, it's a little family gathering."

The officers offered the ladies their arms. They did not need a second asking, and now, entirely reassured, they went off with their partners.

"I am told that there are no better dancers than sailors," prattled the beautiful Madame d'Artigues.

The forger of legal documents, with a courtly inclination of the head, modestly protested.

"A poet said the same thing of German herdsmen." And in careful and measured articulation he quoted the poem.

"Alfred de Musset! That's Alfred de Musset. Oh, I love de Musset."

"How very fortunate. I know him by heart."

They reached the quarter-deck, which was artistically decorated, and where a crowd was quietly waiting for the first strains of the band. The Countess came forward to meet the ladies and thanked them warmly for their kindness and amiability. Facing the band was a somewhat roomy space, and here the first quadrille was danced. One might have imagined oneself in a dancing saloon, or rather in a casino—by the sea, of course.

Nevertheless, after the first polka, the newcomers could not help noticing the somewhat free and easy manner in which the men treated the women with whom they danced, and also the unconventional attitude of these women, who addressed each other in a language that the Marquis du Touchais's friends did not always comprehend. They asked the

Countess and their partners for a few explanations,
and they were freely given.

The feminine element here, it was said, was chiefly
represented by the wives of military overseers, who
traveled with their husbands everywhere, and, of
course, unfortunately became habituated to the use
of slang, owing to their contact with convicts. Moreover, the manner in which they lived on board, the
crowding between decks, had the effect of drawing
this big family closer together, so that nearly all of
them, men and women alike, addressed each other
in tones of familiarity. As a matter of fact the men
and women were extremely gay, and some rather
coarse language was bandied from couple to couple.

Between the dances a general movement was made
to the refreshment bars, which were stormed and
plundered. The visitors noticed the liberality with
which the Captain had provided a most varied assort-
ment of drinks and liqueurs. Some of the persons
present drank out of the bottles; and a struggle waged
round the cases of champagne.

The band struck up again with renewed vigor, and
the dancers entered the fray once more, skipping and
pushing and shouting, while the expressions of
drunken satisfaction on their faces were appalling.
Moreover, the amazing intermixture of all ranks in
an entertainment which tended to become more and
more debauched "passed the comprehension" of the
ladies. They had been longing to depart, but they

were given neither the time nor the opportunity. They were always brought back to the middle of the elated crowd at the moment when they were endeavoring to escape out of the vortex.

And then they received invitations which they neither dared nor had the power to refuse. Carried away on the arms of those whom it would have been difficult to resist, they resumed their places in the eddying throng. The Toper had a way of pressing Madame d'Artigues to his heart which at length greatly alarmed her. Carmen de Fontainebleau and Nadège de Valrieu, who had at first enjoyed themselves, were amazed by certain familiarities.

The three of them, out of breath, asked permission to retire, and they could not understand why the Countess continued to dance with this rabble, and allowed herself to be roughly jostled by couples in an obvious state of intoxication without uttering a protest. The Countess, indeed, was an extraordinary person. She whirled round and round with a smile on her lips, nodding graciously to the women who by chance floated near her during the quadrilles. Did she not notice the awful faces around her? Was she not conscious that the whole business would "end in a row"?

Meanwhile, the naval officer who "knew de Musset by heart," and who had started to recite "Rollo" to Madame d'Artigues during the first waltz, came up and informed the ladies that they could not be allowed to depart like that, for their grace and charm had won every heart, and the entertainment would be shorn of its attraction without them.

The Pick of the Basket continued to express himself in such choice language that the ladies could not pluck up the courage to refuse him anything. Nevertheless, the crush, the noise, the brutish clamor around them had assumed such proportions that they admitted to him that they "felt afraid," and dared not stay longer. The men about them frightened them. Moreover, they were exhausted by the excitement of the shipwreck, and the crew ought really to have some compassion for them.

The forger of legal documents bowed and said:

"There is a way of allowing you to go, and that is, if those ladies," and he indicated Carmen and Nadège, "will perform the items in the programme that they promised us. Until you've danced on the platform, as our men expect, they won't hear of it. Dance at once and you may disappear afterwards. Do you wish me to announce you?"

Carmen and Nadège consulted each other with a glance. They took the plunge. Yes, they would appear on the platform, and afterwards, doubtless, they would be left alone.

"I shall recite 'The Blacksmiths' Strike,'" said Nadège.

"I shall dance my first two love waltzes," said Carmen.

"And you, Madame?" inquired the Pick of the Basket, turning to Madame ·d'Artigues. "You will honor us with . . ."

"Oh, Monsieur, I am not an actress."

"In any case, we should like you to appear on the platform as the men are relying on it."

"Your crew, Monsieur, is really an extraordinary one."

"Oh, you know, Madame, they treat everyone without ceremony, as the saying goes. . . . Obviously they are slightly lacking in reserve, but they are very decent fellows, I assure you. . . . They are merely a little malicious when they have drink in them, and that is why I advise you to give your performance soon."

"Yes, let's get it over as quickly as possible. . . . It's inconceivable that they should be allowed to drink like this on board a ship in the French navy. The whole thing is incomprehensible. Look, look at their faces, and the way they stare at you. It's shameful."

"Come with me," requested the Pick of the Basket.

He hurried them behind the band where the ship's company of actors were dressing and making up for some extraordinary farce which they were to perform. A corner of an awning erected behind the scenes was placed at their disposal in case they desired to collect their thoughts, or to beautify themselves before going on the stage, from which the band had just been cleared. The instrumentalists took their places under the footlights, and the Top announced that the "performance was about to begin," and that Mlle. Nadège de Valrieu of the Odeon Theatre, Paris, Mlle. Carmen de Fontainebleau of the Folies-Bergères Music Hall, Paris, and a society lady, an amateur, would at once appear in different parts.

Amid perfect silence Mlle. Nadège recited "The Blacksmiths' Strike."

The audience listened to the end without stirring, and when it was over, after applauding, shouted to Mlle. Nadège to give them a dance. There was no doubt that they preferred dancing to literature. To save the situation, Carmen appeared. In the ordinary way she danced her numbers very lightly clad, and with the assistance of a veil. In the circumstances she hastily threw over her costume a flowing robe which the Countess lent her.

The moment she began to dance she was encouraged by loud cheers and enthusiastic shouts in slang, which put her on her mettle. She wanted, above all, to get the dance over. She thus appeared to be all the more eager, and truth to tell, seized once more by the demon of her art, she flung herself wildly into her love waltzes, the popular airs of which were sung in chorus by the convicts, swayed by their emotions.

In the whirl of these pagan dances she showed her admirably formed legs, and her success was immense. She did not stop until she was completely exhausted, and she dashed behind the curtain amid shouts of applause and an almost frantic enthusiasm.

"Now, let's go," she said. "It's none too soon. I thought at one moment they were going to rush on to the platform and carry me off."

"Yes, yes, let's slip away," agreed Madame d'Artigues in a trembling voice. "Do you know what I heard just now while you were dancing, Carmen? One of the men, one of the men here with the abominable face of a convict, said to another like him, for they all resemble convicts, every one of them: 'The little girl sets me on fire. . . . Of the three of them I should prefer her to fall to my lot.' "

"Well?"

"Well, what does a phrase like that mean? For my part I fear the worst from such men. . . . I've sent for the Marquis. Why isn't he here? . . . And Robert Bourrelier . . . and my husband? . . ."

"Yes, indeed, where are they? Why aren't the men with us?" asked Carmen in increasingly anxious tones.

"And what's become of the Captain? . . . If the Captain were here . . ."

"Not at all. The Captain frightens me more than anyone," confessed Madame d'Artigues.

"Ah, there you are, you agree with me now," said Carmen as she hastily finished dressing. "Quick, quick, let's make off. Let's go and lock ourselves in our cabins."

"But how are we to get through now. . . . Hark.
. . . It's as though we were besieged."

As a matter of fact the clamour became louder and
louder. The audience wanted the artists to give an
encore, and the Top and Little Buddha appeared.

"Don't go out, whatever you do," said Little
Buddha. "Stay here if you wish to avoid trouble.
. . . They are tipsy, you understand. . . . They all
want to kiss you. . . ."

"But how dreadful! . . ."

"Dreadful," he grinned ominously.

At that moment they could hear the Toper making
an announcement from the stage:

"Comrades, the ladies are tired and ask you to
excuse them (yells). I beg of you to be reasonable
and have a little patience. The *Bayard's* special company will continue the performance, and lots will be
drawn immediately afterwards."

The three women exchanged bewildered glances
when they heard the last part of the announcement.
They dared not impart to each other the feeling of
dread which possessed them. Nevertheless, Madame
d'Artigues, making an effort to appear calm, asked
the officer:

"Are there many prizes in the raffle?"

"No, Madame," replied the officer. "We haven't
very many prizes, but they're splendid ones!"

# CHAPTER XII

AFTER he left the prisons Chéri-Bibi returned to his cabin much exercised in mind by the new attitude of his prisoners, and realizing quite well that the little farce which he was playing with the shipwrecked passengers was drawing to a close. Prompt in his resolutions, as becomes a man of action, he sent for the Toper and gave his orders for the end of the entertainment as far as the ladies were concerned; he could hear the audience over his head singing in chorus.

"That will teach them to speak ill of Cecily."

No sooner was the matter settled than he dismissed the Toper, ordering him to send the Dodger to him.

The Dodger did not come at once, and, beginning to lose patience, he pushed open the cabin door, and his eyes fell upon two men, who did not see him, but thinking that they were alone in that part of the vessel, were chatting over their own affairs. It was Baron Proskof and the Marquis du Touchais. Chéri-Bibi imagined that they were talking about the unforeseen incident which occurred in the Zoological Gardens, and the disquieting considerations which the revolt of the prisoners may have suggested to them. But he was mistaken; he did not know these men. They were talking "women."

We have had occasion, more than once, since the arrival of the shipwrecked persons on board the *Bayard* to refer to Baron Proskof's depressed condition. His melancholy aspect was entirely to the worthy Polish nobleman's credit, seeing that it was not more than two or three days since the Baroness, his precious spouse, was no more, or at all events, since he believed that she was no more. It was to no purpose that Maxime du Touchais endeavored to rouse him from his grief, representing to him that if anyone had cause for sorrow it was he, du Touchais, who had suffered so heavy a loss while the Baron at least still possessed the million francs.

At the moment when their conversation was overheard by Chéri-Bibi, Baron Proskof was launching into a eulogy of his wife.

"She was a woman of superior intelligence, whom I can never replace, nor can you either, my dear Marquis, however much you may try. That Madame d'Artigues makes me quite ashamed. She is not worthy to tie the shoe strings of the Belle of Dieppe, as she was called."

"I quite agree with you, my dear Baron, but what is a poor man to do? One must be sensible. I'm still too young to settle down."

"Do you know what I should do if I were in your place?"

"What?"

"Well, I should return as soon as possible to my wife, and wait quietly until I was positive that the Baroness was dead, for after all we cannot be absolutely sure of anything. . . . Look here, your wife is a very charming woman, and I feel confident that she would be delighted to see you again."

"That's not what the ladies think. You heard what they said at lunch."

"What! Do you take any notice of what those silly ninnies say. . . . Aren't you certain of the Marchioness?"

"Certain of what? . . . Can one ever tell with saints? . . ." sneered the Marquis.

The remainder of the conversation was lost to Chéri-Bibi; moreover, he would have been unable to listen to another word. The Dodger found him as white as a sheet, stretched on his sofa.

"Are you ill?" exclaimed the devoted baker's man. "Shall I go and fetch the Kanaka?"

"No, I want to see his wife first," returned Chéri-Bibi in a whisper.

"The Countess?"

"Yes, the Countess. . . . At once."

The Dodger informed the Countess, who came down in the interval between two Boston two-steps. She betrayed a certain anxiety when she found the Captain so ill.

"Shut the door," said Chéri-Bibi.

"But what's the matter?"

"Something . . ."

He got up and plunged his head into a basin of water, and having thus collected his thoughts, appeared to be much better. The Countess watched him, completely at a loss, as he dabbed the towel on his forehead.

"I say, listen to me," said Chéri-Bibi, sitting down by her side and taking her hands. "I know that you love me, Countess."

"Yes," she answered simply and sadly, "but you don't love me."

"I want to tell you, Countess . . . You were too late, you see, my heart was engaged."

"I always thought as much. . . . It is the worst misfortune of my life."

"Let's be brief, but let's be frank, Countess. Since you love me, will you do something for me?"

"Anything you like."

"Oh, yes, but . . . something . . . something out of the way. . . ."

"Anything you like."

"Well, to begin with, tell me what you and the Kanaka did with the strips of flesh that you cut out of the patient."

"Oh, that," she cried. And she withdrew her hands, and rose to her feet.

"You see, there are things that you won't do for me."

She retreated to a corner of the cabin as if she were afraid now of Chéri-Bibi and dared not meet him, and she said in a hoarse, muffled voice:

"I know quite well what people say."

"Is it true? . . . Tell me . . . me . . . Is it true?" Chéri-Bibi entreated her.

She shook her head so wildly and fiercely that her splendid hair became unconfined and floated in dark waves over her shoulders.

"No, no," she said in a choking voice. "It's not true, it's not true."

"It was mentioned at the Assize Court."

"Oh, that isn't true, either," she said between her teeth. "No, no, they wouldn't have dared . . . they wouldn't have dared. . . . The judge let himself go a little too far, but he at once pulled himself up . . . at once. Our counsel told him that he had no right at all to hint even vaguely at such a thing when he was not certain . . . when there was no evidence. The incident was closed . . . at once. Oh, if you had seen the Court. Women fainted merely at the thought of it. . . . Chéri-Bibi, I love you, and wouldn't lie to you. I tell you again that we didn't do such things. . . ."

She dropped on the sofa beside him and wanted him to take her hands in his, but it was his turn to stand up. He paced up and down the cabin wrapped in thought, and then standing before her:

"It's a pity," he said.

"What do you mean, it's a pity?"

"Yes, it's a pity. I had dreamed of giving you somebody to eat!"

"I know whom you mean," she said as she rose from the sofa and clung to him. "It's the Marquis. I thought during lunch that you were going to do for him."

"Oh no, not at all," he said; "that would have been too good for him. I tell you, Countess, that when I think of him I go clean off my head. I should like to invent sufferings . . . tortures for him. . . . Oh, I believed everything that was said against the Kanaka. . . . I thought that . . . Never mind, we'll say no more about it, since it's not true."

The Countess had an absorbed expression on her face.

"What did that man do to you?" she asked.

"He tore my heart out of me. . . . Do you understand?"

"Oh yes, I understand."

"And then he's too fat, too big, too healthy, too happy, too successful. He wants a particular woman and he planks down a million francs for her . . . he has everything. He's a monster."

"Yes, yes, I understand you. . . . Is he very rich?"

"Rich isn't the word. He has millions . . . millions. What are you thinking about? Why do you turn your head away? Why are your cheeks so pale, and why is there a look of gloom in your eyes? What's the matter?"

"Nothing, nothing."

"I want to know what you are thinking about."

"Nothing, nothing."

"Yes, you are. Something crossed your mind. I tell you that something crossed your mind. I saw a shudder at the thought of it pass over your face. Countess, tell me what the idea is."

"Never. . . . It's too awful."

"Ah, there you are, you see. . . . I insist on knowing what your idea is."

"I should never dare to tell you. You yourself would reject it. Yes, you, Chéri-Bibi, would consider that my idea was too awful. And then it's not merely my idea. It's really a secret between the Kanaka and me; a secret which we keep because, believe me, the scaffold is at the end of it. So you understand why I can't tell you anything."

"I see you want to keep me on tenter-hooks. You are trying to whet my appetite. You don't love me, Countess."

"More than you think, Chéri-Bibi, and it's just because I do love you that I can't tell you anything."

"So it's something more awful than I imagined."

"More awful than what?"

"More awful than cannibalism."

The Countess did not reply for a moment. She was in a state of indescribable agitation. She could not

meet Chéri-Bibi's eyes. . . . At last a few words
escaped her in a murmur.

"Yes, it is much worse than that. Oh, leave me,
leave me."

Chéri-Bibi took her in his arms, and she was but a
poor weak woman. She no longer resisted his desire
to know. Nevertheless, she sent him to the Kanaka.

"I personally don't mind. Listen, my Chéri-Bibi,
I don't mind your knowing it. I won't stand in the
way of his telling you about the frightful thing. I
am certain that you will shrink from it. But if you
ever talk about it, it will cost both of us our heads.
. . . I give you mine, I give you mine. Take it."

She gave him her beautiful face and her white lips
which could not have been more bloodless if the exe-
cutioner had already done his work. But Chéri-Bibi,
who thought only of vengeance, would not let his eyes
fall upon the gift that was offered to him.

"Countess, go and fetch the Kanaka," he said.

She fell back on the sofa in an attitude of despair,
her disheveled head held between her clasped hands
like a Magdalene mourning for her sins, and then she
drew herself up and looked once more at Chéri-Bibi,
wild-eyed.

"I will go," she said.

But first she stopped before a glass and arranged
her disordered locks; and then she hurriedly left the
cabin.

Five minutes later the Kanaka came in. He was

looking yellow and his eyes were bloodshot. He was alone.

"Where's the Countess?" asked Chéri-Bibi.

"She's returned to the dance," answered the Kanaka, who kept his eyes fixed on Chéri-Bibi.

"And we, where are we?"

"We are making for the Gulf of Guinea, and everything is ready for to-night. The wreckage has been set aside for the purpose. We shall throw what is necessary overboard so that it will be believed that the ship went down with all hands. Then to-morrow, at the earliest moment, we shall proceed to fake a disguise for her."

"Do you think that we shall be able to coal and take in provisions at Cape Town without running into danger?"

"It will be quite easy seeing that we have command of the ship, and need stay only for the night."

"What flag shall we fly afterwards?"

"That remains to be considered. Personally, I vote for the Argentine flag. There are some forty of us on board who speak Spanish fluently. And then, as we shan't stop anywhere, no one will want to poke his nose into our affairs. Once we reach the Malay Archipelago . . ."

"I say, Kanaka, what's the matter? You don't seem to me to be yourself."

"The Countess told me, Chéri-Bibi, that . . ."

"Well?"

"Well . . ."

"Come, make up your mind. Can you do anything for me?"

"It's something appalling, Chéri-Bibi, and you wouldn't stand it."

"Tell me what it is."

"If ever you blab, the Countess and I would be done for, when we returned to civilization, which is a possibility that we must always reckon on."

"Do you take me for a spy?"

"No, that I do not, but we've got to be careful. Besides, I must tell you that the thing may not succeed."

"I don't follow you at all, Kanaka, or rather I don't know what you mean; but anyway, tell me, would he suffer?"

"Would he suffer! I should think he would suffer. . . . I'm pretty well certain that you'd say he would suffer too much."

"You don't know me, Kanaka. If you only realized how much I want him to suffer . . . Go on, I'm listening."

The Kanaka went to the other end of the cabin, held his face between his hands, and seemed to be thinking desperately. Chéri-Bibi did not disturb him. At last the Kanaka raised his head. His face was yellower than ever and his eyes were suffused with blood. He was frightful to look upon. It was as though he were already the victim of some over-stimulation, partly cerebral and partly physiological, which had rendered him a hideous brute beast.

He crossed the cabin with tottering footsteps, stretched out his arms, took Chéri-Bibi by the shoulders, looked around to see if the doors were properly closed, and bent over the convict's ear. And slowly, slowly, with pauses and catches in his breath, by fits and starts, he poured into his ear the liquor of his diabolical secret.

Chéri-Bibi seemed in his turn to be lost in a sickly exultation. His shoulders were convulsed, his hands trembled, his eyes became dilated, and the perspiration broke from his brazen forehead in great drops.

At length the Kanaka ceased speaking and drew back, folding his arms. And Chéri-Bibi also folded his arms, and thus they remained for a space of ten minutes gazing at each other in silence. And then Chéri-Bibi fled, closing the door on the Kanaka, who continued to stand erect, his arms folded as motionless as a statue. . . . Chéri-Bibi, in a few leaps, like a tiger, had mounted the deck.

He needed air . . . he needed to think things out. The songs, the choruses, the shouting and the dancing on the quarter-deck drove him away to the forecastle. And here, alone with sea and sky, he shut out the world and communed with himself. He walked in a circle, breathing hard, and he thought in a circle about the Kanaka's secret, which he had determined to know, and which tempted him as the dream of dominion over the world tempted Satan. He lifted his eyes to heaven as was his wont when he appealed to fate; the *Fatum* which he felt was always hanging

over his head, and bearing down with all its irresistible force upon his shoulders.

His exploits were so tremendous that in his ingenuous pride he regarded them as the one and only
preoccupation of time and circumstance. He knew
of no more remarkable or desperate calamities than
his own, and in his cruel but childish imagination he
was allied to those accursed beings in the history of
primitive man—of whom he had read long ago at
school—who were always in direct communication
with the omnipotent God, whom they endeavored
to reach by piling mountain upon mountain, or to
appease by offering up the most terrible sacrifices.

"Why do you subject me to this new ordeal?" he
cried in a loud voice, as if he were addressing one
whom he looked upon as his most relentless enemy.
"Do you not know full well that I could not fight
against this temptation? . . . The very thought of it
burns me like a flaming robe."

He was off once more in his mad tramp round and
round, halting a few moments later to resume his
strange soliloquy. But it was to the Kanaka this time
that he addressed his fervid speech.

"Your words, Kanaka, are easily comprehended.
. . . Even a child could understand them. . . . But
my mind is racked by a deadly torment. . . . Hope
gnaws at the pit of my stomach like a hound! . . ."

He started away again like a man escaped from
Bedlam. Then he stopped once more shouting and
foaming at the mouth. . . . Chéri-Bibi, Chéri-Bibi,

whence come this sudden delirium and anguish without apparent reason? Why those cries of terror and horror to which you give the blessed name of hope? . . . On the poop, between sea and sky, you seem as appalling, as menacing but also as awestruck as was Satan on the mountain before the temptation of Jesus Christ. And then suddenly you collapse! You plunge once more, with lowered head, into the inferno where the Kanaka, turned to stone, awaits you.

Chéri-Bibi pushed open the door of the cabin wherein the statue stood, needing but one word to come to life again. And he threw this word at him.

"Come," he said.

The Kanaka unfolded his arms, held out his hand to Chéri-Bibi, who grasped it warmly.

And they parted without a word.

On deck the entertainment was "in full swing," as the saying goes. Mesdames d'Artigues, de Valrieu and de Fontainebleau, in their tent, were in a state of mind which approximated more and more to a feeling of dismay, for they became aware that practically they were prisoners, notwithstanding the strange words of politeness which the even stranger naval officer lavished on them from time to time. They had in vain endeavored to steal away. On the plea that the intense excitement of the crew would only increase, and that it would be dangerous for them to attempt to go, they were not allowed to move. The tumult of fierce shouting and foul songs reached their ears, and they threw themselves, affrighted, into each other's arms.

They called out loudly for the Marquis and the Baron and Robert and d'Artigues. Thus it was with a sense of relief that they saw Robert and d'Artigues hurrying in. But their joy was of short duration.

Robert and d'Artigues had been as startled as they were by all that they had seen and heard.

After the outbreak in Chéri-Bibi's presence in the cages down below, they determined to obtain some clear idea of the position, and with that object they made their way into certain parts of the ship from which previously, it would appear, they had been deliberately excluded. They had thus been able to witness some rather amazing sights.

To begin with, they noticed that there was an incredible confusion and lack of discipline. Moreover, they had come upon a cordon of convict guards, who prevented them from setting foot into the alley-ways and cabins whence they could hear the cries and groans of women and children; of women calling for their husbands, and children calling to their fathers.

When they sought to obtain some explanation, they were ordered to leave, the men jeering at them in ominous fashion and advising them, in their own interests, to show a little less curiosity in future. Bourrelier and d'Artigues, in trembling voices, had reached this point in their disclosures when Baron Proskof came in. He was in a state of such terror that he could not at first utter a word. Finally, they heard him stammer:

"The Marquis . . . the Marquis . . ."

"What about the Marquis?" asked the beautiful Madame d'Artigues, in anguished tones.

"Well, the Marquis has disappeared."

"How do you mean disappeared?"

"He disappeared before my eyes. . . . I can't explain it at all. I thought he was still with me. We were in the alley-way, not far from my cabin, talking of one thing and another, for we had slipped away from that awful entertainment, and suddenly, when I turned round, he was no longer standing beside me. I looked about, I went into the cabins, I shouted his name. He answered me, but his voice came from the distance, and after a moment he was silent, and it seemed as if he were choking.

"He was undoubtedly the victim of some aggression. The unfortunate thing is that I did not manage to get a clear idea of the exact spot where he was. The ship seems to be run as if the whole business is a matter of play-acting. Abominable things are happening round us.

"Into what sort of hands have we fallen? The convict guards are as much to be feared as the convicts themselves. Besides, where is the Captain? We can't see him. I tried to talk to the officers. . . . They're drunk. . . . It was only with great difficulty that I reached this place. We must get away from here. The whole thing is awful. . . ."

At this point the entrance to the tent was lifted and two of the three sailors belonging to the *Belle of*

*Dieppe*, who had come on board the *Bayard* with them, rushed in. Their mate had just been stabbed in the heart and killed by one of the ruffians who was trying to take his lady partner from him. And as they attempted to avenge him, other ruffians sprang at them, and gave the whole game away. The *Bayard* was in the hands of convicts, and the man who had received them, as Captain, was neither more nor less than Chéri-Bibi. Chéri-Bibi himself!

Madame d'Artigues sank to the floor in a faint. Carmen and Nadège uttered piercing shrieks. At the same moment their improvised tent was flooded by a yelling mob, who carried the three of them on to the platform, where they were exhibited to the fierce curiosity and longings of a crew of raving madmen. . . . They were about to draw lots for them! . . .

Nevertheless, it was beyond doubt that the result of the draw would not be respected. Already those infernal faces were bending over the poor women, clutching them, snatching at them, quarreling over them.

The gang of exasperated convicts who were unable to mount the platform, seeing that the men around had seized the women without further ado, and without a word about the lottery, let themselves go in infuriated shouts and protests. The hapless women were about to vanish under the constantly increasing flood of convicts and be stifled to death when an interruption occurred which saved them.

A meteor passed through the crowd. There was a

tremendous pressure, and convicts fell in heaps from the platform, leaving sufficient room for Chéri-Bibi's immense fists to have full play and to let fly with the force of catapults.

Oh, he was always a brave sight in battle was the terrible Chéri-Bibi! What a number of broken noses, torn ears, black eyes! What bloodshed and shouts and maledictions! But what a splendidly quick clearance. How they applauded him. All the men who were unable to get near the platform, and had abandoned hope of receiving any share in the spoils, cheered him to the echo. . . . And the casualties crawling along the deck were turned into a general laughing-stock. And convicts know how to laugh.

Chéri-Bibi called for silence. He was standing on the evacuated platform in front of the three terrified and trembling women, who hardly ventured to thank their deliverer. For, after all, what was he about to say? To what new torment were they to be doomed?

"My dear pals," said Chéri-Bibi, "I have been thinking things over. As these women can't belong to all of you, they shan't belong to anyone (*thunders of applause*). I shall keep them for myself . . . (*silence*) with the sole object of preventing any harm coming to them . . . (*murmurs*) for I have just pledged myself to land them and the castaways from the *Belle of Dieppe* safe and sound at a time and place which will be fixed at the next conference (*threatening demonstrations. Chéri-Bibi folds his arms*). Who dares to raise his voice when I am speaking? The idiots among you do well to keep their mouths shut, for I have serious things to say to them. We must turn over a new leaf. You must become men of character, self-possessed and steady, because you are rich. The Marquis du Touchais, whom we have had the honor of welcoming on board, agrees, in accordance with my suggestion, to ransom the persons saved from the *Belle of Dieppe* for a sum of five million francs."

At first there was a feeling of stupefaction, not unmingled with fear, before this yawning gulf . . . five million francs. . . . They were dazed. And then they came to themselves and understood, and they burst forth into yells and stamped their feet and danced about like madmen. . . . They wanted to carry Chéri-Bibi shoulder high. He had the greatest difficulty in saying a word, a word to close the mouths of those fatuous imbeciles who never understood anything.

"My pals," he cried, "one last word. It is understood that the Marquis will not be released until we receive the five million francs. It is five million francs, or death" (*tremendous applause*).

"Well, Dodger, what do you think of that?" asked Little Buddha, as he dealt a heavy but friendly blow on the baker man's shoulder, making him wince.

"I know my Chéri-Bibi," replied the Dodger, with a faint smile. "It will be five millions *and* death."

# CHAPTER XIII

DURING the following days a considerable change came over life in general on board. Order and discipline held undisputed sway. Now that the convicts knew that they were rich, they welcomed almost with gladness the necessity of conforming to regularity and method.

They worked with a will for the well-being and safety of the ship.

The *Bayard* was re-christened *Estrella,* and flew the Argentine flag. Sure of his men henceforward, Chéri-Bibi relaxed from time to time the vigilance to which the families of the oversers had up to then been subjected. The women and children were permitted, as before, to play and gossip on the quarter-deck which was reserved for them during certain hours of the day. The prisoners were well treated and allowed out of the cages now and then, so as to have a breath of fresh air on the upper deck. The men with families on board were granted the right to communicate with them.

True, the landing of the prisoners was deferred to some indefinite and far distant date. This and many other matters had been decided at a conference which lasted for some time and to which most of the hot-heads among the convicts were convened.

As a matter of fact it was impossible to set anyone whatever at liberty until the famous five million francs were received. Such a course would have proclaimed to the world, which believed that the *Bayard* had perished with all hands, that she was still sailing the seas with her cargo of convicts.

Later on, when they felt some sense of security and were rich and safely sheltered in the Malay Archi-peligo, they would rid themselves of those embarrass-ing human packages whom they were obliged to main-tain from the ship's stores. Fortunately the provisions appeared to be inexhaustible, and it would be easy to replenish them, by force if necessary, from one of the defenseless towns on the African coast where European civilization had set up its stores.

The main thing was to land, at the earliest moment, Chéri-Bibi's lieutenant, who was to bring back the five millions.

Their choice had fallen on the Dodger, who had given proof of unbounded devotion to his chief, and who had been the main factor in liberating the con-victs. Moreover, it was conveyed to him that convict law would follow him in whatever part of the world he might be, if he failed to run straight and to con-duct himself like an honest man.

The Dodger knew enough of the men with whom

he had to deal to realize that it was impossible for him to escape their vengeance when once they had pronounced judgment. Moreover, he loved but one being on earth, and that being was Chéri-Bibi.

He would have preferred not to be parted from him, but Chéri-Bibi had given the word and there was nothing for it but to obey.

The Marquis du Touchais made every arrangement to render the Dodger's mission an easy one. The Dodger would leave the ship possessed of the necessary papers and instructions. It would be his business to see the Marchioness and a certain solicitor in Paris. Both of them would be apprised by him, and receive written statements from the Marquis, warning them that the slightest indiscretion would cost Chéri-Bibi's prisoners their lives.

The reason why the amount of the ransom had been fixed by Chéri-Bibi at five million francs only was that as a result of the Marquis's representations, it was regarded as impossible for Cecily and the solicitor in Paris to realize a greater sum in bank notes in the comparatively short time—a few months only—which was allotted to the Dodger in which to complete the transaction. The bank notes would have to be changed gradually by the Dodger, before the Marquis's liberation, so that there might be no question later of any trouble over the numbers. In short, they believed that they had omitted no precaution.

For a time they were inclined to entrust this difficult

mission to Chéri-Bibi's sister, St. Mary of the Angels, but not only was the poor girl in an alarming state of weakness, but Chéri-Bibi refused to allow her to be mixed up in this "murderous business," as he called it in moments of nervous strain.

They were steaming at full speed for Cape Town, and life on board was becoming somewhat monotonous when an extraordinary incident occurred which threw the crew in general and the Dodger in particular into a condition of unspeakable ferment.

It may be mentioned that no one had set eyes on the Marquis again, not even his friends who were free to live on board as they pleased. They waited upon themselves, rarely addressing a word even to those with whom they came in contact, and whom, for that matter, they regarded with feelings of dread. But they were not allowed to go near the spot where they were informed the Marquis was confined. No one except the Kanaka, the Countess and Chéri-Bibi was entitled to see him. It was said that the Marquis had been relegated to a large dark cabin, next to the sick-bay, but that he was entirely isolated from the sick' bay itself by a makeshift partition.

Outside the door of this cabin an orderly was posted whose instructions were to fire on any person attempting to approach the door.

Chéri-Bibi made an official explanation of the rea' son of this isolation. The Marquis was suffering from a contagious disease.

It was at first thought that they had to do with cholera or yellow fever or something of that sort, but when they saw the Kanaka and the Countess go backwards and forwards, tending the patient in what was a dangerous illness, and Chéri-Bibi visiting him, without taking any precaution, the crew quickly came to the conclusion that it was not a question of a sick person in the cabin, but of a prisoner representing five million francs who was being guarded with all the honors and attentions due to his rank and fortune.

The thought that possibly the Marquis was really ill, and that his illness might lead to death, did not unduly worry the convicts, for they were aware that Chéri-Bibi had already in his possession the papers containing the Marquis's signature, and that if by ill-luck he were to die, they would none the less receive the five millions even if they were reduced to handing over a corpse in exchange. But the much more simple idea of a carefully guarded prisoner, which occurred to them afterwards, afforded them considerable amusement. And they smilingly asked Chéri-Bibi from time to time for news of the Marquis. Chéri-Bibi himself, however, did not smile.

Far from it. They had never known him so sparing of words. Moreover, he was hardly ever seen, but was waited upon in his own cabin, replying in monosyllables to the Dodger's anxious questions, and never leaving his cabin except to go to the Marquis or visit his sister.

One evening the Dodger, who was looking out for him, feeling more and more perplexed by his curious attitude and his appearance of painful abstraction, saw him go into the Marquis's cabin with the Kanaka and the Countess, but waited in vain for him to come out again. The Dodger was determined to ask a few serious questions, for he feared that Chéri-Bibi might fall ill.

The Dodger's anxiety was greatly increased when, about four o'clock in the morning, he saw the Countess come out of the cabin, her sleeves turned back to the elbows, and her face showing signs of agitation. He ran up to her at the risk of being shot by the orderly on guard. The Countess pushed him aside, hastened to her own cabin, and appeared again, with a small chest which she concealed under a shawl, returning once more to the Marquis's cabin.

Up to eight o'clock in the morning no one had yet been seen again.

At length the Countess appeared accompanied by the Kanaka, who had a peculiar expression on his face. Nevertheless they both seemed quite self-possessed. They answered the Dodger's questions about Chéri-Bibi by stating that he was quite well though slightly exhausted by his work with the Marquis, but there was no cause for alarm.

"You should tell him to be sensible and take a rest," groaned the Dodger.

"Chéri-Bibi is man enough to look after himself," returned the Kanaka in icy tones. And he passed on without another word.

The Dodger stood facing the mysterious cabin whose silence terrified him. No sound emerged from it. Even when the Marquis was in it alone, the Dodger could not pass its precincts without a shudder. And now a terrible anxiety held him in its grip as he thought that Chéri-Bibi, like the Marquis, might never come out of it again. A few minutes later an orderly appeared and requested the Dodger to leave the place.

The morning of the next day passed amid fears that could not but increase. The Dodger questioned the guards who had been on duty at the door, but the men replied that they had not seen Chéri-Bibi go in or out. Where was he? Obviously he was still in the cabin. And what was he doing there? The extraordinary thing was that during the last twenty-four hours no food had been taken into the cabin. The Dodger's alarm was imparted, by degrees, to the entire crew. Chéri-Bibi was no longer to be seen. They wanted to see him. They would have questioned the Kanaka and the Countess, but they too had been shut up in their cabin for hours, and were as invisible as the Marquis and Chéri-Bibi.

Excitement reached its limit when the Toper, in the presence of the officers gathered together for lunch in the ward-room, opened and read a communication which the orderly on duty outside the cabin had just delivered to him. The letter contained three brief sentences from Chéri-Bibi: "You are instructed to obey the Kanaka in all things until you see me again. The Kanaka will merely transmit my orders to you. To obey the Kanaka is to obey Chéri-Bibi." Under the three sentences was Chéri-Bibi's signature; and then followed a few lines in the Kanaka's handwriting:

"The Countess and I are taking care of Chéri-Bibi, who has caught the Marquis's fever through looking after him. Chéri-Bibi's life is not in danger, but it is impossible for us to leave him at the moment. I ask the Toper and the officers to remove any fears entertained by the crew."

The convicts looked at each other askance. The Dodger, who had come in for news, read and re-read the communication. The whole thing seemed so mysterious that no one ventured to put forward any theory. The crew at once found themselves in a state of helplessness, and a heavy gloom prevailed on board. Chéri-Bibi was ill. There was not a man among the convicts who would not have given a limb to save his life. It was certain that cholera was on board. And to think that they had been under the impression that the whole thing was make-believe!

The men who, one after the other, mounted guard at the cabin door exchanged their opinions, and these were now circulating through the ship. The thing that surprised them more than anything else was the unwonted silence.

When the Marquis and Chéri-Bibi were alone in the cabin, the guards did not hear a murmur, though necessarily the slightest conversation would have reached their ears. In the same way, when the Kanaka and the Countess entered the cabin, their visit was not followed by any talk which the guards could hear.

The domestic services were entirely performed by the Countess, and these were reduced to very small proportions. . . . Hardly any food was taken in from outside, and it consisted only of a few basins of herb-tea and a little broth, and even so these were not required every day. It was as though the cabin were inhabited by ghosts.

Nevertheless, on the final day a guard heard terrible gasps. He was not, of course, able to say from whom they emanated.

As may be imagined, the appearance of the Kanaka and the Countess that day was impatiently awaited. Neither of them was seen, though occasionally their footsteps were heard.

The Dodger, who lay awake for several nights, at last gave way to sleep, although he had tried hard to keep his eyes open. He was sleeping like a log when one of his friends who had just been relieved from mounting guard at the cabin door awakened him.

The man had, this time, heard Chéri-Bibi's voice

quite clearly. It was a weary voice which said with a groan—at least the guard thought so—"Not his hands. . . . Not his hands." The Dodger was on his feet in an instant.

"Some accident has happened to Chéri-Bibi, that's a certainty."

Since it was impossible for him to go near the cabin, he would make his way into the sick-bay on some pretense or other and by flattening his ear against the new partition he might perhaps hear something.

He reached the place a few minutes later in a state of terrible anxiety, and as a matter of fact he did hear something. . . . The guard had not been dreaming. Chéri-Bibi was continuing to lament, but—and this was the amazing part—his words, which on every other occasion proclaimed his personal suffering, were now uttered in compassion for the other. For there was no possibility of error; he wanted the other man to be left alone. Therefore, what was being done to him? Chéri-Bibi's voice could be heard saying with a groan: "That's enough as it is. Leave him his hands. It's too awful. Oh no, not his hands, not his hands." And thereupon Chéri-Bibi heaved a tremendous sigh. As to the other man, his voice could not be heard. No lamentation came from him. It was incomprehensible.

Nevertheless the Dodger knew a great deal. During the time that he was associated with Chéri-Bibi, he was the recipient of many confidences from him. And when the Dodger learnt that one of the shipwrecked persons was the Marquis du Touchais, he trembled for the rich nobleman's life. That Chéri-Bibi would be revenged on Cecily's husband, by torturing him or having him tortured, was in keeping with the methods of convicts. But since it was the Marquis who was being tortured why was it Chéri-Bibi who was gasping and moaning? . . . And such gasping!

The Dodger shuddered to the very marrow.

At that moment he recognized the Kanaka's hard voice:

"You know, Chéri-Bibi, you must not talk."

"All right," returned Chéri-Bibi, "I won't say another word, but you've gone far enough as it is. Leave him alone. Don't touch his hands, I can't endure it. No, no, not his hands."

Three nurses, of whom one was a woman, had joined the Dodger, and they listened behind the partition without understanding what it all meant, but they had the sensation that something monstrous was taking place in the cabin.

They would have liked to communicate to each other their impressions, their apprehensions, but the Dodger held up his hand in token of silence, and they resumed their listening.

A hush had fallen once more in the cabin.

They could no longer hear speech, or moan or gasp or sound. A quarter of an hour elapsed and the Dodger and his companions stood up, tired of listening in their cramped positions, when the Countess's voice, which they had not caught until then, reached their ears very distinctly.

"If Chéri-Bibi were sensible," she said, "we could finish the job at once."

"Yes, but he's not sensible," answered the Kanaka. "He has only himself to blame."

And then they distinguished Chéri-Bibi's voice:

"Leave him his hands, leave him his hands. You see yourself how much I'm suffering."

What were they doing to the Marquis's hands, and what had the Marquis's hands to do with Chéri-Bibi's suffering?

It was enough to drive him out of his senses, especially as Chéri-Bibi was moaning again, and at each moan the Dodger felt sick at heart. The poor fellow was almost fainting. Moreover, the remainder of the conversation was not calculated to bring him round.

"Oh, the devils . . . the devils . . . the devils," panted Chéri-Bibi.

"If you talk again," the Kanaka broke in, "I shall be forced to gag you. Countess, pass me the gag."

"No, no, don't gag me. I won't speak again . . . but leave him his hands. Oh, he's had enough of it. How I suffer . . . how I suffer."

The Dodger, who was trembling in every limb, was at the end of his endurance. In a hollow voice which fear had entirely changed he cried:

"I'm here, Chéri-Bibi. . . . Do you want me?"

A great silence reigned in the cabin.

The Dodger took up anew his appeal in more and more despairing and supplicating tones:

"It's I, Chéri-Bibi, the Dodger."

He showered blows on the partition with his fists. But at the same moment someone tapped him on the shoulder. The Toper stood behind him.

The guard had called up the Toper, and by Chéri-Bibi's orders "the Dodger was to be put in irons for twenty-four hours."

"Is it true that you're having me put in irons, Chéri-Bibi? . . . You? . . . I can't believe it. Shout no, and we'll come and set you free. . . . Chéri-Bibi. . . . Chéri-Bibi."

But no answer came from Chéri-Bibi and the Dodger was dragged away.

"Damn it all. . . . What's happening in that cabin," groaned the unhappy man as he went off with the Toper.

The Dodger served his twenty-four hours in irons. As soon as his time was over he hastened to seek information. There was nothing fresh. The Kanaka had not yet left the cabin. The Countess came out for a few minutes, ran to the galleys to warm some broth into which she poured some ingredient, nobody knew what, and returned to the Kanaka without answering the questions that were put to her. She was enveloped in an overall which covered a white smock-frock the lower part of which was bloodstained, and she was wearing gloves.  Her face, it appears, was terrifying to see.  She left in the Toper's hands a written order:

"All's well.  The Kanaka is my man.  Chéri-Bibi."

"They make him believe just what they like, those ruffians," exclaimed the Dodger.  And he asked if any more wails and groans had come from the cabin.

Nothing more had been heard.  Ah, yes . . . the Kanaka's voice was heard telling the guard at the door that the crew would see him during the day, and they needn't worry themselves.

"We needn't worry ourselves!  He's a beauty, he is."

Of course the Dodger did worry himself.

And then in his turn he disappeared.

He went off and ransacked the Kanaka and the Countess's special cabin.  He found the medicine chests and surgical instruments belonging to the doctor who had died on the field of honor, in short, nothing of any importance.  But he did not leave the cabin.  It occurred to him that sooner or later the Kanaka and the Countess would return, and he would not be sorry to overhear their conversation.

With this intention, he hid himself under a bunk, and waited patiently for some three or four hours.  At long last the Kanaka and the Countess came in.  They closed the door.  They had the faces of ghosts who had suffered the tortures or savored the delights of the damned, and they quickly threw off their outer

garments and removed their gloves. They were covered with blood. It looked as if they had come from
a blood bath.

The Dodger, who was of a somewhat nervous temperament, uttered a groan and was on the point of
fainting.

The Kanaka and the Countess at once bent down
and discovered the poor fellow, dragged him from
under the bunk, and stood him as best they could
on his feet.

"What are you doing here?" demanded the Kanaka, whose rage was terrible to see.

His eyes sent forth angry flashes and his teeth were
thrust forward as though he were about to eat the
wretched Dodger, who trembled and leaned against
the bulkhead but who was not devoid of courage.

"I wanted to catch you out, murderer," he cried.
"Cannibal!"

The Countess shot him a blow in the face with all
her might.

"Leave him alone, Ketty," said the Kanaka, making
a grab at the Countess's arm, which had already
started on a second journey. "Leave the poor fellow
alone. Chéri-Bibi himself will see that he's punished."

"What have you done with Chéri-Bibi, you scoun-
drels?" went on the Dodger as he rubbed his smarting
cheek. "Have you eaten him, too?"

This time the Kanaka sprang at his throat, and the
Dodger panted for breath under his clenched fingers.

"Beg the Countess's pardon. Beg the Countess's pardon," he spluttered furiously.

But the Dodger was unable to utter a word. He was choking. His tongue protruded from his mouth like the tongue of a man who is hanged.

"Luckily for you, you villain, we caught you at once. If you had heard a single word of what's no business of yours, your goose would have been cooked. Now clear out!"

He threw him into the alley-way. The Dodger fell his length on the deck and lay there for a few moments before he could recover his breath. The Toper and Carrots, who were passing, picked him up and he told them the story of his encounter.

He went off with them, cursing the Kanaka and his wife, and declaring that things were happening on board which no one could understand, and they would all "suffer in the end." His two "pals" dared not say a word in reply, but he was conscious that they shared his opinion.

The mystery in which the inexplicable absence of Chéri-Bibi was enveloped was beginning to weigh heavily on board; secret meetings were held in every corner. Once more there was a disbelief in an epidemic. Obviously it was not for the purpose of tending patients in a fever that the Kanaka and the Countess were "dressed like butchers."

In short, the crew were agreed that at all costs they must know the truth about Chéri-Bibi. They must see and have speech with him. Such was their general frame of mind when the Kanaka sent to inform the officers that he was waiting to see them in the Captain's cabin.

The officers lost no time in obeying the summons.

The Kanaka received them imperturbably seated at the little writing-table, examining with seeming tranquillity of mind various papers, and the officers were at first reassured. True, the Kanaka was pale and seemed overtired; but all the same he did not have the appearance of a man who was the bearer of bad news.

He opened by referring to their various duties, and asked several questions about the prisoners, the store of provisions and the quantity of coal still remaining in the bunkers. The Kanaka was the only man among the officers, perhaps, who knew anything about navigation; his knowledge was sufficient at any rate to correct the ship's course, and to take command of the old crew who were obliged to continue their duties under pain of death. Therefore as a general rule he was listened to and obeyed.

But on this occasion he had to deal with absent-minded men whose thoughts were concentrated only on Chéri-Bibi. They were surprised that he did not speak of him, since the state of his health was the only question which interested them. Their stupefaction knew no bounds when they received the order to retire.

They remained in their places.

The Toper opened fire.

"Commander, we shall be in Cape Town in a few days," he said with an affectation of great politeness and strict discipline.

"Yes, what about it?"

"Many serious matters will have to be decided."

"Well, what then?"

"We can't decide them without Chéri-Bibi. Commander, our men are very anxious about Chéri-Bibi. We can't go on much longer without knowing what's the matter with him. I felt bound to tell you that. We should like to see Chéri-Bibi."

"Yes, yes. We want to see him," chimed in several voices.

"Impossible," replied the Kanaka laconically.

"Of course," said Little Buddha, "he may not be able to see us all, but we could delegate one of our number to see him. Look here, we're not asking a great deal. Let the Dodger see him for five minutes, and then we shall be easy in our minds."

"Neither the Dodger nor anyone else. It's quite out of the question," returned the Kanaka obstinately.

"Well, in that case, let us speak to him at the door and let him answer us."

"Chéri-Bibi just now can't say anything."

"Why not?"

"Because he can't speak."

"Then let him write and tell us what has happened and set our minds at rest. Should there be anything that must not be known generally, a couple of us only will read the message, and we shall be satisfied."

"Chéri-Bibi can't write."

"Look here, Kanaka, you're pulling our legs," he blazed out, forgetting discipline and losing the dignity which pertained to his new position. "You're not going to leave here until you've given us some explanation."

"You can do what you like, but you'll get no explanation from me."

"We'll force our way into the cabin. . . ."

"You can do as you like, I tell you. Only afterwards don't come and claim the five millions . . ."

"Oh, it has to do with the five millions . . ."

"What do you suppose it has to do with? Let Chéri-Bibi work the Marquis in his own way. There'll be plenty of time to ask him to explain matters when he has made the Marquis fork out the shekels. And now, gentlemen, I won't keep you any longer."

They left the cabin with considerable misgivings. The Dodger did not utter a word. They asked him what he thought of it all. He shook his head and answered that he had his own idea.

The crew became more and more alarmed. How was it possible for Chéri-Bibi to "work the five millions" if he could neither speak nor write?

Next day, after the Kanaka and the Countess were shut up with Chéri-Bibi and the Marquis for half an hour, extraordinary howls were heard proceeding from the cabin. It was like a dog baying at death. Men crowded into the alley-way and all eyes were fixed on the door while the howls grew louder—louder and more frightful. Only a wild beast or a madman could howl like that. And this time they clearly recognized the Marquis's voice, particularly when mingled with the yells they caught the sound of words babbled in pain though they could not grasp the sense of them.

And then the howls changed to shrieks, to fierce barking, to wild sobs. And then suddenly they stopped.

The crowd of convicts stood in the alley-way for another quarter of an hour with a look of terror in their eyes. And by slow degrees, as nothing further was heard, they melted away.

Later in the night more groans were heard, and these also came from the Marquis. They did not hear Chéri-Bibi's voice again. And it was this which produced a greater strain of anxiety than when the groans came from him.

The Dodger, gloomy and sullen, did not leave the deck, nor did he answer anyone who spoke to him.

One evening the lookout man cried: "Land on the port bow!" and the Dodger said with a sigh: "At last!"

Some minutes later the Kanaka came to meet him.

"Dodger, we're near land," he said. "In a few hours we shall be at Cape Town. You know that we are to land you a little below Malmesbury. Pack up your traps, my lad. We shall give you all the necessary papers, and you'll find the complete scheme of what you've got to do written out in Chéri-Bibi's handwriting. Are you ready?"

"No," returned the Dodger, who had been nursing an idea.

"Why not?"

"Because I reıuse to take upon myself this job until I've had a final interview with Chéri-Bibi."

"You've made up your mind?"

"I've made up my mind."

"Can I tell Chéri-Bibi so?"

"By all means, Kanaka. . . ."

The crew were soon aware that the two men were at variance, and they considered that the Dodger was in the right. Excitement was general, and there was no doubt that the most reckless among them were inclined to take extreme measures when the Kanaka came back and said simply:

"Chéri-Bibi will see the Dodger before he goes."

The crew gave way to shouts of joy and cheers.

The Dodger left them to pack up his things in a state of great emotion. It was quite dark when the Kanaka came to fetch him. The Dodger followed him trembling in every limb. At last the cabin door was opened; and the Toper, Little Buddha, the Top and Carrots waited outside to hear the result of the interview.

When he first entered the cabin the Dodger could distinguish absolutely nothing. No light was burning. Then gradually, as his eyes grew accustomed to the darkness, he saw by the faint glimmer that filtered through the port hole, the upstanding outline of the Countess, and afterwards, at his right and left, two bodies lying on bunks, or rather two mere shadows deprived of all power of movement.

He could not have said which was Chéri-Bibi and which was the Marquis.

The sound of Chéri-Bibi's voice soon put an end to his doubts.

"Sit down here, Dodger."

A chair was drawn up, and as he dropped into it he whispered:

"Chéri-Bibi!"

"So you wanted to see me before you go, my dear fellow."

"My dear Chéri-Bibi. . . . Have you been very ill, then? . . . Are you getting better now? . . . Give us your fist, old pal."

"No, no," interposed the Kanaka. "Stay where you are, you mustn't touch his hand. You mustn't touch him."

"It's not allowed," agreed Chéri-Bibi. "You see I'm suffering from some contagious disease . . ."

"I can't see anything, it's too dark," groaned the Dodger. "I'd like to see your face . . . to make sure that you're not off color."

"You can't have a light. I can't allow it for the present," broke in the Kanaka again. "He mustn't tire his eyes."

"But, good Lord, what's the matter with you?"

"I'll tell you that later on, Dodger. . . . Now we must talk of serious things. . . . And be quick about it, for the Kanaka, who knows his business as a doctor, won't give us more than five minutes."

"Five minutes. . . . How weak your voice is. . . . I can scarcely recognize it. . . . You must have had a bad time, old man."

"He is weak. . . . That's quite true. . . . Don't tire him," said the Kanaka. "Get on with it."

"As to the Kanaka," said Chéri-Bibi, speaking with some difficulty, as if it hurt him to move his jaws and he was too exhausted to articulate his words clearly. "You must tell the Toper and the others that the Kanaka has looked after me well and saved my life, and they must carry out his orders in any and everything. . . . Now listen carefully. The Kanaka saved my life. That's worth a bit. He must have a million francs for himself."

"The others will never agree to that," said the Dodger.

"You needn't tell them and they won't know about it. The Marquis, who is very generous and whom the Kanaka has also looked after well, agrees with me that 'it's worth a million.' You'll see it all set out in the papers. It's six millions that'll be handed over to you, one million for the Kanaka apart from the other money. . . . Now listen to this: By the time you come back I hope to be well again, but if I am not . . . we must look ahead . . . if . . . if I'm dead . . ."

"Don't talk like that . . . don't say that. . . . I'd much rather stay behind . . ." groaned the Dodger.

"Well, if anything does happen to the Marquis or me, or to both of us, you will be carrying out my last wishes by giving the Kanaka a million francs without letting anyone know about it. . . . Is that understood?"

"That's understood," agreed the Dodger in solemn tones. And he turned towards the other body lying in the darkness on the opposite side, but the Marquis was as motionless as if he were dead.

"You are artful and have your wits about you," went on Chéri-Bibi with a sigh. "If you follow the instructions that I've written out, you won't run into any danger, and it will be as easy for you to get the money as it is for a workman to draw his wages on pay day. You will be put ashore to-night. Don't show yourself for a couple of days, and then we shall be some distance away. If anyone asks for your papers you can say that you left the *Estrella* while she was coaling to go on the spree, and you haven't got any. They made you drunk and you're a Frenchman who wants to be sent home. . . . You'll pull through right enough."

"Yes, you needn't worry about that. I wasn't born yesterday, you may be sure. Everything will be all right, never fear."

"I know you, old man. You have a knack of getting through difficulties. You musn't dawdle. We'll give you five months to the day. Five months from now we shall wait for you for two or three weeks at Palmerston in the Northern Territory of South Australia. It's a nice little place which I know well, and it's as quiet as can be. You can write to me as instructed in the papers, addressing me *poste restante*. To get back you must take the China boat and stop at Batavia. There is a service of steamers between Batavia and Palmerston. Do you follow me?"

"I understand. . . . Five months. . . . That's a long time without seeing you."

"Afterwards you shan't leave me, my dear old Dodger."

"Have you finished?" asked the Kanaka.

"Oh, give us another minute longer, you know," begged the Dodger, who felt an inclination to weep.

Chéri-Bibi seemed to make an effort, and he said with a deep sigh:

"You will have the luck to see Cecily. . . . Well, have a good look at her . . . look at her for me. . . . And when you come back you'll be able to tell me if she is as beautiful as ever."

"Well, he doesn't trouble himself much about the Marquis," thought the Dodger. And he turned his eyes once more to him, but the Marquis still maintained his deathlike attitude. "I don't like the look of it," he said to himself. . . . "Sure enough he's kicked the bucket already. . . . Why doesn't he stir?"

But the Kanaka interrupted his reflections and made him get up.

"Good-bye, Dodger."

"Good-bye, Chéri-Bibi. . . . I'd very much like to

shake hands with you before I go. . . . Isn't there any chance?"

"No," said the Kanaka.

"All right, all right. I'm off. Good-bye, Chéri-Bibi, good-bye. . . . Get better soon."

And he allowed himself to be put outside the door as he burst into sobs.

The *Estrella* stopped that night. A long-boat was lowered and soon landed the Dodger on a lonely part of the coast.

"Good luck," cried the Kanaka, who had accompanied him so far.

"Good luck. . . . Look after Chéri-Bibi and you can count me as your friend."

The long-boat's crew were already pulling hard for the *Estrella*, whose lights could be discerned a few cable-lengths away.

"A million francs," said the Dodger to himself, thinking of the Kanaka. "Well, there's a sudden death merchant who doesn't look after the poor for nothing. . . . His prescriptions cost a bit!"

And he plunged into the bush.

●    ●    ●    ●    ●    ●    ●    ●

## EXTRACT FROM *THE TIMES*

(From our Special Correspondent)

SINGAPORE.

"It is officially announced that an end has been made at last of the notorious *Bayard* and her convict crew. The French cruiser *La Gloire,* which was on her track during the whole of last year, and from which she succeeded in escaping in the many groups of island of the Malay Archipelago, came up with her in the Molucca Sea, near the Sula Islands. *La Gloire* at once opened fire. A quick engagement ensued, and the *Bayard* was blown up. Three-fourths of the crew were drowned. The remainder, who had taken to the boats and were attempting to escape, preferred to be shot rather than to surrender. *La Gloire* picked up over a hundred dead bodies, among which they were able to identify the leader of the gang, the Kanaka, and the Countess, his terrible wife. It is known that the Kanaka took over the position of Captain of these abominable pirates after Chéri-Bibi's strange disappearance. Thus ends the astounding organisation which has occupied the attention of the whole world for such long months, and which terrorised the entire China Seas; but the fact remains that the infamous Chéri-Bibi is still at large; for on the best of authority it can be stated that he left the *S. S. Bayard* some weeks before she was sunk."

The amazing circumstances in which Chéri-Bibi was able to impersonate the Marquis du Touchais, and the further adventures of this extraordinary character are told in "The Return of Chéri-Bibi," which will be published shortly.

www.ingramcontent.com/pod-product-compliance
Lightning Source LLC
Chambersburg PA
CBHW030243030726
47493CB00023B/568